HOW ELVIS

SAVED

QUEBEC

Ronald Sutherland was born and raised in the largely French-speaking East End of Montreal. He taught at l'Université de Sherbrooke and founded the discipline of Comparative Canadian Literature. He has published numerous scholarly articles and books, humorous vignettes for newspapers and two novels, one of which, *Lark des Neiges* (Snow Lark) in paperback, became the feature film *Suzanne*.

* * *

For my late brother-in-law and dear friend,

KEITH WILKINS,

who brightened the lives of all who knew him.

How Elvis Saved Quebec

by

Ronald Sutherland

Borealis Press
Ottawa, Canada
2003

Copyright © by Ronald Sutherland
and Borealis Press, 2003

All rights reserved. No part of this book may be used or reproduced in any manner whatsoever without prior written permission except in the case of brief quotations embodied in critical articles and reviews.

Canada

We acknowledge the financial assistance of the Government of Canada through the Book Publishing Program (BPIDP) for our publishing activities.

National Library of Canada Cataloguing in Publication Data

Sutherland, Ronald, 1933-
   How Elvis saved Quebec / Ronald Sutherland.

ISBN 0-88887-224-0

   1. Title.

PS8587.U8H69 2003   C813'.54   C2002-905532-6
PR9199.3.S88H69 2003

Cover design by Bull's Eye Design, Ottawa, Canada
Photograph of Ronald Sutherland by Sophie Nöel de Tilly

Printed and bound in Canada on acid free paper

Contents

Chapters

1	1
2	15
3	22
4	27
5	40
6	54
7	61
8	74
9	81
10	99
11	117
12	128
13	135
14	147
15	158
16	179
17	195
18	227
19	248
20	266
21	273
22	285
Glossary of Quebec French	291

Chapter One

It was a stop sign sure enough. The distinctive octagonal shape could be recognized even by complete illiterates. And Canadians in general, Frank speculated, would soon have to recognize stop signs by their distinctive shape alone. The lettering on the sign he was looking at had been obliterated with red and blue paint. He presumed that, like the first stop sign he had seen in French Canada, just over the border from Ontario, it had once had both the French *ARRÊT* and the international STOP printed on it.

Driving farther into Quebec Province and through the City of Montreal, he had noticed the STOP on many signs was blotched out by blue paint. Then on the outskirts of the Village of Saint-Alphonse de Chadley Nord, the *ARRÊT* had been covered by red paint. This time, in the village itself, the sign had been given a double whammy—defaced by both red and blue. Then on the sign identifying the town, North Chadley was spray-painted in red over the French name and—strangely, thought Frank—the word *OUI*, French for Yes, had been superimposed several times in bright blue.

Candidate for a Ph.D. in Anthropology at Wayne State University in Detroit, Frank Collins did not know what to make of it all. After only a few hours in the country, mainly driving along the Trans-Canada Highway, he was beginning to think that Canadians were a little ... well, more peculiar than he had imagined they would be. He had believed that he was getting a marvellous bargain in gasoline until he checked the fuel gauge in his car and realized that he had bought litres and not gallons. The mental arithmetic of converting from the kilometres indicated on the road signs to proper miles had at least helped to pass the time during the long drive. Yet twice when he asked for directions, the Canadian garagemen, seeming to ignore their own system, had spontaneously given him distances in miles. Then when he had stopped at a roadside diner after crossing the border into the Province of Quebec, instead of normal ketchup the waitress had brought him a bottle of plain vinegar for his French-fried potatoes, which she called *"des chips."*

But Frank's most alarming experience had been on the highway just before arriving in St-Alphonse. In fact, when his prized 1972 Buick Regal with air conditioning and genuine leather upholstery was buried in five or six feet of snow in the roadside ditch, he had come close to abandoning his research project and returning to the relatively civilized Motor City before he had even seen the town.

Not that Collins hadn't been forewarned about Quebec drivers. He had even read in some anthropological study that the two population groups in North America currently being charged the highest automobile-insurance rates, presumably because they were the continent's worst drivers, were the Chinook Indians in the American West and Quebeckers in Canada. The explanation for the Chinooks was that they were culturally maladjusted, collectively frustrated and consequently bombed out of their minds much of the time. Still, despite the warnings, Frank was taken completely by surprise when the image of a grey pickup truck with red fenders emerged out of the blowing snow about ten or fifteen feet in front of his eyes. He had been staring straight ahead through the windshield, almost mesmerized, mumbling encouragement to the skinny wiper blades as they strained to maintain a wedge of visibility. The driver of the truck had neither looked to the left nor stopped when he or she arrived at the highway from a side road. Frank's leg, the pile-driver leg of a 260-pound former football lineman, stiffened as he rammed the brake pedal. The Buick slithered from side to side like a snake on loose sand, then it plunged at an angle into the ditch. Through the side window in the instant before the car sank beneath the surface of the snow, Frank saw the grey pickup truck with bright red fenders rolling merrily away. It was an old Ford.

By lowering the window and clearing the snow with his hands, Frank managed to open the door enough to squeeze out and clamber to the road. He trudged to a farmhouse a mile or so back, and the farmer either deciphered Frank's shaky French or else divined what had happened. After sitting the stranger beside a huge pot-bellied stove to warm up and pouring him a glass of potent hooch which he called "*whiskee blanc*," the farmer went to the barn and got his tractor and a chain. He had Frank's car back on the road in a few minutes, and when he noticed the Michigan licence plates, he absolutely refused any payment. The farmer's generosity, good will and *whiskee blanc*, which after lighting a fire in Frank's stomach was now causing a tingling sensation in his fingers and toes, improved the fledgling anthropologist's mood to some extent as he continued his daring expedition into the icy heartland of rural Quebec.

Frank Collins' first view of St-Alphonse de Chadley Nord, which used to be called, in fact still is called simply North Chadley by a lot of its residents, was from the crest of a hill. He gazed down at a genuine picture-postcard town, a cluster of snow-capped clapboard houses around the outlet of a banana-shaped lake, except for one curious, mosque-like brick building halfway up the hill on one side. Another part of the scene which the American graduate student found curious was that parked on the ice about midway between the shores of the frozen lake was a car.

"What the hell is that car doing there?" Frank asked the innkeeper when he checked into the small hotel in the middle of town. From a plaque near the door he knew that the man's name was Wilton Wadleigh. He was handsome, with the facial features of a Rudolph Valentino, a sturdy build and thick, straw-coloured hair which flowed back over his head in perfectly orchestrated waves. Frank estimated him to be about thirty years old and could not help noticing his steely blue eyes.

"What car do you mean?" Wadleigh responded.

"The one on the ice in the middle of the lake."

"Oh, that's just a piece of junk."

"But what's it doing out there?"

"Ed Wilson—he owns the garage in town—is taking bets."

"Taking bets?"

"Yeah. Everybody places bets on the hour and the day that the heap will sink in the spring."

"Oh, I see."

"Biggest excitement we have around here," the innkeeper continued. "The locals all stand along the shore for days, staring out at the lake, working themselves into frenzies like a bunch of teeny-boppers at a rock concert, until the bloody old jalopy goes under."

Frank nodded his head.

"Know what the average age of the population of North Chadley is?" asked Wadleigh.

"I have no idea yet," Frank replied. "I know the national . . . "

"Deceased!" The innkeeper roared with laughter, slapping his thighs, and Frank managed to muster a sympathetic chuckle or two. Then Wadleigh explained that during the long winter, the population of North Chadley was about 600 people, many of them retired and elderly.

"There's no jobs here, no industry, no nothing. Fifteen bucks."

"Fifteen bucks?" inquired Frank.

"For the room."

"Oh yes, of course, the room."

"How long you planning to stay?"

"I'm not sure yet. It depends on how my research project goes."

"Aha. So you're after the silver up to the old Eustis Mine."

"No. I don't know anything about silver."

"Is that a fact?"

"I'm in anthropology, the study of people and their customs and beliefs."

"Then you've come to the wrong place, buddy."

"How is that?"

"The people around here ain't got no customs and beliefs."

"They . . . they must have," Frank responded hesitatingly.

"Nothing to speak of. Except them goddamned, foaming-at-the-mouth Separatists, like Clémentine, who runs that two-bit café in front of here. But what they got are not really beliefs. They got delusions. Anyway, you should have come here during the summer. When the summer people move in, the population jumps to about 2,000. A few of them still come all the way up from the States."

"Is that right?"

"Sure. Most of them big houses along the shore were originally built by Americans. And you know something? They're not really houses."

"Not really houses?"

"Some of them have sixteen or twenty rooms, but they're only summer cottages. No insulation or nothing and built on cedar posts just like they were in Georgia or Alabama or one of them places down South. No use whatever in the winter."

"But the town is pretty evenly divided between English-speaking and French-speaking people, isn't it?"

"Now it is. Used to be mostly English. But ever since they built that damned university over in Brooke, the French have been pouring in. Bloody professors. Cheap bastards. Don't eat or drink out much. And when they do, they tip a lousy quarter. Say, you're not a professor, are you?"

"No, I'm only a student."

Frank was standing by the counter of what appeared to be, because of the numerous bottles of liquor on shelves and glasses suspended upside down from an overhead rack, a bar-salon. The innkeeper was behind the counter, which obviously also served as a front desk for the inn. Nobody else was in the bar-salon when Frank had arrived, but now a woman—in her sixties, Frank guessed—entered and plunked herself down at one of tables without removing her overcoat. She exchanged cheery greetings with Wadleigh, who called her

Marge and reached for a gin bottle. A few moments later a man with swarthy skin and coal black hair, wearing heavy flight boots and a parka, also came into the bar, nodded to the innkeeper and headed for a table on the opposite side of the room. While the man was taking off his parka and throwing it over a chair, Wadleigh told Frank that he was "some kind of Indian" who had come for the ice-fishing on the lake and who didn't say much. The innkeeper added tonic to the gin he had poured, opened the refrigerator to get an ice cube and a bottle of beer, then shouted, "Lisette!"

A dark-haired woman in a tight black skirt slit to above the knee, a white blouse and a dainty waitress apron, emerged from what appeared to be a kitchen off to one side of the barroom. Frank could not help noticing how shapely she was—generous, rounded buttocks and good legs, a tiny waist, prominent bust—as she stretched over the bar stools to pick up the tray with the bottle of beer and the gin and tonic.

"This is the wife, Lisette. She's the barmaid and the cook and the floor show around here," said Wadleigh, chuckling.

"How do you do, Mrs. Wadleigh," said Frank.

"Bonjour, Monsieur. Happy to meet you," the innkeeper's wife replied, smiling at Frank and allowing him to take note that her face was as captivating as her lush figure, although in a way which was almost a contrast. It was the face of a little girl, a pixy face, with large, bright eyes, a turned-up nose and a mouth which seemed to be set in a kind of pout. The combination, thought Frank, was an image of assured, defiant femininity, which was probably just as well, because her husband did not convey the impression of being overly sensitive or considerate.

"I should mention," said Wadleigh as his wife left with the tray to serve the two customers, "that the wife can whip up a pretty good breakfast. In fact, to let you in on a little secret, that's how she first got her hooks into me."

The innkeeper chuckled again, winking at Frank, and added, "We also serve snacks and light meals."

It turned out that there were not many rooms at the inn, which, Wadleigh explained, used to be a feed mill, accounting for the huge, rough-hewn beams across the ceiling and the wide, unpainted planks in the walls, ceiling and floor, giving the bar-salon a sort of frontier ambience.

"Take a look," said the innkeeper. "Some of them planks are over a yard wide. You don't get lumber like that any more. That's why I left them in their natural state."

Frank noted the uncommon width of the planks, at the same time catching a glimpse of the equally uncommon protuberance of Mrs. Wadleigh's hips in comparison to her tiny waist as the young woman strutted across the room holding up a tray in one hand, and he could not restrain himself from briefly visualizing how *she* would look in the natural state.

Wadleigh and his wife apparently lived in the suite above the bar-salon, and the other rooms, four in all, were at the back of the inn and reached by separate doors from the outside. Frank made arrangements to rent one of these rooms for $65 a week.

Once he had settled into his room, Frank took a walk around town, and he was impressed by the peace and tranquillity. It was as quiet as downtown Detroit, except that in the case of the giant American city, the quietness was the result of stark terror. People were afraid to walk the streets, and if they were obliged to for some reason, then they tried to be as inconspicuous as possible. The downtown of North Chadley, spread along the lakeside road on each side of the bridge over the outlet stream, consisted of a café, a snack bar, two churches, a general store, a hardware store, a gas station, a bank, a post office, a grocery store and a large old folks' home. Actually there were two bridges, one for the road and the other, constructed of large timbers, for the railway track. The second bridge, Frank learned from an old man standing on it with a fishing pole, was used mainly for fishing, but every two or three days a train did pass through town carrying granite for tombstones from a quarry down near the border of the adjoining "Granite State," Vermont.

Frank Collins was also impressed by the large, stately houses of North Chadley, which were scattered along tree-lined lanes winding up the hillsides on each side of the lake. Along the small river were more modest wooden houses where, as Frank soon found out, the French Canadians used to live when they first trickled into town, but which were now occupied by a mixture of working people. Smoke drifting from the chimneys and icicles hanging from the snow-covered roofs indicated which houses were being lived in, as did the shovelled walks and cars in the driveways. As he wandered around getting his first look at the town, Frank was still asking himself if he had made the right decision to drive some 800 miles to a remote little village in the Eastern Townships of the Province of Quebec in the middle of the winter. The icy wind sweeping across the empty expanse of lake caused him to shiver and turn up the collar of his coat and was not exactly reassuring.

The idea of coming to Quebec, in fact, had not been

Frank's own. Completing a Ph.D. in Anthropology at Wayne State University in Detroit, he was desperately in need of a dissertation subject. Anthropology departments, he realized too late, like the child-bearing women in Third World countries, were guilty of over-production. Had he known sooner, he might have gotten into nuclear-night theory, destruction of the ozone layer, acid rain or something of the sort with a promising future. But after finishing three years of courses, he had no choice now but to shoot for a diploma and hope that it would turn out to be a meal ticket. Professors and students in his department tried to offset their anxieties by joking about the situation. In the South Sea Islands, Margaret Mead's old stomping ground, anthropologists, they quipped, were now studying the courting and mating customs of one another. The typical Inuit family in the Arctic now consisted of father, mother, two children, snowmobile and resident anthropologist. It was Frank's department chairman who suggested St-Alphonse de Chadley Nord, which he had himself visited a couple of times and where a friend of his happened to live.

"Quebec Province is undergoing extraordinary infrastructure transformations," the chairman remarked to Frank. "The French Canadians had been economically and psychologically subjugated by the English ever since the British Conquest in seventeen something, but now they are finally reasserting themselves, which is generating conflictual ethnic-group interfacing. They've elected a government which platforms the actual separation of Quebec from the rest of Canada, and they've even made French the only official language of the province."

"Yes, I know," Frank replied, and he told the chairman that his grandfather on his mother's side was a

French Canadian who had come to Michigan as a lumberjack. Frank had learned about Quebec and had even acquired some French when he was a small boy and "grandpoppa" was still alive. He used to love to climb onto the old man's lap because he always had a supply of candies, or *bonbons* as grandpoppa used to call the little animals made of maple sugar which one of his sisters sent from the family farm back in Quebec. The department chairman speculated that a detailed analysis of the social evolution in a community which was changing from English to French might result in an acceptable doctoral dissertation, and he suggested that North Chadley might be the ideal community to investigate.

"The last time I was there," said the chairman, "a number of the English appeared to be almost panic-stricken, a reaction not entirely dissimilar from that of white Americans in the more affluent suburbs of Detroit when a Black or a Hispanic moves into the neighbourhood. Some residents of North Chadley were actually making plans to move elsewhere, even though they would have to take considerable losses on their property, because the rise in the Separatist movement has apparently depressed values. It's a buyer's market up there in Quebec, Mr. Collins. If for some reason your projected dissertation fails to make the grade, then you could consider dabbling in real estate perhaps. Did you know that half the population of Florida are accredited real-estate agents?"

Frank had the disquieting impression that his department chairman was trying to get rid of him one way or another, but he was in no position to ignore the advice being offered. And he was genuinely interested in the homeland of many of his ancestors. Other ancestors had been Irish, but it was a well-known fact that Ireland was not amenable to anthropological or any other kind of rational analysis. The chairman told Frank that institutions would be his primary focus of study.

"And what about the institutions?" Frank asked.

"Check Louis Althuser and Richard Adams. Or Robert Redfield, Everett C. Hughes. Then there's Horace over at the U. of Chicago, Horace Miner, who did a book on a Quebec town called Saint Denis, if I'm not mistaken. Social stability is dependent upon the relationship between the people of a community and their institutions—schools, hospitals, churches, brothels, bowling leagues, legions, blind pigs, service clubs and so forth. The present Quebec government, being committed to independence, has centralized control of a lot of the institutions which used to be in local hands as it were. These institutions used to operate exclusively in English, as if the French-speaking people didn't exist. Now they are being forced to use French, sometimes only French. You can imagine the effect on unilingual English nervous systems."

Frank did all the background reading, packed his bags, changed the oil in his Buick Regal to a lighter grade for cold weather, installed two recap snow tires and left for Quebec. Being an only child and having lost both his parents, he left no immediate family back in Detroit. He had recently gotten a "Dear John" from his girlfriend of many years, who had taken up with a computer consultant, probably despairing that anthropologists in general and Frank in particular had any hope of success in the contemporary U.S.A.

When he got back to his room behind the inn and opened the door, Frank was startled by a flash of black moving past his legs. He searched for the light switch, then he saw a large black cat calmly step into the open suitcase on the floor and settle itself on top of his clothes. Leaving the door open, he attempted to shoo the scruffy beast out of the room, but the cat darted under the bed. The wind was howling and blowing snow through the open door. The cat came out from under the bed and slowly crept toward the suitcase again, watching Frank with its luminous yellow eyes. When it settled itself on his clothes once more and began a loud, raucous purring, he decided that he could not throw any living creature out into such a stormy winter night, even if there were a remote chance of catching it, and he closed the door.

Lying in bed, Frank resolved that he would get rid of the cat first thing in the morning. It was a female, a bag of bones with a bloated belly, probably starving. Frank recalled that he had put two little containers of seven-percent cream in his coat pocket when he stopped at a roadside diner for a coffee on the trip from Detroit. His mother had repeatedly banged into his head when he was a child that it was sinful to leave anything on his plate, and he had developed the habit of slipping whatever he didn't consume into his pockets. The consequence, when he was a child and his mother served asparagus or boiled cabbage, was soggy pockets. Now he still managed to mess up his clothes fairly regularly when little packages of ketchup or relish or barbecue sauce burst open, but he could not break the thrifty habit. He got out of bed, fumbled in his coat pocket and offered the cream to the black cat, which lapped it up eagerly and resumed its loud purring.

Back in bed, Frank had a few moments of uneasiness as he pondered the fact that a black cat had crossed his path. He was not given to foolish superstitions, he reassured himself. On the other hand, as a trained anthropologist he knew that often the rituals and beliefs and taboos of various tribal communities had significance, indeed power which baffled the scientific Western observer. His own mother would never invite thirteen for dinner.

Then again, the black cat had not really crossed his path, had it? It had simply rushed past him through the door. And he was showing it hospitality, so it was bound to be on his side. Whatever, he would straighten everything out in the morning. It had been a long, tiring day.

Chapter Two

Awakened by the cat meowing at the door, Frank looked at his watch and was surprised to see that it was almost eleven o'clock. He had slept in. *I must have been more tired than I realized*, he told himself. The long drive, then trudging through the snow out of the ditch and to the farmer's house had worn him out. All because of a reckless idiot behind the wheel of an old Ford pickup with red fenders. He'd recognize that truck if ever he should see it again. Then there was the air of North Chadley. Compared to breathing the thick smog of Detroit, it was like being in an oxygen tent. There were all the trees to soak up the carbon dioxide, and the wind off the lake blew away what little smoke came from the house chimneys. Frank got up and stepped over to open the door. *Well that takes care of the cat problem*, he assured himself, as the creature trotted across the threshold and out of his life.

He had brought with him from Detroit a hot plate which he intended to use to prepare some of his meals, but first he would have to go to a grocery store and lay in supplies. This morning he would check out Lisette's acclaimed skill at making breakfasts, even if he had to do without the appetizing preliminaries crassly alluded to by innkeeper Wadleigh. He washed, got dressed, putting on his favourite thick woolen shirt in Wallace tartan, then stepped over to the door. As he opened it, he saw the same black flash that he had seen the night before. The damned cat had darted around his legs and was back in the room. Frank decided that he needed a coffee and something to eat before trying to tackle the devious animal.

He opted for pancakes and local maple syrup, which he found especially delicious, bringing back memories of grandpoppa's *bonbons*. He recalled that the maple sugar candies had been in distinctive shapes, one a maple leaf, another a *fleur de lys*, and another, the one which used to fascinate him the most, a little man something like one of the Walt Disney seven dwarfs wearing a long tuque and carrying a rifle. His grandfather had explained simply that the man was a *patriote*, presumably a reminder of the 1837 Rebellion against the British authorities, and it occurred to Frank as he was demolishing his second plate of pancakes that Quebec nationalism had been around in one way or another for a long time. The "Separatists" mentioned bitterly by Wilton Wadleigh yesterday were nothing new. They were just the latest manifestation of a deep-rooted yearning that had never been allowed to fade away, even though Quebec, or Lower Canada as it used to be called, had joined the Canadian Confederation in 1867 of its own free will. But Frank knew from his reading that the province was planning a Referendum on independence in the near future to settle the issue once and for all. It was just as well, he reflected, a sensible and civilized way to proceed, allowing people to weigh the pros and cons and pick the best solution. And maybe it would let the STOP/ *ARRÊT* signs go back to being neutral traffic regulators.

After thanking Lisette and paying his bill, Frank wandered over to the grocery store. He resolved that he had to get himself some boxes of cereal and other light fare like fat-free yogurt if he didn't want to balloon to over 300 pounds eating at the Inn. But Lisette's hearty breakfast had fortified him well against the brisk wind off the lake. He was pleasantly impressed that the four people he passed on his way to the store, people he had never seen before, all greeted him with a cheery Hello or *Bonjour*.

Back in his room, Frank made several futile attempts to grab the black cat, then he gave up and arranged his dissertation documents on the desk in the room as the cat settled back in his suitcase. He told himself that later he would unpack the suitcase and put it away, and maybe the scruffy beast would get the message. He could also complain to innkeeper Wadleigh, who would surely have to do something. Back in Detroit, Frank had lived in rooms and flats infested with cockroaches, including a giant variety with wings, and once even a rat, but a cat was a bigger intrusion. A cat presumed that human beings were there to accommodate it. Still, before starting to look at his papers, Frank poured a bit of the milk he had bought at the grocery store into the empty cream containers. The cat would soon be gone, so there was no point in treating it meanly. He intended to work at his desk for a while then drop over to see William Martin, the friend of his department chairman who lived in St-Alphonse de Chadley Nord.

Martin, he knew, was a history professor at the French-speaking Université de Brooke, a small city fifteen or so miles away. He was a heavy-set, bearded man in his late forties, with an American wife acquired in the same way as the American wives of many other male academics throughout the world—a girl he had met while studying at a graduate school in the United States. Martin, Frank also knew in advance, had five daughters in their teens, an old yellow dog, three or four cats and a loud voice. Frank heard his voice before he met the man himself. When he arrived at the door of the Martin home, one of the daughters let him in.

"Daddy and our neighbour, Mr. Jackson, are having a little chat in the kitchen," she said, after he had introduced himself.

"What the bloody hell do you mean you're going to vote yes in the Referendum?" Martin was shouting at Jackson as Frank stood in the doorway taking off his coat and boots. "Don't you realize, you damned idiot, that if the Separatists win the Referendum, it will mean total chaos?"

"I doubt that, Bill," replied Jackson, a slim, aristocratic-looking man a little older than Martin.

"Goddammit, Gord, there are two things you people from Ontario never seem to understand—the tribal nationalism of extremists in Quebec, the very people you want to put in the driver's seat . . ."

"Quebec nationalism has been around a long time," interrupted Jackson, "and it's not going to just go away. I think we should give them a chance. I'm curious to see what would happen . . ."

"I'm telling you what will bloody-well happen! They'll try to separate Quebec from Canada, and all hell will break loose. The second thing you don't seem to understand is that the English minority in Quebec will fight back furiously, and that will bring in redneck volunteers from all the other provinces, even from the States. Everybody will be forced to take sides, even though the majority don't want to. It'll be the French against the English all over again."

"I don't see why."

"You don't see because you haven't lived here most of your life like I have. So you're ready to let raving fanatics take over."

"Not at all, Bill. I want the will of the majority."

"Christ! Don't you see that you're being suckered in? You and all the other bleeding hearts from outside Quebec who support the damned Separatists, even though you're not really Separatists yourselves, you're giving an extremist minority the means to manipulate the majority. You have the perverted idea in your heads that you're supporting a noble cause, helping the downtrodden and all the rest of the bullshit. Then when the roof caves in, you'll all go back home and forget about Quebec."

"I don't intend to leave Quebec."

"You may have no choice. The only way the Separatists can achieve their ultimate goal is to generate fear and hatred among French Canadians of everything associated with English Canada, and that includes you."

"I don't see that at all."

"You don't see because you're a damned fool!"

"And you're turning into a blockheaded redneck!"

Martin's daughter brought Frank Collins into the kitchen just as her father rose from his chair and reached for Jackson, yelling, "You bastard! Who do you think you're calling a blockheaded redneck?"

As both men scrambled to their feet, knocking over a glass full of beer, Frank shifted his bulky frame between them.

"Who the hell are you?" shouted Martin.

"Dad, this is Frank Collins," said Martin's daughter nonchalantly. "He's from Detroit. He's going to do a Ph.D. dissertation on North Chadley."

Both Martin and Jackson stared at the huge newcomer.

"You're going to do what?" asked Martin.

"A study of the social evolution of this town for my

doctorate in Anthropology," Frank replied.

"As you can see," remarked Jackson, smiling, "there hasn't been a great deal of social evolution around here."

"Right," said Martin. "Some people in this town are very backward."

"Even retarded, you might say," added Jackson, positioning his chair and sitting down again.

"You're from Detroit?" asked Martin as he offered Frank a chair and sat down at the table again himself.

"Wayne State, sir, where you once studied, I believe. I also believe that you know my department chairman, Russell Howard."

"Of course. Known Russ for years. How is he?"

"Fine. He sends his regards to you and all the family. Actually it was his idea that I do my dissertation on St-Alphonse de Chadley Nord."

"I can't imagine what you'll find to do," said Jackson. "This is a dull little dormitory town. Nothing much happens."

"It seemed quite lively to me a few moments ago," said Frank.

"Just a neighbourly discussion," Jackson responded.

"Sure," added Martin. "Gord here and I have the occasional small difference of opinion. But it doesn't mean anything really. We're colleagues and old friends. By the way, this is Dr. Gordon Jackson, professor of history at Brooke University."

"How do you do, sir."

"Would you like a beer?" asked Martin.

His daughter stepped over to the refrigerator and took out three bottles of beer, which she opened and handed to the three men at the table.

"I have the impression," commented Frank, "that the

people of Quebec are becoming quite . . . uh . . . concerned about the upcoming Referendum on independence."

"A little, perhaps," said Jackson, leaning back in his chair and taking a sip of his beer. "But we're Canadians, you know. We don't get emotionally involved in political issues the way you Americans do."

"That's right," added Martin. "We quietly and calmly weigh the platforms, then we go out and cast our ballots. That's exactly what we'll do in July when the Referendum comes up . . . "

He was interrupted by a loud siren, and both he and Jackson jumped to their feet, the latter explaining to Frank that they were members of the North Chadley Volunteer Fire Brigade. A moment later the telephone rang, and Martin's daughter rushed out of the kitchen to answer it.

"Dad! Mr. Jackson!" she shouted from the study. "It's the Café Québec Libre! They're trying to burn it down again!"

Chapter Three

Several people, including Frank Collins, watched as the volunteer firemen backed up their truck, unrolled a hose and doused the flames from a stack of papers and cardboard boxes piled against the wall at the back of the Café Québec Libre. Melting snow had prevented the fire from doing more than scorch the clapboard of the building, but the owner, an Amazonian woman with long, coal-black hair and eyes like burning embers, was in a righteous fury. Brandishing a rolling pin in one hand and a butcher knife the size of a claymore in the other, she was threatening the spectators, who retreated en masse each time she rushed forward a few steps.

"*Maudzite gang de têtes-carrés! Enfants de chiennes!*" she shouted in a voice which would have drowned out a rock band. "You wait! Soon we get rid of hall you Henglish *bâtards!*"

Like some enraged Scottish chieftain driving back the hordes of Sassanack invaders, she swung the butcher knife over her head, her tartan skirt and white apron swirling around thick, sturdy legs and her long hair whipping in the wind.

"*Fini! Caput! Toute-foké!*" she yelled.

Frank noticed that a large number of blue and white *fleur-de-lys* Quebec flags decorated the café, attached to the window sills, balconies and every other variation in the architecture. He also noticed that innkeeper Wilt Wadleigh, whose small hotel was directly behind the Québec Libre and was contrastingly decorated with red and white Canadian maple-leaf flags, was standing in his doorway with a large fire extinguisher. He had a smile on his face, however, and he seemed to be enjoying the spectacle.

Then something happened which struck Frank as rather strange, considering that Bill Martin was presumably an avowed, staunch federalist and the café owner was making no secret of her arch-separatist, anti-English feelings. Martin walked over to the screaming woman, whose rage had now expanded to include not only those who had tried to torch her café and the English-speaking residents of the town but the entire cross-section of the world's population contaminated by any trace of Anglo-Saxon blood, and she immediately put down her weapons and embraced him. As the other firemen rolled up the hose and shovelled the debris into garbage cans, Martin escorted the woman inside the café, and Frank, his curiosity whetted, followed them through the door.

Before long he was seated at a table drinking coffee with Martin, Wilt Wadleigh's French-Canadian wife, Lisette, the café owner herself, whose name turned out to be Clémentine, and a man called Giovanni, who was apparently Clémentine's assistant or perhaps her husband. The latter was wearing an apron and spoke to Frank briefly in fluent English. The rest of the conversation was in rapid Quebec French, and Frank had trouble following, but he soon gathered that Bill Martin and Clémentine were old acquaintances who had been brought up together in the largely French-speaking, working-class East End of Montreal. At one point Bill mentioned to the café owner that if she'd stop hanging Quebec flags, *OUI* Referendum posters and pictures of independentist politicians all over the inside and outside of her damned café, she would have less trouble with the local hotheads. She reacted by jumping up and pointing her finger at Lisette, shouting that she, Dame Clémentine, had more right to manifest that she was a true *Québécoise* than Wadleigh and his *"vendue"* woman had to fly the red banner of Canadian oppression outside their lousy little hotel and hang *NON* Referendum posters all over the inside to ruin their customers' appetites, when they had any customers.

Giovanni and Bill remained silent as the two women engaged in a shouting match, each accusing the other of treason, treachery, betrayal of her own people, slovenliness, sluttishness and the incapacity to cook a proper meal. Then Clémentine made a remark to Lisette which Frank was not sure he understood correctly. She seemed to accuse the younger woman of luring the "Arabs" to her inn by showing off her *"queue,"* which, so far as Frank knew, meant a tail. But whatever the meaning of the word, Lisette's face flushed, and she rose to her feet and headed for the door without replying. Frank could not help noting again how exquisitely shaped she was, with a trim waist yet a virtual cornucopia of hips and bust. She was not tall, but she projected a disproportionate sensual presence. It was as if, Frank mused, she had been designed by a demon, who had started off with the standard model then had titillated himself by adding extra flourishes in the strategic locations. Gazing at the retreating figure, the American anthropology student decided that there was no mystery about the considerable amount of intermarriage and cohabitation between the so-called English and French in Canada. A woman like Lisette could devastate any language barrier, to say the least.

Eventually Frank was properly introduced to Clémentine and Giovanni, who turned out to be her common-law husband. After finishing their coffee, he and Bill Martin left the café.

Back in his room a little later, looking over his notes and attempting to make sense of what he had witnessed during his first few hours in St-Alphonse de Chadley Nord, Frank Collins found himself scratching his head. The issues seemed clear enough—in about three months' time there was going to be a Referendum to decide whether Quebec would remain a province in the Canadian Confederation or become an independent nation. The wording of the Referendum question had not yet been announced by the Quebec Government, but presumably the people would be asked to vote "yes" or "no" as to whether or not Quebec should separate, accounting for the Separatist *"OUI"* posters and the Federalist *"NON"* posters. Theoretically the English were the Federalists and the French were Separatists. Obviously, however, some French Canadians, such as Wadleigh's wife, were Federalists, and some English speakers, Gordon Jackson for example, were Separatists, or at least supported the Separatist cause. Then there were all the people in-between, half French and half English like Bill Martin, or some other mixture like Giovanni, possibly the majority of the current population. Bill's attitudes were clear, but what about Giovanni and the others? Despite what Jackson and Martin had implied, Canadians, so far as Frank could determine, were hardly remaining calm and collected about the upcoming Referendum. Arson, threats, flags, posters, condemnations, two professors who were supposedly old friends coming within a hair of belting one another—and no doubt it would all get even more intense as the Referendum date drew closer. The lid could blow off. In fact, Frank speculated, if Canadian nationalism was as low-keyed and wishy-washy as he had been led to believe, the country may have little hope of surviving the crisis. The loss of the vast territory of Quebec, twice the size of Texas, situated right smack in the middle of the country, would split the rest of Canada into two widely separated parts, and Frank had read that parts of these parts, the western provinces, Newfoundland and the Maritimes, already had movements afoot to go it alone or to join the U.S.A. Perhaps, thought Frank, he may have arrived in Quebec at a historic moment, he may well be a witness to the nation's disintegration. But whatever the case, he was an outsider, a scholar with a research project to complete, and he would have to be careful not to become personally involved in the Battle of Canada. How Canadians chose to bugger one another was none of his business, except as an neutral observer.

With regard to what was Frank's business, the doctoral dissertation, he would first have to put together an account of the history of the area, which meant days or weeks of going over the town and county records, old newspaper files and everything else he could lay his hands on. He had already read a book called *The North Chadley Story,* written by an elderly lady, but it was a collection of reminiscences about her family and other people of consequence in her mind who used to spend their summers in the village rather than a proper historical study. Another elderly lady, Miss Jeannie McVicar, according to Bill Martin, who had lived in North Chadley all her life, was the person with the most information about the town. Frank knew she was a "Miss" because when Bill was telling him where she lived, he remarked, "Quite an old doll she is. Been engaged to Joe Larose for more than 50 years. Must be the longest marriage engagement in history."

Chapter Four

From the large veranda in front of the rambling old McVicar house it was possible to see the entire length of Lake Missawappi, and in the distance both the Green Mountains of Vermont and the White Mountains of New Hampshire. Frank Collins stood for a few moments enjoying the view and catching his breath after the long climb up a winding road almost to the crest of the hill. He did not want to be panting when he met Jeannie McVicar, because he had heard that although she was well into her seventies, she still walked down to the general store and back for her newspaper every day. As he gazed out over the white expanse broken by patches of dark brown leafless maples, oaks and walnuts and green cedars, spruce and pine, from the corner of his eye he noticed that he was being observed from behind the curtains, so he took a deep breath and knocked on the door. Jeannie McVicar was a tall, statuesque lady. She had a broad, handsome face with strong features and blue-green eyes, accentuated by the upsweep style of her white hair.

"How do you do, young man," she said, smiling as she held open the door.

"How do you do, Miss McVicar. My name is Frank Collins, and I'm a graduate student in Anthropology at Wayne . . ."

"Yes, I know."

"You do? But how . . ."

"In a small town like this everybody knows everything. Will you come in, Mr. Collins? I was just about to have a cup of tea and some scones with blackberry jam. My own blackberry jam, I might say. You've come just in time to join me."

"It would be a pleasure, Miss McVicar."

The spacious living room was graced with what Frank took to be antiques, including a spinning wheel, a loom, a wooden cradle and a grandfather clock. Frank almost dropped his hat when the clock struck a resounding bong which reverberated among the china figurines and silver trophy cups on top of the mantelpiece over the fireplace, also rattling the rows of dishes along an ornamental moulding high up the walls.

"Don't be alarmed, Mr. Collins," said Miss McVicar. "That's just the old clock. It actually belonged to my grandfather, and my father brought it over from Scotland 85 years ago. Joe keeps it going for me. He's marvellous with his hands, is my Joe."

"You mean Joe Larose?"

"Yes, of course. You'd never imagine it, he's such a big hulk of a man, but he also fixes wristwatches and plays the fiddle. You're quite a good-sized man yourself, aren't you? I'd better see if I can find some sandwiches and muffins to go with those scones."

"Please, Miss McVicar, don't go to any trouble for me."

"It's a pleasure, young man. I don't get many visitors away up here in the winter, you know."

As he settled into a comfortable, stuffed chair and his hostess served the afternoon tea, Frank noticed that she was wearing a diamond engagement ring, and since Jeannie McVicar was anything but shy and retiring, one compliment on his part was sufficient to elicit the whole story. She had indeed been engaged for almost 50 years, ever since Joseph Jean-Jacques Georges Larose, on bended knee as it was supposed to be done, proposed to her the night that the two of them won the ballroom dancing championship of Quebec in 1933. They were drinking champagne, compliments of the championship committee, in an elegant Montreal restaurant at the time, and it would have been highly inappropriate, Jeannie commented with a warm glow on her face, to reject the proposal and the ring.

"He was God's own handsome man," she said, "although his English was a little unpolished. It still is, I'm afraid. Poor Joe, he never did learn to read or write. But they say we made a good-looking couple on the dance floor."

Jeannie showed Frank the 1933 Championship trophy and a number of other cups and prizes on the mantelpiece above the huge, field-stone fireplace, where maple logs were crackling and radiating scented warmth into the living room. Then she dug out a photograph from a secretaire made of intricately inlaid walnut and rosewood. Elegantly beautiful in a ballroom gown which complimented her stately figure, with long, seemingly strawberry blond hair, Jeannie McVicar was in the outstretched arms of a man in a tuxedo with a mass of black, wavy hair and huge shoulders and chest.

"Joe was very strong," Jeannie remarked. "His father owned a woodlot just outside of town, and when he was only about ten or eleven years old, Joe used to go lumbering with his older brothers. Old Amos King—he's dead now, poor soul—who built most of the stone retaining walls you see around the village, used to hire Joe because he was the only fellow who could lift some of the stones. He learned to curse from Amos, I'm afraid. Curse in English, that is. But for a big, heavy man he was incredibly light on his feet. Danced like a leaf in the autumn wind, did Joe."

When Frank was fumbling for words to ask Jeannie why she and Joe had been so long engaged but had never gotten married, she divined what he wanted to know and provided a candid explanation.

"I had known Joe since I was a young girl and he used to come up here to do jobs for my father, such as building the rock garden out back. I used to love to watch him stripped to the waist. I'd hide behind the curtains in my bedroom upstairs. Then one night he showed up at the highschool dance. But the Laroses were Catholics, I mean Quebec Catholics. None of your watered-down English or American R.Cs. Quebec Catholics in those days, it was often said, were more Catholic than the Pope. Crucifixes, gory pictures of the Bleeding Heart on the walls, every living creature including the cats, dogs and canaries at mass on Sunday, Weeping-Jesus and Holy-Mary statues all over the place, ugly grottoes made of plaster and painted underwear pink on the front lawn."

"And I take it you were not Catholic," said Frank.

"To Joe's mother and father, we were known simply as Black Protestants." Jeannie then went on the explain that the McVicars were staunch Scottish Presbyterians, once again quite distinct from the pale variety in the United States and elsewhere. Predestination, original sin and depravity, the Doctrine of the Elect, Roman Catholics frying in hell, eternal damnation being too good for the majority of human beings and all the rest of it. Jeannie's uncle was actually an ordained "minister of the Kirk," who just before the turn of the century had been "called" from Scotland to serve three small congregations in Canada, one in North Chadley and the other two in nearby communities.

Her father, Angus, came over with his older brother. He had been an apprentice machinist in Scotland, and after exploring the possibilities in Brooke for awhile, he formed a partnership with a French-Canadian blacksmith named Louis Morin. Within a year the two of them had a thriving business, Morin and McVicar Machinery Inc., and Jeannie's father was able to bring his fiancée over from Scotland.

Just before Jeannie was born, Angus McVicar bought the house on the hill. Unfortunately, however, her mother died in childbirth. Her uncle Robert, the minister, moved in with his brother, and by the time Jeannie was in her teens, she had taken over the housekeeping for both men.

When Jeannie and Joe were engaged, his parents were already in their sixties, the Reverend McVicar had retired except for preaching guest sermons to keep the devil at bay, and her father was close to retirement.

"So Joe and I decided to keep the fact that we were engaged to ourselves," Jeannie continued, "until his parents and Uncle Bob died. We were afraid that to make the announcement would wipe out the whole lot of them prematurely. The Laroses did pass on within the next five or six years, but Dad lived till 75, and Uncle Bob didn't die until 20 years ago. He was 88 years old."

"And why didn't you and Joe get married then?" asked Frank.

"Habit, I guess," replied Jeannie, gazing at the fireplace. "We had gotten so used to doing things on the sly, as it were, that we just kept on, and the years passed. You know, my Uncle Bob never knew that I was a ballroom dancer. He was dead set against dancing of course."

"Wouldn't he have read about the championship in

the newspapers?"

"He never read newspapers. The only books he ever read are in that little bookcase over there."

Frank got up and stepped over to the bookcase. It contained a huge, leather bound Bible lying on its side, a concordance to the Bible, a copy of something called the *Westminster Confession,* John Bunyan's *Pilgrim's Progress,* an old dictionary, two histories of Scotland, *The Works of John Knox* edited by Laing, John Knox's *Historie of the Reformation of Religion within the Realme of Scotland* and Muir's *John Knox: Portrait of a Calvinist.*

"A little heavy on the Knox," observed Frank. "You mean these are the only books your uncle ever read?"

"The only ones I ever saw him read."

"What about Robert Burns and Walter Scott? I thought they were the great favourites among the Scots."

"To Uncle Bob, Walter Scott was frivolous. I found that out when I had to read *Rob Roy* for school. Scott wrote romances instead of dealing with serious matters and fundamental truths. And Burns—well so far as Uncle Bob was concerned, Burns was a degenerate womanizer who was even forced to sit on the stool of repentance several times."

"Forced to sit on what?"

"The stool of repentance. In the churches of Scotland, they used to have a stool up near the pulpit. Anyone caught sinning—and in those days, just about everything apart from breathing, working hard and praying was a sin—would be forced to sit on it during the sermon as an example to the congregation."

"Something like the scarlet letters of the New England Puritans."

"Yes, along those lines. People who take religion too

strictly can be very cruel, I'm afraid."

Jeannie became more and more talkative as the afternoon advanced, especially after the refreshments graduated to a second course of excellent sherry and Scottish shortbread. Frank was beginning to feel quite at home in the old McVicar house, fetching logs for the fire from the back shed, sprawling in the comfortable stuffed chair, and having to do nothing more than make a remark now and again to maintain the flow of local information.

Mentioning that the opportunities for young people must be somewhat limited in such a small town as North Chadley, he learned about the notorious Elspeth Parker, and by the time the story was over he was both fascinated to meet the woman and apprehensive that their paths might cross. Elspeth apparently had the morals of an alley cat, but without the feline restrictions to periods of heat and creatures of the opposite sex. She also apparently had weak genes. Each of her five children was the spit and image of its father, and each of the five fathers, including one of the town's four current clergymen, according to Jeannie, was a local man with highly distinctive physical features. Henry Ralston, for example, had an outsized forehead, and Mel Carson had a shock of flaming red hair. Yet somehow Elspeth had managed to stick two different men for the support of the same child and three others for support of another of her offspring. At the same time, she was also collecting both unemployment insurance and social welfare cheques while working full time as a cleaning woman for a well-heeled lady from New York City. Before long, however, she had modified her status from housekeeper to the American woman's lover. A "wee besom of unusual flexibility," in Jeannie's words, and a talent for milking the Canadian system of social benefits as well as anything else within striking distance. Elspeth was at the moment vacationing with her latest conquest on the beaches of the balmy Caribbean Islands.

Skill at wheeling and dealing combined with total innocence of stifling inhibitions in personal relations seemed to run in the Parker family. Elpeth's cousin, Wyoming Parker, used to operate the local garage on a lease from the owner. He was a big, sloppy, jovial man with unruly blond curls who had manifestly fathered Elspeth's first child, who had himself now grown into a big, sloppy, jovial youth with unruly blond curls. But Elspeth had not troubled Wyoming for child support, commented Jeannie, because, after all, he was family. She nailed old Ned Barton, the town accountant, for that one, and rightly so, because a presumably respectable professional man of his age should not have been fooling around with a sixteen-year-old girl and even buying her fancy lace underthings, which she brazenly hung out on the clothesline behind the Parker hovel for all the world to see.

The baptism of the baby, which Jeannie attended as president of the Village Improvement Society, caused a bit of a commotion in the Anglican church, she told Frank. The minister, a rather stuffy Englishman, the Reverend Barnabas Buxton of St. Bartholomew's, at first refused to perform the rite, but he was persuaded to do so by a couple of the lady parishioners, in the interests of town propriety and the salvation of the innocent infant's soul. He took exception, however, to Elspeth's wish to call her baby Chuck.

"You mean Charles?" he asked the young mother.

"No way, Rev," she replied. "Just plain Chuck."

"But Chuck is merely a diminutive of Charles.

Therefore, young woman, you wish to have this child baptised Charles."

"No goddamned way, Rev. I detest Charles. Chuck it is."

"But my dear young woman, Chuck is not a legitimate name."

"Well this little runt's not a legitimate baby. So let's get the show on the road, your holiness."

And Elspeth, in her usual perverse way, prevailed over the flabbergasted clergyman. Her cousin Wyoming, however, was eventually obliged to leave town. He got to be too much for North Chadley. Everyone had warned Professor Jackson, a perfect gentleman, that it was a mistake to leave his nearly new radial tires at Wyoming's garage when the latter offered to store them after installing snow tires on Jackson's car, but Jackson had just arrived from Ontario and was a trusting soul.

"What tires?" Wyoming Parker had responded with his look of incomprehension and his wide, boyish grin when Jackson inquired in the spring.

But the final straw, to Jeannie McVicar's mind, was the Christmas tree which Wyoming sold to Mr. Reginald Richmond, a retired businessman who was probably the richest and most influential man in town. Mr. Richmond didn't like any of the trees Wyoming had for sale when he arrived at the door a few days before Christmas Day. The old man explained that he was having his family visit for the holidays and that he wanted a perfectly shaped Norwegian spruce, like the ones in the terraced garden behind his house. Later that night Wyoming came back, and this time he had a perfectly shaped Norwegian spruce. Delighted, Mr. Richmond paid him double the usual price for the tree to compensate for the time he had spent scouring the bush in deep snow. It was not until the following spring, when old Richmond went out to his back garden to look at the crocuses, that he noticed a sawed-off stump where his favourite spruce used to be. That afternoon he bought the garage which Wyoming operated, and the next day it was being run by Ed Wilson.

Before Frank left, Jeannie McVicar told him about a mysterious gentleman who had bought the old Buckley property next to hers and was making her repeated offers for her own place.

"He's some kind of Arab," said Jeannie. "Says he's a businessman into high technology and the like. But I don't know. I find him a trifle arrogant and aggressive."

"You're not thinking of selling, are you, Miss McVicar?"

"No, of course not. I have everything I need here. But I do find it a bit strange that this Arab fellow should be wanting to buy so many properties. Joe tells me he's having a huge house built on land he owns down the lake, a couple of miles outside of town. Now what do you suppose he's up to, Mr. Collins?"

"I have no idea, Miss McVicar. But if ever I get a chance to talk to him, I'll try to find out."

"Yes, I wish you would do that. Then be sure to let me know."

Frank got to meet the mysterious Arab sooner than he might have expected. Passing by the Café Québec Libre on the way back to his room, he saw a chauffeur-driven dark-green limousine parked by the door. Frank walked on by, noting that the chauffeur, whose swarthy complexion suggested that he could well be Arabic, was ogling a girlie magazine tucked inside a newspaper. Frank continued a few paces, then telling himself that after all it was a public café, he let his curiosity get the best of him, turned around and entered the Québec Libre.

Clémentine was standing by the kitchen door with her hands on her hefty hips, while Giovanni stood a little behind her. The Arab gentleman, as Jeannie McVicar had referred to him, certainly looked every inch a gentleman. Dressed in a perfectly fitting, three-piece, dark-brown suit, he was a slim, darkly handsome man not much older than Frank, with a large emerald ring on his index finger.

Frank's attention, however, was soon drawn away from the businessman to his blonde secretary, a rather stern-looking woman in school-marmish glasses, wearing a trim jacket-and-skirt ensemble almost like a uniform. There was a luster about her hair which made its flaxen colour look natural, even though she had it tied up in a bun. She had slim ankles, Frank noted, and her lips, accentuated by a hint of lipstick, were somewhat incongruously sensuous. In fact, despite the general propriety of her appearance, the Arab's secretary was to Frank's mind quite a captivating lady, one he might well be interested in getting to know.

As Frank sat down at one of the tables, the Arab shrugged his shoulders and turned to leave the café. On his way out he gave Frank a penetrating glance, but the blonde secretary was putting away her note pad in her purse and did not seem to notice Frank at all. In the next few minutes Clémentine explained, talking to Frank in accented but fluent English, that Monsieur Gabib, as she called him, wanted to buy her café. He was also trying to get Wadleigh's Inn, the gas station and the hardware store, and he already owned the marina. Maybe it was a good thing, Clémentine speculated with a wide grin, because it would get rid of a few of the *maudzits*

Anglais. She herself would never sell her café, but an *Anglais* would sell anything if the price was right. Wadleigh for sure would be selling the Inn as soon as the numbers were to his liking, and no doubt he would throw in his sex-pot wife besides, if the Arab upped the offer enough. Which quite likely he would if Lisette kept wiggling her outsized *queue* right under his nose.

When Frank inquired about Gabib's secretary, Clémentine dismissed her as an *Anglaise divorcée*, as cold as a witch's tit, who had no time for anything except her job and her three kids. Musing that a full-time job and three kids would be more than enough to keep anyone busy, Frank took his leave, but once again his return to his room was interrupted. To his astonishment, as he passed by the door of the bar-salon, he heard what seemed unmistakably to be Elvis Presley belting out "Blue Suede Shoes." But he knew that the Inn did not have a juke box or sound system of any sort. There was a small raised platform in one corner of the room where a guitar player occasionally entertained on Saturday nights.

Frank walked through the door and stopped in his tracks as he looked upon what appeared to be a reincarnation of the late, famed singer performing on the small platform. The distinctive face and sideburns, the gyrating hips, the gaudy costume, the ornate guitar—the resemblance was uncanny. Frank stared, mesmerized, until the number ended. The singer then leaned his guitar against the wall and came over to the bar, where Lisette smiled and handed him a bottle of beer.

Noticing Frank, Lisette reached into the refrigerator and brought out another bottle of beer. Then she introduced him to her brother, Danny, adding that he made his living doing imitations of Elvis Presley.

"Elvis was incredibly popular in Quebec," she said. "We hold the championship. Quebeckers bought more Elvis records than any other group in the world."

"Really?" said Frank, still staring at Danny.

"He does look a lot like Elvis, doesn't he?" Lisette continued. Frank thought that he saw her wink at her brother as she spoke.

"I'll say he does. It's amazing."

"Danny played the part in the movie on Presley's life."

"I can understand why. Do you come here often, Danny?"

"Only when I find out that my brother-in-law is away. I'm afraid that he and I don't get along too well."

When Frank finally got back to his room, the black cat was waiting for him by the door. He had bought more milk and cat food during the day, just in case she did show up again. After she had had her fill, she spent a few minutes preening herself, and Frank noticed that she no longer looked scruffy. Her stomach was still bloated, but with her now glowing black fur and yellow eyes like a pair of piercing fog lights, she resembled a miniature black panther. She jumped on the bed for him to pet her, purring a raucous appreciation, then curled up in the open suitcase.

Chapter Five

After his long conversation with Jeannie McVicar, Frank Collins decided to spend a few days researching the history of St-Alphonse de Chadley Nord in the archives of the Brooke Historical Society, the county Records Office and the microfilm files of local newspapers in the library of l'Université de Brooke. His enthusiasm had been especially spurred by a few remarks Jeannie had made about the American connection, that Jefferson Davis, for instance, President of the Confederate States, had once spent some time in the vicinity and that Confederate soldiers had established local bases from which to launch hit-and-run attacks over the border against St. Albans and other unsuspecting, presumably remote-from-the-front-line towns in Yankee Vermont during the U.S. Civil War.

Jeannie had also mentioned the Fenians, a fanatical Irish group in the U.S. who were obsessed with the notion of liberating Ireland by capturing Canada, then forcing some kind of exchange with Great Britain, presuming that London really gave a damn about Canada. Recruited in the teeming Irish ghettos of Boston, New York and other American cities, sporadically supported by riotous fund-raising rallies at Hibernian Halls across the U.S., literally thousands of displaced Irish patriots had nipped at the Canadian border. A typical encounter, according to Jeannie, was the "Battle of Goodwin's Gulch." The attack was supposed to be a surprise, but the Fenians had been congregating at the border town of Horton's Mill for two weeks previously, demolishing heroic quantities of booze, which had to be brought from the Canadian side when American supplies ran out, dancing jigs in the street, singing sentimental songs about the "Auld Sod," flying a Republic of Ireland flag which had been sewn by the Irish ladies of Ryan's Mill, Massachusetts, skirmishing with the local men and doing their best to molest the Yankee ladies of Horton's Mill.

The Canadians, of course, were fully aware of what was happening, but no one knew quite what to do about it. Since the U.S. Government had passed the Neutrality Act, forbidding any citizen to take up arms against a friendly nation not at war with the U.S., it was hoped that the American authorities would eventually disperse the boisterous members of the Fenian Brotherhood. But according to one newspaper report Frank read, the American authorities, namely the county sheriff and his two or three deputies, did not know what to do either.

When the news came that 500 or more Fenians had finally stumbled across the border and were heading in the general direction of Brooke, brandishing a large green flag with a sunburst and a golden harp, and had already stolen two horses and a half-dozen chickens, Canadian officials obviously had to do something. They summoned the only group resembling a military unit in the region, the cadet corps of a private boys' academy. Up the road to Brooke, Jeannie told Frank, staggered the Fenians, and down the road to meet them marched the cadets, carrying old muskets ordinarily used for drills. Night was falling by the time the two opposing forces entered Goodwin's Gulch.

The captain of the cadet corps ordered his boys to load their muskets, which they all tried their best to do. But when they began to move forward toward the enemy, who were now judiciously marking time, one cadet tripped and dropped his musket. As the resulting explosion echoed through the darkening gulch, apparently both the cadets and the Fenians turned and ran for their lives. By the afternoon of the following day, the two stolen horses had found their way back to their owner's farm, the Fenian leaders had been arrested by a beefed-up sheriff's posse, the rest of the Brotherhood were on trains back to Boston and New York, the cadet corps of the private academy had become the first such corps in Canada to receive battle ribbons, and all that was left of the six chickens were the bones and the feathers.

Frank Collins discovered in his research that the Eastern Townships of Quebec had not been settled by United Empire Loyalists, as seemed to be commonly believed, but mainly by simple squatters from the more densely populated regions of New England. What happened to the original Missawappi First Nations people was something of a mystery. They had been there, participating in raids and having their own villages razed to the ground in the customary manner during the struggle for control of their land between the British and French, then between the British and Americans. According to Frank's sources, the survivors of these skirmishes either succumbed to the various diseases imported from European centers of civilization, or were assimilated, or else wandered off to join the remnants of other tribes in reservations in the North. One small reservation of Missawappi Indians did reportedly exist on the south shore of the St. Lawrence River. In none of the documents consulted by Frank was there any mention of treaties with the Missawappis or of land purchases. He found a few references to village sites, including that of North Chadley at the outlet of Lake Missawappi, then nothing. Thus the original inhabitants of the Eastern Townships of Quebec, who had been caught in the middle and decimated as the white colonizers fought among themselves and recruited Indian allies to collect enemy scalps and do most of their dirty work, would not be around, Frank mused, for the latest confrontation over their former territory, the battle to separate French and English Canada.

American squatters had settled in North Chadley before the end of the 18th Century, and it seems that they were less than enthusiastic supporters of the British colonial regime. One Taylor Wadleigh, no doubt an ancestor of the current innkeeper, Frank speculated, was even arrested and sent to prison in Montreal for supporting Papineau and Nelson and their so-called *"Patriotes"* during the Rebellion of 1837, a popular uprising against the appointed and often corrupt British governing authorities.

By the middle of the 19th Century, the Missawappi Valley Railroad had been built, linking the tiny settlement of North Chadley with the Grand Trunk Railroad between Montreal and Portland, Maine, and with the Connecticut and Passumpic Railroad into the population centers of the U.S. eastern seaboard. North Chadley then became conveniently accessible to Americans. Frank's sources indicated that Lake Missawappi, with its deep, clear waters teeming with perch, trout, bass, salmon and gigantic sturgeon, was "discovered" by a doctor from Baltimore, Powhatan Clark, in 1886. By 1895 the summer colony consisted of two dozen well-to-do families from the sweltering cities of the American South, including the Atkinsons, founders of the Coca-Cola Company, who arrived in style each summer in their private railway cars. Frank was amused to read one account of the incursions of Southerners which claimed that they closed the curtains in their railway cars while passing through New England so that they would not have to look at Yankee territory. Other accounts explained one of Jeannie McVicar's remarks which had mystified the Anthropology student. She had said that her clergyman uncle used to grieve constantly about the ungodly emotionalism of the Black people in the North Chadley Baptist Church, how they pranced and wiggled and sang and shouted "Yeah Lord" and "Sweet Jesus" during religious services. These African-Americans, Frank concluded, were the servants who came north with the wealthy American families. They had been birds of passage.

Many of the large clapboard houses in North Chadley, painted white and ornamented by green, blue or yellow shutters, with lofty ceilings and spacious verandas, had thus been built by Americans, or at least to the specifications of summer visitors from the U.S. And as innkeeper Wadleigh had told Frank, they were indeed perched on cedar posts and had no insulation, indifferent to the cold realities of the Canadian winter. As time went on and the road systems improved in the U.S., while concurrently the railroads were allowed to deteriorate, many of the original American owners sold to Canadians from Brooke, Montreal, and even Toronto, who proceeded to dig out basements, install furnaces, add double windows, and insulate, to winterize their homes.

Meanwhile North Chadley developed into a thriving summer resort, and the local people soon learned to provide the required services, or if not exactly required, then presumably desired. Four steamboats offered excursions and moonlight cruises on the lake. Five hotels were built, with casinos, bowling alleys, poolrooms, golf courses, tennis courts, riding stables and bathhouses on the lakeshore. In the large rooming house which would eventually become a pottery, the Misses Maloy, aided and abetted by several other accommodating young misses, provided a specialized service which, according to Jeannie McVicar, inspired her Uncle Robert's most awesome sermons, sparkling with such resounding ecclesiastical phrases as "great whores of Babylon," and "fleshpots of Sodom and Gomorrah." The Misses Maloy, however, were Roman Catholics and therefore were deprived of the benefits of Reverend McVicar's exhortations on their behalf.

Reflecting on the town's history, Frank Collins could easily see why Wilt Wadleigh was so disappointed with the current state of St-Alphonse de Chadley Nord. The town simply was not as lively and profitable as it used to be. Frank, in fact, was the only guest at Wadleigh's hotel. The innkeeper was nevertheless determined, he confided to Frank, to become a millionaire before the age of 35, whatever he had to do, and he had a number of schemes in mind. The last townsperson to make real money, according to Wadleigh, was his grandfather, who had divided up his farm on the hillside into lots, each with a separate 21 feet of lakefront down below. And even though he set the condition that buyers sign an agreement never to keep hogs, the lots were sold, because most of the buyers were retired professionals interested mainly in peace, quiet, and privacy. By then the majority of the summer people were also aging, the professors from l'Université de Brooke were beginning to trickle into town, and the French had arrived to take the various available service jobs. His grandfather, Wadleigh added, once everything was sold, had headed for Naples, Florida, with all five of the girls who worked for the Maloy sisters and was never heard of again. At least not until he died and Wilt's father and two uncles began battling over the last will and testament. "But what a way to go, eh?" Wilt had muttered wistfully.

After three weeks of reading, checking records and talking to various people in town, Frank decided that he had a fairly good idea of the history of North Chadley. It had been the site of an Indian village without doubt— during dry spells when the water level of Lake Missawappi fell a few feet, artifacts such as arrowheads, flint knives, and fragments of earthenware pots, could still be found in the exposed mud along the shore. Squatters from New England arrived toward the end of the 18th Century, by which time the Indians had largely disappeared. The attraction of the site was that a grist mill could be built on the river draining the lake, and the first name used by the Yankee settlers was "The Outlet." Half the working people in the current town—carpenters, mechanics, plumbers, gardeners, roofers, painters and such—could trace their ancestry back to these American pioneers. The other half of the working people were French Canadians who had been attracted when the town was at the peak of its prosperity. Readily finding jobs at the hotels, on the steamboats, or as handymen and maids for the wealthier townsfolk, they built Quebec-style houses along the river. Although clapboard-sided like the American houses, these homes were rectangular rather than square, smaller and narrower, with relatively tiny verandas in front, and more sharply sloped roofs to avoid the build-up of snow which required the residents of hillside houses to have the snow removed several times a winter. The houses built by the French-Canadian newcomers, moreover, were painted a variety of flamboyant colours—pink, blue, turquoise, yellow—in contrast to the uniform, pristine white of the older homes.

The colour contrast between the French and English houses, Wilt Wadleigh pointed out to Frank with his usual chuckle, was the same as that between the underwear worn respectively by French and English girls, but Frank felt that he was unfortunately in no position to evaluate the accuracy of this observation, given the parameters of his research project and the fact that electric dryers had now generally replaced clotheslines.

Apart from the working people who provided the services in town, the population of North Chadley now consisted mainly of retirees and professionals such as professors, doctors, and lawyers, about half French-speaking and half English-speaking and three-quarters bilingual, who commuted to and from their places of employment in the nearby city of Brooke.

There were also a few oddballs, Frank learned. He had met a cleaning woman called Margery Miller, a divorcée in her sixties, who quite regularly stopped by the bar of the Inn after she finished her day's work, at about the same time that Frank took a break from his research. She was a compulsive talker, dedicated to the dissemination of information, notably the juicier bits of local gossip. After Frank had bought her a gin and tonic on a couple of afternoons, she had come to regard him with special affection. When she learned that he was engaged in research on the evolution of North Chadley, her enthusiasm was boundless, and she told him that in the interests of "real high-falutin research," she felt duty-bound to tell him all she knew, which was a "damn sight more than a lot of other people." She had herself, she confessed, often thought about writing the story of North Chadley, but since she didn't have enough schooling to write properly, she would content herself by making sure that Frank got everything right. When Marge was talking, he occasionally took out his notebook and wrote in it, which never failed mightily to impress her. He soon came to recognize that when she bent over the table and lowered her voice, he should brace himself for dirty details about one villager or another.

Yet Frank was somewhat startled when Margery bent over the table, lowered her voice and got around to telling him about Wilt Wadleigh's wife, Lisette, a hard-working, congenial young woman whom he had come to like and respect. He also, of course, admired her physique, and he found his eyes drawn as if by a powerful magnetic force to her bulbous rump and exquisitely-shaped legs every time she strode through the bar-salon in her high-heeled shoes, holding up a tray of glasses and dishes. He repeatedly marvelled that such a tiny waist could explode into such round, firm, generous hips, and he was even toying with the idea of one day conducting a scientific analysis of the body structures of French-Canadian women, with perhaps an annex on the diabolical accentuation effected by high-heeled shoes. One afternoon in the bar he had overheard two truck drivers comment on Lisette. The peculiar hybrid Quebec expression one of them had used was *"ben-stackée,"* and that expression often popped into his mind when he looked at the innkeeper's lady. She was in fact heading for the kitchen, and he was looking, when Margery Miller bent over the table.

"Pity about them two," she said in a low voice as

soon as Lisette was out of sight.

"What two?" asked Frank.

"Wilt and his wife. It ain't what you'd call a proper marriage, you know. Being as how they both look like movie stars, you'd think they'd be a perfect match, wouldn't you? It's a pity."

"Well, I have noticed that he dominates her quite a bit. She works hard. But he does push her around."

"Wouldn't you if your wife was cheating on you? Though I'm sure he doesn't know about it. And with his own cousin besides."

"What do you mean, Marge?"

"And he's such a nice boy, is Wilt. I knew his mother well, you know. They finally had to put the poor soul away in the loony bin up to Montreal, but she had a heart of gold, did Lucy."

"But Marge, I can't imagine a woman like Lisette..."

"Well I *know,* Frank. Because I clean for that weirdo Morton Wadleigh one afternoon a week. He's Wilt's cousin, and he's something else, I'm telling you. The lights are on, but there's nobody home. He inherited a pile of money from his grandfather on his mother's side, and he went to college and got all kinds of degrees, and everybody figured he was a genius. And do you know what he does? He says he's an artist and an inventor, but he just sits around that house 24 hours a day. A man 50 years old or more, with all that education and money, and so far as I know he hasn't done a damn thing 'cept collect gloves."

"Collect what?" asked Frank, leaning toward Margery now.

"I saw it with my own eyes. He had an old trunk in his bedroom that he usually keeps locked. But one day when I was changing the sheets on his bed—you know, he's got one of them king-sized beds, and he sleeps in it all by himself, and it's a damn hard job to change the sheets on a bed that size. Anyway, I notice that he's left the trunk unlocked. So I take a quick peek, figuring that there might be sheets and blankets, maybe even pillow slips in that trunk, and what do I see? I tell you, Frank, he's something else, that Morton."

"And what *did* you see, Marge?"

"What do I see? Well I'll tell you what I see. I see a whole pile of long white gloves, the kind that reach right up to the elbow, like fancy women used to wear in the old days. And there's also a bunch of dirty pictures."

"Dirty pictures?"

"Pictures of naked women. But I didn't get more than a glance at them, because he came back to the room and locked the trunk. 'Gotta guard my treasures,' he says. Them were his very words. Treasures? Long white gloves? Now don't you figure that's a bit weird for a man who lives like a damn hermit in a cave and don't do nothing?"

"Maybe it's a fetish of some sort."

"A what?"

"A fetish. Some people become obsessed with certain objects. Hats maybe, or shoes. Underwear is quite common. Usually a fetish is quite harmless. It's simply an oddball way of getting your kicks."

"Well there ain't nothing oddball about the way Morton gets his kicks. Nothing unusual at all. Same old way men've been doing it since they climbed down out of the trees."

"What do you mean, Marge?"

"I mean he pays Lisette."

"You mean she . . . uh . . . sells herself to. . . ."

"That's exactly what I mean. She goes over there

once a month or so, maybe more. Twice she arrived before I had finished cleaning up the place. The mess he makes, you can't just sort it out in ten minutes, you know."

"But Marge, just because she visits her husband's cousin once in a while doesn't mean. . . ."

"Listen, Frank, I *know*. One time just before she come over, I'm dusting off his desk, and do you know what I see? A cheque made out to Lisette Wadleigh for $100. Now why do you figure he'd be paying her $100? For whistling Dixie? For baking bran muffins? And me that scrubs his floors on my hands and knees and does his dirty laundry and shovels out his pigsty of a kitchen, do you know what he pays me? A lousy $12 for half a day. Not half an hour, mind you, half a day. It's not easy for decent folk to make a decent living, let me tell you. A woman can rake in a hell of a lot more laying on her back in a kind-sized bed than scrubbing a hardwood floor on her hands and knees. As soon as I win the lotto, I'll never scrub another floor. That's for sure."

"Still, Marge, what you've told me doesn't necessarily mean that Lisette. . . ."

Margery leaned over a little closer to Frank and cast a glance toward the kitchen door. "I *saw* her, Frank," she said in a low voice. "I saw her with my own eyes. One time I had to go back because I forgot my cigarettes. The price of smokes these days, you can't afford to leave them anywhere, you know. And I hear they'll be going up again soon. It's a damn shame the way they make us pay an arm and a leg for the only simple pleasure. . . ."

"And what exactly did you see, Marge?" interrupted Frank.

"Well, as I was saying, I had to go back there for my

cigarettes, and I just happen to look through the living-room window before I knock on the door. There's a big veranda in front of the house, you know, and you have to walk right past the living-room window to get to the door."

"I know. And what did you see?"

"I see that Lisette Wadleigh standing there in the middle of the living room as sure as the Lord made little green apples. And I swear she was as naked as the day she was born."

"No kidding?"

"Without a word of a lie, Frank. Standing right there in the middle of the living room she was, as brazen as a bantam hen, and not wearing a stitch."

"Really? Completely nude?"

"Well she may have had on a pair of those little bikini underwear. But that's not really wearing anything. It's terrible the underwear they sell these days. I mean, why bother wearing anything at all? And oh yeah, I nearly forgot. She had on a pair of those long white gloves. From the trunk I told you about."

"Long white gloves," Frank repeated, glancing toward the kitchen door.

"I tell you, Frank, I couldn't believe my eyes. Her a married woman with a fine, handsome husband and all. Of course, her mother was even worse, you know. Madie was her name. She was one of them strip-teasers. Used to dance in Montreal and some place in the States. Only she didn't just tease men. A fellow over to the Legion used to tell about how one time she went to a military base called Goose Bay, away off in the bush in Labrador with about 2,000 men stationed there. He says she stayed for a week and came back with $10,000. But you know, Frank, the French ain't got the same morals like we got. It's a well-known fact."

"But on the night you were talking about, Marge, what about Morton? What was he doing while Lisette was standing there?"

"Well right then he was just sitting in a chair staring at her with a silly grin on his face. But. . . ."

As Lisette finally emerged from the kitchen, Margery Miller sat up in her chair and started talking about the weather. Frank gazed at the young woman with new wonder, shaking his head slightly. The words *"ben stackée"* rang in his head, accompanied now by involuntary phantasms of pink flesh and long white gloves.

Back in his room, Frank fed the black cat, which had now clearly decided to settle in with him. He called her Mirabel, after the huge airport north of Montreal which was commonly considered to be a white elephant. It was appropriate, he amused himself by thinking, that a black feline which was a white elephant so far as he was concerned should be called Mirabel. Besides, the name had a melodious ring to it. He wondered if perhaps he might be overfeeding his uninvited guest, since she seemed to be getting fatter and fatter, and although she had the admirable habit of scratching at the door when she wanted to go out, presumably to relieve herself, she now was usually back at the door within a minute or two, and she seemed content to spend most of her time in his suitcase. Frank wondered what his dissertation director back in Detroit would say if he found out that his student was spending a good bit of his field-work time in Quebec operating a cat house.

Chapter Six

Frank Collins met his first certified, full-blooded Separatists, not counting Clémentine and possibly Gordon Jackson, when he dropped in at the Café Québec Libre one afternoon for a coffee and a couple of Clémentine's delicious maple doughnuts, which he had discovered would evoke pleasant memories of his childhood and grandpoppa. Three men and a woman were talking animatedly with the café owner as Frank entered the door, but they stopped abruptly and cast caustic stares at the large newcomer. Frank felt decidedly uncomfortable, as if he had stumbled into an occupied women's washroom by mistake, but as soon as the jovial café owner introduced him as an American graduate student come to do research in Quebec, the hostile expressions on the faces dissolved. The four people rushed over to shake Frank's hand and identify themselves.

The oldest, a slightly built, white-haired man with thick glasses, was a dean from l'Université de Brooke, Michel Bertrand. He was, he told Frank, the chairman of the local OUI Committee, one of many such committees set up across the province to politicize the population and to make sure that everyone would do the right thing and vote for independence from Canada. The second man, Marcel Tremblay, about forty years old with a great stack of frizzy brown hair, was a Brooke professor of sociology who lived in St-Alphonse. The third man, a ferocious-looking individual with a black beard and moustache who was almost as big as Frank, described himself simply as a "party militant."

The lady was Marie-Ange Monet, "a woman of a certain age," as Frank had heard it put in French, whose residual beauty was locked in a struggle with pounds of bulging blubber. Within moments she managed to communicate to him that she was a Paris-born French professor who had begun her career back home teaching his compatriots, namely Americans posted to France, that she was divorced, that she lived in town alone, that there were many things which she could teach a young American such as himself, and that he was more than welcome to come up and see her some time.

The four members of the OUI Committee sat down at the table with Frank as Clémentine brought him his coffee and doughnuts. Bertrand and Tremblay spoke fluent English, and although, as they explained, they had both sworn never to speak the English language again, that vow applied only in the company of English Canadians. They seemed determined to seize upon the opportunity of the American anthropology student's presence to explain the Separatist cause to the United States of America. For her part, Madame Monet seemed determined merely to seize the American. Neither she nor the blackbeard had any problem with vows, since neither could speak much English. They nodded as the two older men did the talking, and Marie-Ange Monet, who had seated herself by Frank's side, simultaneously lent emphasis and distraction to the main points by periodically clutching his muscular thigh.

"We intend to do precisely what you Americans did in 1776," said Michel Bertrand, "and for many of the same reasons. For 200 years now we have been abused and exploited by the English. . . ."

At this point the black-bearded man grunted "*mau-*

dzits Anglais," a Québec expression which Frank knew was similar to "Damned Yankee," and which, repeated whenever the word English was uttered, would be the blackbeard's principal contribution to the conversation.

"For the French of Canada," Dean Bertrand continued, "Confederation has meant the institutionalization of an inferior status. We have been the hewers of wood and the drawers of water. Our language, our unique culture, our religion have been veritably in a state of siege."

"Did you know," interjected Tremblay, "that right here in the Province of Québec the average salary for francophones was eleven percent lower than that for anglophones?

Did you know, *mon ami,* that any French Canadian who hoped to rise above the level of common labourer in the workforce right here in French Canada had to learn English? Even the common labourer had to know enough English to understand the foreman. That's why the slang of the working people, which is sometimes called *'joual,'* has deformed expressions such as *'une jobbe steadee, le boss, watch out, l'overtime, l'union, toute foké'* and so on. The language has been contaminated and brutalized."

"That's why," added Bertrand, "it is essential that we liberate Québec before it is too late, before there is nothing left to preserve. We have to purify our culture, eliminate the extraneous and contaminating elements. Take Montreal, for example. It is an appalling disgrace, a hodge-podge of Japanese cameras, German cars, Chinese and Italian restaurants, clothes from Korea and Taiwan, McDonald's, *Poulet frit à la Kentucky,* British scotch, Irish pubs, Greek and Portuguese wine, Jewish bagels and smoked meat, Danish pastries. A visitor can have no idea that he is in *l'État de Québec."*

"But would separating Québec from Canada change that?" ventured Frank.

"*Bien entendu.* Of course it would," said Bertrand. "All these things have happened because the English have been in charge of Quebec ever since the Conquest. The real control has been in the hands of a small Anglophone minority, people with absolutely no interest in our culture. Nor in their own, for that matter."

"You can find them all in the late afternoon having cocktails at the St. James Club in Montreal," Tremblay remarked.

"Some sort of private association?" asked Frank.

"*Mais oui,*" replied Tremblay, "very elite, very exclusive, very English."

"You mean that French Canadians are barred, like Jews and Blacks used to be from a lot of organizations in the United States?"

"No, not exactly. There are French-Canadian members. But they are worse than the English. They are not true Québécois, they are the '*Vendus.*' How do you say it—Sold-outs?"

Frank nodded.

"We have nothing against the English, you understand," said Bertrand. "But they are not like us. They are single-minded, ruthless, cold, interested only in making money. Even when they marry, they marry uniquely for money. They have no sense of beauty, charm, finesse, taste. Every year they hold a big debutantes' ball at the Ritz Carlton Hotel in Montreal, and you should see those young women—large, awkward creatures with long horse faces and large horse teeth. No wonder English bosses all have Québécoise secretaries and divans in their private offices."

"But surely, Monsieur Bertrand," said Frank,

"you're talking about a tiny proportion of the English elite. What about all the. . . ."

"They're all the same," interrupted Tremblay. "It's what we call '*la mentalité anglo-saxonne,*' and it is an alien, ugly thing that has been imposed upon us too long. The time has come, *mon ami,* for us to make our declaration of independence, just as you Americans did some 200 years ago."

"*Maudzits Américains,*" muttered the blackbeard by way of variation.

"*Non, non!*" Bertrand quickly remonstrated, waving the comment away with both hands. "We love the Americans. We have profound admiration for the United States, and at the moment we wish to imitate American history, we wish to do exactly what you Americans did when you fought for and won your independence."

"But don't you think," commented Frank, "that your objective of splitting up the country might be more closely parallel to the circumstances of our Civil War, when the Confederate states of the South tried to break away from the Union, rather than to the war of Independence?"

"No, no, no!" exclaimed Tremblay. "We have never been a true part of Canada. A lot of the English, especially those in the western provinces like Alberta and British Columbia, will be happy to get rid of us now that we are refusing to be exploited like domestic animals in a barnyard. We must now stand up for our rights, and we believe that the average American will understand and support us. Don't you think so, Monsieur Collins?"

"It's hard to say," Frank replied. "To tell you the truth, the average American probably doesn't know much or think much about Canada."

"That is the reason we are talking to you now," said

Bertrand. "We are sure that once Americans realize the truth about what is happening here, they will be behind us one hundred percent, *n'est-ce pas?*"

"We are proposing an economic association with English Canada," added Tremblay, "after we have established the sovereign *État de Québec*. But if the Canadians refuse to cooperate, as some have already intimated they will do, then we will negotiate an economic association with the United States. Personally, I think that is what we should do in the first place. Several prominent members of our party already have condominiums in Fort Lauderdale or summer chalets at Old Orchard Beach. We have always been closely connected with your country."

"But we still have a fight on our hands," said Bertrand. "The English will of course try every trick they can think of. They will threaten to take away investments, transfer all the money to Toronto, move the Sun Life Building, put the Expos in another city, reduce Québec to a banana republic. Nevertheless, as you Americans say, we shall overcome. Because we love Québec. Because we are willing to fight for Québec, which is our *patrie*, our homeland."

The dean had raised his voice for emphasis as he spoke the last two sentences, and this moved the black-bearded man to turn to Tremblay.

"*Qu'est-ce qu'il a dit?*" he asked.

When Tremblay quickly translated, the big man rose to his feet.

"*Vive le Québec libre!*" he shouted, and to make sure that everyone understood that he was not simply complimenting the café, he pounded his fist on the table top. The cups, saucers, creamer, sugar pot and utensils, like an audience in the palm of a great orator's hand, all responded with a clattering hop, and two cups crashed to the floor. Clémentine, who had been hovering in the background, rushed over with a broom and raised it in the air as if she were about to strike the culprit, who immediately sank back into his chair.

"*Maudzit fou!*" she yelled.

"*Non, non, calmez-vous,*" said Dean Bertrand, standing up and taking Clémentine by the arm. At this point, however, the blackbeard jumped to his feet again, believing, Frank presumed, that the dean was intervening on his behalf and thus giving him the go-ahead.

"*Vive le Québec libre!*" he repeated at the top of his voice, and this time he swung his brawny arm across the table, liberating most of the remaining dishes for a brief moment until they shattered on impact with the hard reality of the floor. In the commotion that followed, with loud screams and both Bertrand and Tremblay hanging onto Clémentine's arms as she attempted to wield her broom with seemingly homicidal intent, Frank noticed the café owner's boyfriend, Giovanni, signalling to him to escape into the kitchen. As he sidled in that direction, Madame Monet was suddenly clinging to his arm.

"*Sauve-moi.* Give it to me a hand. S.O.S.," she said to him.

Frank escorted her into the kitchen, and Giovanni closed the door.

"They're all nuts," he commented in fluent English, nodding toward the outer room, "and this one's a man-killer. Wore out three husbands, she has."

By then Marie-Ange Monet had collapsed into Frank's arms.

Chapter Seven

When Frank Collins got back to his hotel, he found the Wadleighs in a state of excitement.

"Look at this!" Wilt exulted, holding up five crisp new $100 bills. "The A-rab"—he stressed the first syllable and pronounced it to rime with day—"gave me this just to be on call during the next three days."

"The who?" asked Frank.

"The A-rab, Mr. Gabib. Haven't you heard about Mr. Gabib? He's got excellent taste, that A-rab. He likes my new Lincoln, and he wants me to be available in case some people he's expecting need to be driven around town."

Frank had heard about Mr. Gabib, of course, had actually even seen the man, but he was intrigued to know what Wilt Wadleigh had to say about the mysterious newcomer. He soon found out that Gabib's major distinguishing feature, to Wilt's mind, was that he seemed to have unlimited amounts of money. He had arrived in North Chadley about two years previously, staying for three months at the expensive Missawappi Manor, a small country inn down the lake on the outskirts of town which was fronted by white pillars and was allegedly an exact replica of Thomas Jefferson's mansion in Virginia. The manor was filled with old spinning wheels and antique furniture. When he visited the place briefly, Frank saw muskets, primitive snowshoes, oxen yokes, tomahawks, a seven-foot stuffed sturgeon and yellowing photographs on the walls of the lounge, dining room, and bar. He also saw the rates, which precluded any possibility of his taking up residence among these artifacts.

Within a few days of his arrival, according to Wadleigh, Mr. Gabib had hired a private secretary, none other than the local inscrutable blonde, Norma Duffin. An expert stenographer—shorthand, typing, filing, the works—but tight-lipped and reserved, who infuriated the town gossips by never telling anybody anything, Norma was divorced and raising three children. She had, said the innkeeper, at one time or another been linked by the frustrated gossips to every man in town with half a hormone, although never with a shred of evidence, and when her statuesque form was seen strutting into the Missawappi Manor every weekday morning at 8:30 a.m. and not emerging until sometimes 8:00 or 9:00 p.m. at night, the whole town, naturally, knew what was going on.

Margery Miller, the cleaning lady who had worked for almost every family in North Chadley with the means to hire help and thereby had gathered more dirt than ever she had removed, had expressed definite views about the affair. "They try 'em out first," she had informed Lisette, who repeated her words to Frank, "then they drug 'em and ship 'em back to Arabia for a hoorem. There's even a name for the dirty business. It's called blonde slavery."

"Then I guess I'm safe," had been Lisette's reply.

"No way," Marge had continued. "They'd just dye your hair. None of us is safe, Lisette. It shouldn't be allowed. The police should do something before it's too late and all the women in town have been kidnapped and drugged and shipped away."

Besides Norma Duffin, a local real-estate agent called Earl Morton also spent a lot of time at Mr.

Gabib's hotel suite during the latter's first sojourn in North Chadley, and rumours spread that the Arab was thinking of buying property. Which property, however, was a matter of wild speculation. Prospective sellers did not say much, their minds no doubt concentrated by stories of Mr. Gabib's untold wealth and profligate spending habits. Bus boys, maids, and waitresses, at the Missawappi Manor all reported receiving $100 tips, and the chef, who on a hunch and a tip from his Lebanese brother-in-law prepared a rack of lamb in addition to the roast of pork scheduled for the main dish one day, got a bonus of $500 for his initiative. The menu at the Missawappi Manor had subsequently begun to omit pork and to lean heavily on various lamb and mutton dishes and at least once even featured goat meat.

Lisette, too, had received a large tip, although she seemed a little embarrassed to talk about it. But innkeeper Wadleigh provided Frank with the details.

"He came in here one afternoon with a couple of his A-rab buddies, so I made her change clothes before serving them. She's a little thick-headed at times, this broad is. Almost had to whack her to get her to do it. The damned fool doesn't seem to understand how to turn her God-given goodies into a nice piece of change. Like wearing those high-heeled shoes. She keeps bitching that they hurt her feet when she's waitressing. Well so what? That's a small price to pay for what they do for her legs and arse. Ever notice how sexy her arse wiggles when she walks? Like two cats in a gunny sack."

Frank nodded, then lowered his eyes.

"Well that's one thing I know about them A-rabs," Wilt went on, "they keep their own women all bundled up and in bloody veils, but they sure as hell like to see as much as they can of ours. That's why I got her to put on this little waitress costume I picked up in California. Had a feeling it would come in handy one of these days, and sure enough, it did the trick. It's got a skirt so short that when she bends over just a bit, it shows off her whole backside, and the top part is so low-cut that she might as well be topless, which is exactly how she would be working in here, just like in a lot of the places in Montreal, if I didn't think the old fogies in town would come down on my back. Can you imagine the money I'd make if the boys could gander at that pair dangling before their eyes while they're guzzling their drinks? Lisette, go up and put on that costume and show this dude what I'm talking about."

"No, Wilt," Lisette replied firmly.

"Come on, doll. Like I've told you a thousand times —if you've got it, use it. Because you won't always have it."

"Look, Wilt, it doesn't matter. I know what you mean," interjected Frank.

"Okay then," said Wilt, "suit yourselves. But I'll tell you something—them A-rabs was impressed. Sat there bug-eyed the whole time. Didn't drink nothing and hardly ate, but they left her a $200 tip. Now any way you look at it, that's good business, right? All they did was look at her, after all, and there's no harm in looking, is there?"

Frank nodded, and Lisette remained expressionless. Frank understood now what Clémentine was alluding to when she made her remark about Lisette wiggling her *queue* under the Arab's eyes.

"And I'll tell you another great idea of mine," Wilt continued, his eyes beginning to glow with enthusiasm. "You know how the Catholic Church in Quebec used to run the whole show, then in the last few years it went right down the drain. Well people still remember how the Church used to slap them around, and they get a kick out of taking a crack back. My idea is to have Lisette and two or three other well-stacked waitresses dressed as nuns—the wimple, big crosses dangling around their necks, rosaries, the whole caboodle. Except for one thing —their dresses would be mesh or completely transparent. I'd call it the Convent. . . ."

"Wilt," said Lisette, "I've tried to explain to you. It's sick. It's sacrilegious."

"What do you mean sacrilegious? Why did God give people natural urges unless he wanted us to follow them? Answer me that."

"What if you have the urge to kill somebody? Is it all right to do it then?"

"That's different," Wilt replied. "I'm talking about normal urges."

"You're talking about men's urges," Lisette replied. "What about women's?"

"Women are all by nature exhibitionists. They enjoy strutting their stuff and watching men drool over them. That's a fact."

Frank did not agree with Wilt's statement, but he decided to avoid getting into an argument, especially since Lisette seemed uninterested in pursuing the discussion. Frank asked about Mr. Gabib again.

The rumours about the properties Gabib was supposedly trying to buy, Wilt then explained, became as rampant and varied as the speculations about the men in Norma Duffin's secret life. The two marinas, the restaurant, the gas station, the hardware store, the old Buckley estate on the hill, several of the larger houses, a large tract of land down the lake, and the Missawappi

Manor itself had all been mentioned one time or another.

"Then one morning we woke up," said Wilt, "to find out that the son of a bitch had actually bought them all, everything except the goddamned Missawappi Manor. He owned half the town, he did. Earl Morton had been acting as his front man, and for his lousy pieces of silver—made himself a mittful I guess—he'd sold the town right out from under us."

Mr. Gabib then immediately began construction of a multi-million dollar personal residence on the tract of land down the lake and a four-storey brick building halfway up the hill in town. By the time the latter was near completion, according to Wilt and Lisette, the whole town was in a panic, and the residents behind the new building, who discovered that they no longer had a view of the lake and the setting sun, were epileptic. It had always been understood that no commercial buildings would be erected in the residential area of town, and a bizarre, four-storey office complex which blocked the view was as unthinkable as a mid-town piggery or a nuclear waste dump. But there it was, like a painted lady in a scarlet mini-skirt and black-mesh stockings in the front row of a church choir. The North Chadley Ratepayers' Association des Propriétaires de St-Alphonse de Chadley Nord was quickly organized, and to everyone's consternation the lawyers hired to investigate the situation reported that Mr. Gabib's enterprises, although in dreadful, alien taste, were perfectly legal.

The municipality had never enacted zoning laws of any sort. Everything was simply understood. A town meeting was hastily called, and lo and behold, according to Wadleigh's account, who should show up but the A-rab himself, flanked by two similarly foreign gentlemen, apparently architects or engineers. To the utter astonishment of the assembled townsfolk, the three wise men from the Middle East rose and went to the front of the room as soon as the meeting was called to order, launching forthwith into an unbridled celebration of the architectural magnificence of the four-storey office complex, seeming to take for granted that the locals must share their appreciation. Obviously they had no idea that the form of the new building was just as appalling to the residents of North Chadley as its size. To the minds of Lisette and Wilt Wadleigh, it resembled some sort of Arabian mosque, such as they had seen in pictures, with encircling arches at the ground-floor level, domes and spires, all in gleaming pink brick. The structure stood out like a festering wound among the white clapboard houses of the town, each demurely clothed in cedar hedges and ornamental shrubs. Not a blade of grass had been left in the yard surrounding the office complex; it was entirely surfaced by gaudily coloured patio squares and white sand.

The inside of the building, according to Wilt, was as outlandish as the exterior. Lavish oriental carpets hung from the ceilings and walls, large mirrors were everywhere, great chandeliers like upside-down maple trees, spiralling staircases, plush divans in dark leather, velvet draperies, statues of turbaned warriors on horseback brandishing scimitars, censers in silver and brass holders, marble drinking fountains.

"When I went over to see Norma about a catering job," said Wilt, "she was sitting behind a little desk in an alcove at the top of one of the twisting staircases. So I made a remark about the place looking to me like a Burmese brothel, which is just an expression, because I don't know what the hell a Burmese brothel looks like. And you know, Norma started laughing so hard she nearly fell out of her chair. It seems a guy from Pakistan had come in to see her that very morning. This guy walks up the stairs, stands in front of her desk for a few moments, then quite matter-of-factly he says to her, 'You know, Madam, the last time I saw a place like this was in Burma, and the madam was sitting at a little desk at the top of staircase exactly like where you're sitting.' So there you are, sometimes we know more than we think we know."

"Maybe the idea of brothels is in the subconscious mind of all males," remarked Lisette with a wry smile, but her husband was not paying attention.

"I'll tell you one thing about that A-rab and his buddies," he went on, "they're bringing real money into this town."

"But doesn't it worry you?" asked Frank.

"Whattaya mean, worry me?"

"All the property he's bought up. I'd heard about one marina and the Buckley place up by Jeannie McVicar's, but I didn't realize that he'd also grabbed the snack bar, the gas station and the hardware store. That means that apart from the Québec Libre and your place here, he now owns just about the whole downtown area. Don't you wonder what he's up to?"

"Frankly," replied Wilt, "I don't give a damn what he's up to. I've already got a price for this place in mind, and as soon as he gets close enough, then whammo...."

"Not so fast," interjected Lisette. "Remember that I own 50 percent of this hotel, and I'm not interested in selling. I want to stay here."

"Now why the hell do *you* want to stay here in this little pisspot of a town, tell me that?" Wilt asked his wife. "You're dirt here, you know that."

"No, I don't know that. And even if I did. . . ."

"Come on now, stop pretending. Everybody knows what your old lady was."

"I don't care what some people think. There are men in this town who worshipped her as a goddess, despite whatever she might have done. She was part of this town."

"Yeah, but I won't say what part."

"Then keep your mouth shut. And no matter what you think, I'm not going to sell my half of the hotel."

"We'll see about that," responded Wilt.

Observing the two Wadleighs, Frank could not help but recall Clémentine's comment that Wilt would throw his wife into the deal if the price was right. It was amazing really, he mused, that a man lucky enough to be married to such a doll should have so little appreciation of her. Well perhaps he did have an appreciation of her, but only as a marketable commodity. He seemed to believe that Lisette's considerable physical assets were not hers but his to exploit. Out of the corner of his eye, Frank had been noting that the mysterious Indian he had seen the first time he had been in the bar salon was sitting there again, maintaining his usual silence but obviously listening attentively to the conversation and every once in a while gazing over, longingly it seemed to Frank, at Mrs. Wadleigh. But then what man, apart from her husband, didn't?

"And what do *you* think about Gabib buying up the town, Mrs. Wadleigh?" asked Frank.

"It's a mystery to me," she replied. "Obviously he has some plan in mind, but I'm not sure what it could be. I've heard rumours of an Islamic Studies centre. I've also heard that he intends to tear everything down and build a new town of his own."

"That would be a tragedy," said Frank. "This is certainly one of the most beautiful little towns I've ever seen."

"A town is a bloody town," commented Wilt, who began arranging bottles behind the bar.

"You're right, Frank," said Lisette, ignoring her husband, "but what can we do about it? We can't stop people from selling if they want to."

"There is one thing that might be done."

"What's that?"

"The people in town, as you and Wilt have just explained, realize now that it was a mistake not to have adopted proper zoning restrictions. But it's not too late to correct that and protect what's left. You could get the townspeople together and pass zoning and building bylaws in the town council. That would be a way of preserving the special character of the town. I've seen it done in many places in the States."

"Frank," said Lisette anxiously, "I wish you would explain that to some of the big shots, like Mr. Richmond and Mr. Martin and Monsieur Tremblay."

"But I'm an outsider too, Mrs. Wadleigh. It's really none of my business. Although I did mention it to Bill Martin not long ago."

"And what did he say?"

"He said that he was too busy with the Referendum. First the country has to be saved, then they can start thinking about the town."

"Damn that Referendum! It may be too late then."

Further conversation was precluded by the arrival of a group of customers. After finishing his beer, Frank wandered out of the inn and without thinking found himself heading toward the bizarre mosque-like building halfway up the hill on the east side of the village. As he strolled along, he realized that his curiosity had been whetted—he wanted to find out what the Arab had in mind. But he had to admit to himself that Mr. Gabib's blonde secretary was also occupying his thoughts. His encounter with her at the Québec Libre, brief and one-sided as it was, had set off an alert signal which continued to flash at the back of his brain.

Just as Wilt Wadleigh had described, Norma Duffin was sitting behind a desk in an alcove at the top of a winding staircase. She was wearing a prim, high-necked white blouse and a beige jacket. The golden luster of her hair left no doubt that she was a natural blonde. Frank was startled when she looked up and said, "How do you do, Mr. Collins."

"Uh . . . how do you do, Mrs. Duffin. I didn't think that you would know my name."

"It's a small town. When an outsider moves in, we all soon know about it. What can I do for you, Mr. Collins?"

"Do you also know that I'm doing research for a Ph.D. dissertation on the evolution of institutions in North Chadley?"

"Yes, I've heard something to that effect."

"Well, I'd be interested in interviewing Mr. Gabib."

"For what reason?"

"Because the way it's going, he may have a profound effect upon local institutions."

Norma Duffin lowered her glasses to the tip of her nose and looked over them at Frank. She had light-blue eyes. The strong features of her face made handsome a more appropriate term to describe her than pretty or cute. There was nothing of the saucy, pixy quality which made Lisette so instantly attractive to a man, and of course she wasn't wearing a slit skirt and form-hugging blouse.

"I'm afraid, Mr. Collins, that Mr. Gabib does not think in terms of local institutions. He has his own institutions. His affairs here are strictly business."

"Maybe so, but surely he realizes that the town of North Chadley will soon be ... well ... pretty much his to control. The lives of all the villagers will be affected."

"Unless you've got property to sell, Mr. Collins, my boss will not be the least bit interested in talking to you."

"Then what about yourself, Mrs. Duffin? I"m sure you could provide me with a lot of useful information."

"Not me, sir. There's no way I can help you."

"I don't believe that for a minute."

"Mr. Collins, you can sure save yourself a great deal of trouble...."

Before Norma Duffin could finish the sentence, Mr. Gabib emerged through a door to the right of her desk. Looking at the Arab and at the same time catching a glimpse of himself in one of the wall mirrors, Frank could see that he and Gabib were contrasts to each other. Norma's boss was as slim and suave and nattily dressed in a three-piece suit as Frank was bulky and sloppy in a pair of blue jeans and a heavy windbreaker. Frank also noted the way Gabib looked at his private secretary. There was more than a hint of intimacy, even of possessiveness in that look, it seemed to him. The rumours around town were no doubt well founded. Norma's services to her rich, handsome boss had to exceed the strictly secretarial. It was the old formula of money, power, and sex. Put the ingredients together and there's bound to be a chemical reaction. Mr. Gabib pointedly did not address Frank.

"What does this man want?" he asked Norma.

"He's doing a Ph.D. research project, sir."

"A what project?" Gabib cast a scornful glance at Frank.

"A doctoral dissertation, I believe it's called. Mr. Collins is a graduate student. And he would like to interview you, sir."

"Impossible. I'm much too busy to play school games."

"That's what I told him, sir."

"Then why is he still here?"

"Because I haven't had time to leave," Frank responded. "But that is about to be resolved."

As Frank turned and started down the staircase, Gabib went back into his office. In the mirror at the first landing, Frank could see Norma's reflection. She was watching him with what, if he hadn't known better, he might have misinterpreted as interest.

Frank stopped at the bar-salon to pick up a couple of little containers of coffee cream for Mirabel. The big Indian was still there, sipping a beer and gazing wistfully at Lisette, who was perched atop a bar stool with one leg on a rung and the other extended alluringly through the slit in her skirt. At that moment, Frank felt a strong bond of sympathy with the other man. He almost decided to join him and attempt to start a conversation, but it was now getting on in the evening, and Frank went back to his room to make himself what to him was a gourmet dinner of macaroni and cheese with Italian sausages.

Chapter Eight

By the middle of March there was still not the slightest sign of spring in the village of North Chadley. Back in Michigan, Frank knew, the crocuses were already in full bloom and the tulips were six inches out of the ground, but here in the foothills of the Canadian Appalachians, the lake was still frozen solid. Betting on when the old car on the ice would sink had not even begun. The snow, like Frank's notes, just kept accumulating, but that did not disturb him, because he knew that he would not have to make any sense out of it eventually—the snow would melt and be gone. His notes, on the other hand, were a different matter. He had a mass of information, but he knew that he would need a lot more, particularly on the nature and function of local institutions—the churches, Legion, Village Improvement Association, school board, Missawappi Club and the new Ratepayers' Association des Propriétaires.

The last organization differed from the others in that it was completely bilingual and was composed of about an equal number of English and French. Frank resolved to question Bill Martin, its president, about it and at the same time, somehow, to piece together the whole truth about the Arabian invasion, even if the Arab chieftain himself and his playmate blonde secretary refused to cooperate.

Meanwhile, the Referendum issue was heating up rapidly. Marcel Tremblay had confronted Reginald Richmond in front of the post office, and the two might have come to blows if Jeannie McVicar had not happened along and intervened. Tremblay had reportedly made uncomplimentary remarks about the Missawappi Club, of which Richmond was a prominent if not a particularly active member, denouncing it as an elitist, racist, despicable clique of the overprivileged *Anglais*, a cancer in the village which would be summarily amputated as soon as Quebec gained its independence.

Frank knew that the Club was a long-established, private social and recreational organization. A fee of $1,000 or $1,500 was charged to join and an annual rate of $500 to use the clubhouse facilities, which included a hall and bar, a beach, a pier with a diving board, sailboats, canoes, water skis and surf boards, as well as hired camp counsellors to babysit children left there for the day by their parents. Money alone, however, did not ensure membership. Any person or family wishing to join had to have the endorsement of three current members in good standing then be approved by the executive committee.

The Missawappi Club held teas, regattas, dances and parties of one sort or another throughout the summer months. Local people out for a stroll, or sitting on their front verandas, or perhaps out fishing on the lake, often heard the music and sounds of revelry coming from the clubhouse late into the night, as Frank Collins had already found out for himself. Fishermen complained about drunk teenagers swamping their rowboats as the "spoiled brats of the rich" sped back and forth between the Club pier and their parents' lakeside chalets at full throttle in their high-powered motor launches, which also scared the fish. And so far as Frank could determine, if not by official policy, then by force of habit and circumstances, the Missawappi Club was a bastion of the English language. French-Canadian workers in town, like their English counterparts, could never afford to join, and either the endorsement rule or lack of interest was still keeping the more affluent French from seeking membership.

One evening in a conversation at the Inn bar with cleaning lady Marge Miller, who occasionally worked at the Missawappi Club for receptions and the like, Frank learned that most of the Club members were in fact well-to-do "summer people," who had permanent residences elsewhere, perhaps in Montreal or Toronto, and who came to their vacation chalets only during July and August, thus tripling the population of the tiny village of North Chadley in those months. Even if they could find the necessary cash, according to Marge, the working stiffs in town could never round up the required endorsements. "What high-falutin lady," said Marge, "wants to rub elbows socially with the slob who scrubs her floors and cleans her toilets?"

"Besides," Marge went on, "I hear tell of a lot of hanky-panky among them people. They're not like us. Got no morals whatsoever. The husbands ain't to home most of the summer. They dump off their wives and kids for the season while they stay in the city to do their jobs, and I got a pretty good idea what that amounts to. Men are all the same. And I guess them wives have a pretty good idea what their men are doing too. After a while they get bored, so they mosey over to the clubhouse to knock back a few with somebody else's husband or whoever happens to be around. Then the next thing you know ... Mrs. Wilkinson—her man's a bigshot lawyer in Montreal and they have a chalet down by the Manor— she's even got a poem about it."

"A poem?" inquired Frank.

"Yeah, so she does. Recites it every time she ties one

on. It's about a woman at a party, and I've heard it so often I can remember the whole thing."

"I'm curious to hear it, Marge."

"Here it is, then: Your martinis are truly delicious,
But I can only drink two at the most.
Three I am under the table,
And four I am under the host."

"Not bad," Frank chuckled.

"And let me tell you, Frank, she puts away a fair number of martinis, that Penelope Wilkinson, if you know what I mean. She don't seem to think no more about it than if she was having a cup of coffee or changing her clothes. In fact, she's much fussier about her clothes than she is about her men. He'll be all tied up with an important case in Montreal, and his friends, or what's supposed to be his friends, whip down here to relax. And boy can she show them how to relax. But I really don't understand what the men see in her. She's no great beauty, I'll tell you. She's as skinny as a garter snake. I'll bet the makeup she slaps on weighs more than she does."

"Some women simply have sex appeal, Marge, even if they aren't particularly beautiful by the usual standards. They send out certain signals, something like a bitch in heat, I suppose. And men respond."

"Yeah, but this bitch is always in heat."

"That's one of the basic differences between human females and the females of most of the other species."

"What do you mean?"

"All I mean is that human beings are not restricted to certain specific periods. They can turn it on or off when they like."

"Well, I guess that's true enough. Anyway, they got two kids, ten and twelve, and they're both spoiled rotten—a huge playroom packed with every toy you can think of, electric trains, little racing cars with those remotor controls, all them games they run on the TV set. They even got their own VCR. Would you believe it? Their own VCR. Now when I win the lotto, that's one of the first things I'm gonna get me, a VCR."

"It's a good thing to have all right. A lot of good movies are available now."

"But you'd never believe them kids, Frank. Two little boys that look like those pictures of cherububs you see in Bibles—big blue eyes, blond curls, toothy smiles, a look as innocent as the morning dew, and they're both rotten to the core. They must have 500 of them kids' movies—you know, Walt Disney and Star Wars and D.T. or E.T. or whatever it is—and you know what they do? They sneak into their mom's bedroom and steal the filthy movies she hides in her drawer under the jewelry box. And I know they're filthy, because I checked a couple out when the family was down to Cape Cod one weekend."

"That's fairly normal," said Frank. "Youngsters are always more interested in the forbidden fruit. Actually, I suppose all ..."

"Normal! Holy Baldheaded! Them kids ain't the least bit normal. Last year the oldest one locked his little brother in a closet and set it on fire. If old Joe Larose hadn't been working on the roof and heard the screams, the kid would've been dead for sure. They had to rush him to Montreal for skin grafts and everything."

"My God! Where was the mother?"

"Out in the motorboat with a jug of martinis and what they call a QC, a Queen's Consultor, which she says is some kind of hotshot lawyer."

"I see."

"I just can't figure it out, Frank. Them kids has

everything, and they're still rotten. The oldest one should still be in diapers. I have to change his bed every time I go over there, which is twice a week. And let me tell you, after three or four days the smell of that piss would gag a maggot."

"It sounds as if the children are emotionally insecure, which wouldn't be unlikely if the father is away a lot and the mother has ... uh ... extracurricular interests."

"Extracurr ... ic ... ? What does that mean, Frank?"

"It means out of the ordinary, outside the usual run of things."

"You mean foreigners? Well you're quite right—she's got a few of them too. One time there was this Japanese or Chinese guy. She told me that he was a conductor of one of them big sympathy orchestras. He came up to see her from the States somewhere. I don't remember his name, but I can sure remember ironing his pants."

"Ironing his pants?"

"Because he fell in the bloody lake. He was a short little fellow, and I guess Mr. Wilkinson didn't know that she was carrying on with him. Anyway, Mr. Wilkinson comes down from Montreal by surprise, and she spots his car coming through the gate from the bedroom window. So she's got to get rid of the other guy in a hurry. And whiles she's out front welcoming her husband and stalling him, I have the job of getting her fancy man down to the dock and into one of the canoes."

"Really?"

"Oh yeah. And I tried my best. But I guess he don't know nothing about canoes. Besides, he's trying to button up same time as he steps off the dock. What do you call them sticks those sympathy orchestra conductors wave around?"

"Batons, you mean?"

"Yeah," said Margery, chuckling. "Well, I guess right then that little Japanese man was wishing that he'd kept his baton in his pants. He puts one foot in the canoe and goes arse over kettle into the lake. He looked like a drowned rat when he climbed back onto the dock."

"And did the husband catch him?"

"No, not that time anyway. I put him in the rowboat and brought him back to my place. And that's how I ended up ironing his pants after I'd run his stuff through the dryer at the laundromat. And him standing there the whole time wearing my pink bathrobe and muttering to himself in Japanese. Or was it Chinese? Anyway, one of them yellow people."

"And what happened to him finally?"

"He's still conducting orchestras, as far as I know."

"No, I mean what happened to him that day?"

"Oh, she came over and picked him up eventually. I offered him a bite to eat, but he didn't have no appetite. I guess she figured out some way to get away from her husband. He divorced her finally, did Mr. Wilkinson, and now she's taken up medication with one of them Indian googoos."

"You must mean meditation, transcendental meditation."

"Yeah, that's it—transcontinental meditation. With another foreign type. You hit the nail on the head about her being extracurbicular."

"Will you have another gin and tonic, Marge?"

"Don't mind if I do, Frank. I've got some more stories to tell you."

"They'll have to wait, Marge. I must get back to my room and get a little work done, I'm afraid."

Chapter Nine

As the weeks passed and Mirabel got fatter and lazier and spent most of the day in his suitcase, Frank discovered that he no longer had to seek out people to interview. The news had spread around the village that he was writing a book about North Chadley, and all the townspeople seemed to want to talk to him, presumably to provide him with personal accounts, just in case other personal accounts may have distorted the truth, particularly with regard to themselves. Frank had repeatedly tried to point out the scholarly, impersonal nature of his research project to several people, but few paid any attention. Bill Martin, of course, being a university professor, understood the nature of doctoral dissertations and that the vast majority of them, once completed, accepted and filed, were plunked on a shelf in the university library to be consulted only by graduate students from time to time or else completely forgotten. Frank regularly visited the Martins to discuss his progress. Bill was an astute critic, and his wife, Sue, a middle American with whom Frank had a lot in common, always made him feel right at home.

More important perhaps, considering the daily challenge of keeping his 260-pound bulk adequately nourished, Sue Martin was an excellent cook and was always ready to throw an extra bag or two of potatoes into the pot. The only disconcerting element in the Martin household was that the five daughters got into ear-shattering battles with each other over one taking another's clothes, one staying on the telephone too long while another was expecting an important call and other such momentous issues. At the height of their fury they seemed almost homicidal. In an instant any one of the Martin girls could transmogrify herself from a sophisticated, well-spoken, polite young lady into a snarling, screeching, scratching, tigress. And to complicate matters, Frank would inevitably be called upon by each of the girls simultaneously to justify her particular position against the others.

"Can you believe what she's saying? Have you ever heard anything so ridiculous, Frank?" one girl would shout at him.

"Me! Me ridiculous! Tell her, Frank. Go on, tell her the truth," another would interject.

And Frank would straddle the wobbly fence of diplomacy, trying desperately to avoid taking sides. But often it made no difference. Each of the boisterous Martin girls seemed so absolutely assured of the rightness of her own convictions that she could not imagine the possibility of doubt on the part of any reasonable person. Thus although Frank did not utter a sound, change his expression or make the slightest gesture, his corroboration was simply taken for granted.

"You see! Frank agrees with me!" one or another of the girls would loudly proclaim. "Frank says you're a lying bitch. Frank's shocked out of his tree by the way you carry on. And he's an anthropologist. He's studied cannibals and head-hunters and freakos and primitive maniacs of every kind."

Frank Collins, in fact, was not shocked, but he did occasionally marvel that such a tight-knit family of bright, gifted people, who were obviously bound together by strong emotional ties and shared values, could escalate their internal spats to such hysterical heights.

He recalled the statement of Caribbean anthropologist Sidney Mintz that conflict can actually be integrating, and observing the Martins it occurred to Frank that Mintz might have been on to something, provided, of course, that the conflict did not get out of hand.

The written invitation to dinner at the Richmonds' was delivered to the Inn and handed over to Frank by a smiling Lisette Wadleigh.

"I see that you are ascending the social ladder, Monsieur François," she commented in her slightly accented, precise English. "Soon you will have no time to speak with us peasants."

"I'll always have time to speak to you, Madame Wadleigh," he replied sincerely, thinking Sweet Mother of God, she sure is *ben stackée*. And although he had long since dismissed Margery Miller's story about the innkeeper's wife and the eccentric cousin as malicious gossip bred of jealousy and passing over the hill, a phantasm of Lisette adorned by no more than white gloves and dark nylons flashed across his mind, causing him to feel a slight twinge of guilt. After all, he reminded himself, as a disciplined scholar, he should be devoting his intellectual powers to something other than mentally undressing pretty *Québécoises*.

On the other hand, he ruminated further, pioneer anthropologists never had occasion to do any mental undressing when they were investigating native tribes in the jungles and the South Seas—the women were generally running around stark naked to begin with. And the anthropologists took plenty of photographs besides, many of them to appear in *National Geographic Magazine,* which is why that publication came to be jokingly labelled "the Black man's *Playboy*." Still gazing at Lisette, Frank wondered if the young woman had any suspicion of what was happening to her in his mind. She was looking at him inquiringly.

"Are you wondering how to get to the Richmond place?" she asked.

"Yes, you're right. I have no idea where they live," he replied with relief.

"I'll explain it to you," she said.

The Richmond estate was on the edge of town, and the lake road actually ran through it. On one side of the road was a large boat house and pier; on the other side was the white, clapboard house with a spacious veranda, a two-car garage and a shed which was probably used to store gardening tools. A tall, white-haired man in his seventies, Reginald Richmond greeted Frank at the door, let him hang up his coat and deposit his overshoes in the vestibule, then invited him into the parlour for a pre-dinner cocktail. Mrs. Richmond came in to be introduced, but she immediately left to supervise in the kitchen. Frank caught a glimpse of Margery Miller when Mrs. Richmond opened the kitchen door, and he speculated amusedly that he could no doubt have found out much more than he needed to know about the Richmonds without even leaving the bar in the Inn.

Prompted by his guest, Mr. Richmond allowed that his family had been in the world of finance for generations. The first Richmond to come to British North America had received a grant of 1,000 acres where the City of Brooke now stood. He had rather foolishly sold the five acres which were to become the prime-real-estate downtown area of the city to two brothers called Ira and Amos King for 100 gallons of their moonshine, but then he had had no idea at the time that the parcel of land would become prime real estate.

"It's comical in a way," Mr. Richmond told Frank.

"Everyone takes for granted that the main artery of Brooke, which is called King Street, was named for one of the British monarchs. But in point of fact it got its name from a couple of disreputable moonshiners. And by rights it should be called Richmond Street. Mind you, that still doesn't give those fanatics in Quebec City the right to change the name to *Rue du Roi*. Or to change Katevale to *Ste-Catherine*. Or North Chadley, or any of the other names chosen by our ancestors, who worked hard to pioneer this area, and who were proud to speak English. I'm sorry, young man, but it makes me furious to think about it. I mean they're tampering with history, with traditions, with a sacred trust. How dare they? Have you ever heard of such despicable behaviour?"

Frank almost replied that he had often heard of such behaviour, that in fact it was commonplace, reflecting that the settlers of the Eastern Townships, like all relocating populations throughout the world, had never hesitated to change many of the previous Indian place names to suit themselves. But he noticed that Reginald Richmond had become slightly flushed with rage, and he simply nodded his head in a semblance of accord as the older man continued.

"But let me tell you, Mr. Collins, we're not going to stand for it. We beat them once before, and if necessary we'll do it again. We're keeping our rifles oiled and the powder dry, don't you worry. We will not let them push French down our throats."

"Do you really think that's what the Quebec Government is trying to do, Mr. Richmond?" asked Frank quite innocently.

"Good Lord, young man!" Richmond replied, his voice rising to match his blood pressure. "Just go into Brooke and try to buy a pair of socks. I was in a store just the other day, a store where I've been shopping for at least 50 years, and would you believe it? The clerk refused to talk to me in English. She actually refused. 'I don't speak English,' she said. In perfect English. The man who founded that store, I don't mind telling you, was a close friend of my grandfather's. If he were alive today, I'd have had that insolent salesgirl fired on the spot."

"It is unfortunate," commented Frank.

"Unfortunate, you say! It's a damned disgrace! We're being pushed around like dogs. They're trying to ram French down our throats. Do you realize that all businesses in Quebec have been given a time limit to make French their working language? My own trust company, founded by my grandfather and expanded by my father and run by me for the past 30 years, and I'm being told what I have to do. Well, Mr. Collins, I'm not going to stand for it. I've added a French equivalent to the name of the company, which I really don't mind doing because a number of our clients are Francophones, but now they're trying to force me to drop the original English. And if we want to have bilingual signs, then the French lettering has to be twice the size of the English. Have you ever heard of anything so absurd? Well, I absolutely refuse. I've hired lawyers, and I'll take it to the Supreme Court of Canada if necessary. I intend to fight."

"You say that you have French clients, Mr. Richmond. How do they feel about all this?" asked Frank.

"They want nothing to do with it, I'm sure. They're entirely satisfied with the way the company had been handling their affairs. They dislike the hotheads as much as I do, and they're all quite fluent in English of course. It's not that I have anything against the French, you understand. I've lived here all my life. I have never had any prejudices. I quite like French individuals . . . although sometimes I think they should never be allowed to gather in groups larger than one person."

Frank smiled, again nodding his head.

"The French in Quebec don't seem to realize what we've done for them," Mr. Richmond went on. "We're the ones who built this province, founded businesses, took all the risks, constructed factories, canals, roads, bridges. Left by themselves they would still be wearing tuques while they chopped wood and tended trap lines. They'd be a curiosity in North America, a sort of tourist attraction, five million *habitants* surrounded by hotdog stands and Holiday Inns."

"But surely, Mr. Richmond, there were French business leaders who contributed to Quebec's development."

"Damned few, I'll tell you. All you have to do is look over the list of top executives in Quebec, back in the 1950s say, to know that. And the ones who did do something were the ones who learned to speak good English and to adapt to the realities of the business world."

"I see," said Frank.

"They have only themselves to blame. They let the Church run their lives, and all the Church wanted was to keep the men ignorant farmers and the women pregnant. Leave commerce to the English and Jews, because they were all going to hell. Did you ever hear about the Revenge of the Cradle? That was the Church's idea, you know. Reverse the British Conquest by overwhelming the English in population. When I was a boy, I knew of families with as many as 24 children."

"Holy Mary! Is that a fact?"

"They bred the women like animals on a farm, they

did. Married them off at the age of 12 or 13, then a baby every spring same way as the cows. And if spring came around and a woman wasn't pregnant, the priest wanted to know why not."

"Isn't it ironic?" said Frank. "I was just reading the other day that now the birthrate in Quebec is the lowest in North America—only one point four children per child-bearing woman. The pendulum seems to have swung completely to the opposite side."

"That's right. Because the Church has lost control," said Richmond, seeming to calm down a little as he refilled Frank's glass and his own with Scotch and soda, even showing a hint of a smile. "The French girls are still as . . . uh . . . lively and . . . uh . . . willing as they always were, I'm sure. But now they know about the pill and tubal ligations to keep from having babies. We have eight young, more-or-less married women in the office, and only two of them have children. Marie has two boys, and Louise has a little girl, I believe. Four out of the eight are separated or divorced from their husbands, but I have no doubt that they're living with other men. That seems to be the general practice these days."

"Yes, it's not unusual any more. Changing mores," commented Frank.

"Anyway, what the French do in bed is not my business," Richmond continued, "but what they are trying to do to my business does concern me. And I don't like it one bit."

"Perhaps the Referendum will settle the situation," said Frank, unwittingly provoking the older man to new apoplectic heights.

"The Referendum!" shouted Richmond. "The Referendum is a damned fraud! Have you seen the question that will be asked? In today's paper, it was. And they've decided to hold the wretched thing on July 14th, probably figuring that a lot of the English will be off on vacation and won't bother to vote."

"July 14th..." repeated Frank, reflecting, "... why that's Bastille Day."

"It's what?" asked Richmond.

"France's national holiday—when the notorious prison called the Bastille was stormed during the French Revolution. In 1789, I believe."

"So that's it. I'm not surprised. And do you know what the question is going to be? They're going to ask the people if they want the Government of Quebec to begin negotiations with Ottawa for what they call "sovereignty-association," which is a term clearly invented to dupe the population. Apparently they've found out from the public-opinion experts that the vast majority of French Quebeckers do not want anything to do with separating from Canada. So they're trying to fool them all by calling it something else. It's a fraud, I say, an abominable piece of trickery."

"I didn't know about the question," said Frank. "Haven't had a chance to look at today's papers yet."

"They're trying to take the people in by the word twisting," Richmond went on, "they're trying to make the public think that if the YES side wins in the Referendum, it will mean nothing more than the beginning of talks with the Federal Government. Quebec will not separate, they say, until there is another Referendum. Can you believe the hypocrisy and deviousness of these people?"

"What do you mean?"

"Don't you see? It's a trick. That gang of raving Separatists have no intention of holding another Referendum. All they want is to con the people into voting

YES. There won't be any negotiations. The Federal Government will refuse to negotiate with Separatists. They're bound to refuse. They can't very well be expected to sit down and discuss the dismemberment and disintegration of the nation they were elected and sworn to govern and uphold, can they? Then as soon as the Federal Government refuses to negotiate, the Separatists will announce that they tried their best, but there was nothing for it, so they are now unilaterally declaring Quebec an independent state. And that will be the end of the ball-game. Of one inning, anyway."

"Do you really think that will happen, Mr. Richmond?"

"It could happen. The masses of people are not too bright, you know. They could be fooled, then wake up and find themselves in a banana republic without any bananas. You Americans, of course, preserved your union by fighting a civil war, but Canadians are different. Our Federal Government is unlikely to consider any kind of military intervention. And a lot of Canadians, especially in the West, would probably be happy to get rid of Quebec."

"And what about yourself, Mr. Richmond? What would you do if the Separatists win the Referendum and Quebec actually becomes an independent country?"

"I would have no choice, Mr. Collins. I would move my company to either Toronto or Calgary. As you probably know, Sun Life and a lot of other companies have already left. A YES in the Referendum would be the signal for all the others to leave. The bags are packed. And what's left of Quebec would be an economic basket case. It would serve those Separatist fanatics right. Within a year there would be chaos, the masses of unemployed would be storming the National

Assembly and burning it down."

The conversation continued during the roast-beef dinner, with Frank discovering that Mrs. Richmond had even more extreme and pessimistic opinions than her husband had. She roundly condemned French Canadians in general as ingrates and sheep, having been so long dominated by the Church that they were quite incapable of thinking sensibly for themselves. She warned Frank against all the professors at the French-speaking Université de Brooke, including William Martin. When Frank responded that he was certain that Professor Martin's allegiances were strictly federalist, Mrs. Richmond dismissed the idea as preposterous. Everybody knew that the Université de Brooke was a hotbed of Separatism, and most of those professors were degenerates in any case, she pointed out to Frank. They all worked in French, which spoke for itself. When she found out that Frank was staying at the Inn, she also warned him against Wilton Wadleigh, who was a good local boy, but with insanity in the family, and who was being manipulated by that French woman who managed to get her claws into him.

"Lisette seems to me to be a lovely person," Frank could not keep himself from saying.

"Maybe so," Mrs. Richmond responded, "but I wouldn't trust her. I wouldn't trust any of them. I knew her mother, you know, Madeleine Something or Other. Well I didn't know her personally, but I knew all about her. The whole town did. She was a tramp, I'm sorry to say. She went to Montreal when she was no more than 16 years old, supposedly to work as a salesgirl for the Dupuis Frères department store. Then a chap from town who was up in Montreal happened to go into a bar which turned out to be one of those strip-tease places, and who should he see up on the stage taking off her clothes but little Madeleine. Isn't that right, Reginald?"

"I believe so, Edna," Mr. Richmond replied.

"Then the next thing we knew," Mrs. Richmond went on, "she was out in Las Vegas in the United States. Madame Larose, who was Madeleine's aunt, used to tell everybody that she was just a showgirl at a fancy big place called Satan's Palace...."

"You mean Caesar's Palace, dear," Mr. Richmond corrected.

"Whatever. We all knew what she was really up to, especially when she came back driving a new car and dressed to kill. She was just a showgirl all right."

"You shouldn't forget, Edna, that she was working to support two children. You have to give her credit for that," said Mr. Richmond. "She did send that young Lisette to a good private boarding school run by one of the religious orders. Would you care for a drop of brandy, Mr. Collins?"

Frank accepted the brandy while Mrs. Richmond continued.

"But what about the boy, Reginald? Would you believe, Mr. Collins, that Madeleine had a child with that singer Elvis Presley?"

"You mean *the* Elvis Presley?" asked Frank, thinking, My God, Lisette's brother is the spitting image of Elvis. Could it really be possible?

"Indeed. Although I can't see that it is anything to be proud of. Apparently Elvis Presley was performing in Las Vegas and Madeleine happened to catch his eye. So he had her delivered to his hotel suite, I was told."

"Like sending out for a pizza," chuckled Mr. Richmond.

"I've read someplace," said Frank, "that hundreds,

perhaps thousands of women claim to have children fathered by Elvis Presley. It's much the same, I believe, with all famous singers and actors."

"Perhaps so," Mrs. Richmond continued, "but Madeleine used to show people gift cards signed by this Presley fellow, and she also had photographs of herself and him together. And besides, the boy turned out to be a carbon copy of Presley, I'm told. She couldn't have done that all by herself, could she? He's a singer now too, they tell me. Makes a living doing imitations of his father in the various nightclubs. Although you'd think he'd be ashamed to tell people that he owes his existence to the fact that his mother was a common prostitute who happened to catch the eye of Elvis Presley. Reginald, slow down on that brandy."

"Now, Edna, you don't know that she actually was a prostitute," said Mr. Richmond, recharging his and Frank's glasses.

"What else do you call women who sell themselves?" his wife replied.

Frank thought about saying that perhaps Madeleine Poulin had not sold herself but had accommodated the singing star for nothing, but he had misgivings about how his hostess would react.

"Maybe she simply got carried away by the glitter and glamour of it all," he said finally. "I believe that happens to young women sometimes."

"Come on now, Mr. Collins. She had already had one illegitimate child, Lisette, and God knows who her father was. But you're right about those French girls getting carried away. They seem to get carried away the moment they lay their eyes on a man. That's why I'm against mixed marriages. Men are slaves to their physical desires. They can be lured too easily by girls like

Madeleine, then they end up caught before they know what's happening to them."

"What about the other way around?" asked Frank.

"What other way around, Mr. Collins?"

"An English-Canadian woman and a French-Canadian man."

"Oh, that seldom happens. English women generally know better."

"What about Jeannie McVicar and Joe Larose?"

"What about them?"

"Haven't they been engaged for a number of years?"

"Engaged? Miss McVicar and Joe Larose? Why that's absurd, Mr. Collins. They've never been engaged. Years ago, as I recall, they did a little ballroom dancing together, but that was strictly an artistic partnership."

"I see," Frank responded, although he didn't see at all, having heard the truth from Jeannie McVicar herself.

"Quite unthinkable," Edna Richmond went on. "Joe used to work as a handyman for the McVicars. Her father was very successful in the machinery business, you know, and her uncle was the Presbyterian minister here in town. And a dour Presbyterian he was indeed. Miss McVicar may have kept Joe on as a handyman after her father and uncle died, but there was never anything more than that, I'm sure. Isn't that right, Reginald?"

"Quite likely, dear. Joe has worked for everybody. There's not much he can't do with his hands. Would you care for another brandy, Mr. Collins?"

"Reginald, will you please stop trying to corrupt this young man. I'm sure Mr. Collins would prefer a nice cup of coffee now. Wouldn't you, Mr. Collins?"

"Yes. I'd love a coffee," Frank lied. He had in fact seldom had occasion to drink expensive brandy, and he was finding it quite to his taste. When Edna Richmond left the room to fetch the coffee, her husband winked at him conspiratorially, then reached over with the bottle and filled his glass to the brim. After replenishing his own glass, Richmond signalled to Frank, and they both downed their drinks in one gulp.

"I don't mind telling you," said the older man, gazing upward with a broad smile, "that woman my wife was telling you about, Madeleine, she was a real beauty. She had every man in this town drooling when she walked by. Her daughter, Lisette, looks a lot like her."

As his hostess poured the coffee from a silver pot, Frank's head began to spin slightly. When he closed his eyes, visions of Lisette floated enticingly across his mind. Then to his own surprise he was seeing Elvis Presley gyrating on a stage and belting out "You ain't nothin' but a hound dog," followed by a chorus line of showgirls kicking up their legs. One of the girls was the image of the innkeeper's wife.

"Are you feeling all right, Mr. Collins?" asked Edna Richmond, yanking Frank from his reveries.

"Oh yes, Mrs. Richmond. I feel fine," he replied, opening his eyes. "By way of curiosity, what happened to that woman Madeleine you were talking about earlier?"

"She died. Came home with cancer of the pancreas, and she was gone within a few months. A dreadful disease it is."

Before the visit was over, Mr. Richmond explained to Frank that the English language in Quebec was being irreversibly corrupted and deformed. In a few years, the new "Frenglish," as he called it, the consequence of Quebec anglophone professionals being inundated by oceans of Government directives and such, would prevent the nominal English left in the province from communicating with other English-speaking North Americans.

"Listen to this," Richmond said, picking up a pamphlet from an end table. "'Because of recent manifestations, the director-general of the school has appointed two special animators to meet with teachers on disponibility to examine the syndicate's demands for extra classes.' This is a newsletter from the high school. The English high school, mind you. Do you have any idea what it means, Mr. Collins?"

"I'm not sure," Frank replied. "I know that director-general is what we call a school principal, and I believe that animator is used for moderator or organizer."

"You see what I mean. Pretty soon English Quebeckers will need to have interpreters in the rest of the country. Now they all say *dépanneur* instead of corner store, *inscription* instead of admission, *autoroute* instead of highway, and God knows what else. I tell you, Mr. Collins, it won't be long before they're incomprehensible to people from the outside such as yourself."

Frank acknowledged Richmond's point that Quebec English was acquiring a French flavour of its own, but he remained unconvinced that it was in any danger of being transformed into an inaccessible dialect like London Cockney or Detroit jive talk, as the older man seemed to fear. In fact, Frank speculated, what was happening to Quebec English was much the same as what had happened to Quebec French when English was in a dominant position, as Marcel Tremblay had illustrated to him a few days earlier. The tables had been turned. Special animator was the same sort of thing as *un bon boss*.

Reginald Richmond, Frank also learned before the

evening was over, did not have a high opinion of the Arabian businessman, Mr. Gabib, who had recently invited him and two other local men of affairs to an afternoon meeting at his lavish new home down the lake.

"Would you believe," asked Richmond, "that all he offered us to drink was tea?"

"I can understand that," said Frank. "Moslems have strict laws against drinking alcohol."

"Be that as it may, Mr. Collins. Let the man live as he likes. But in this country he'd be well advised to follow our customs and show a little respect for his guests."

"You didn't think he showed respect?"

"He treated us like schoolchildren. He actually gave us a lecture on how Canadian businessmen were all a bunch of fumbling idiots and how, if we went along with him, he would be generous enough to lead us down the road to success. Bear in mind, Mr. Collins, that besides myself, he was talking to John J. Finlay and Jefferson Pierce. John owns the Penobscot Complex in Detroit, three or four farms in the Kentucky bluegrass, not to mention a fair bit of downtown real estate in Montreal and Toronto. Pierce's holding company has a chain of hotels, a chain of newspapers and a chain of shops in airports around the world."

Evidently the meeting between Gabib and the local businessmen was a total fiasco. When Gabib began to lose patience and shout at them, the three Canadians simply got up and left. Richmond knew that Gabib had bought a lot of property in town, but he was not particularly concerned. He was convinced that the man really did not know what he was doing and was therefore no threat, apart from the effect he was having on property values. But then, according to the mayor of North Chadley, that effect was a counterbalance to the drop in values caused by the Separatists, who were the real threat to the country.

    When Frank got back to his room, Mirabel rubbed herself against his legs and kept on meowing until he poured some milk into her saucer. Watching her lap up the milk, he began to worry about how fat she had gotten. It was not normal for a cat to be so bloated, he told himself. Perhaps he was feeding her too well, but she was so demanding that there was nothing else to do. It might be a good idea, he reflected, thinking of Lisette's mother, to take the cat to a vet to find out if there could be something wrong with her. But she certainly seemed happy enough.

Chapter Ten

It was Bill Martin who invited Frank to accompany him to a meeting of a new organization, CAPIQ, in the town hall. Bill explained that CAPIQ meant *"Canadiens anglais pour l'indépendance de Québec,"* and that he was curious to see who, apart from his own mixed-up neighbour Gord Jackson, these English-Canadian Separatists could be. Bill met Frank in front of the Inn, and the two men strolled through the town leisurely. Spring was finally in the air in North Chadley, the musky aroma of things becoming unfrozen. The sunshine of the lengthening days of late April was melting the snow, and the water was flowing down the hillsides onto the lake, creating patches of dull grey mush. The old heap of a car, however, as Frank and Bill could see, remained defiantly on the surface, like some shrunken deformation of the Titanic proclaiming the superiority of man-made machines over the forces of nature. The betting on when the car would sink, according to Bill, was now in full swing at Ed Wilson's garage, the townsfolk all having a go at guessing when the inevitable would occur.

Marcel Tremblay, the local OUI committee official whom Frank had met at the Café Québec Libre, also speculated about the inevitable when he introduced the president of CAPIQ to a gathering of eight people in the town hall, counting Frank Collins, Bill Martin and, curiously enough, the stone-faced Indian Frank had seen at the Inn when he first arrived in town. Regressing to his quite fluent, at once flowery and slang-sprinkled English for the occasion, Tremblay pronounced a ten-minute discourse on the entire history of the world, pointing out the inevitability of cohesive collectivities forming their separate, distinctive nations—the Greeks, the Jews, the Romans, the Huns, the Turkeys, the French, the English, and so on and so forth. It was likewise inevitable, he said, that the *Québécois* would form their own nation, as any reasonable son of a bitch could see. Nourished by the minerals of consanguinity, cohabitation, shared memories, determination to survive, purity of spirit, bloody-mindedness, and the life-sustaining sap of a distinctive culture, the bud had swollen to the point of bursting, and it was inevitable that the lily would soon blossom. The English of Quebec, according to Tremblay, could either go along with the sacred process of self-determination or else futilely attempt to bugger the inevitable. Unfortunately, as indicated by the small audience, in which there was at least one well-known, goddamned Federalist spy, the majority of English in Quebec were anti-French reactionaries, concerned only to conserve their fat-cat status. But the meeting was at least a start, Tremblay concluded his remarks, and the President of CAPIQ, Mr. Trever Treadwell, was a veritable beacon in the Anglo-Saxon darkness.

Trever Treadwell then rose to speak. He had a strong British accent, which Bill identified to Frank as Yorkshire, and he began by describing how throughout the world cultural minorities were now struggling to preserve their uniqueness and to assert themselves. It was all part of the anti-imperialist crusade. It was the duty of all right-thinking people to join that crusade, to help the down-trodden and oppressed. Frank noticed Marcel Tremblay wince when Treadwell went on to mention that French Canadians were in a particularly pitiful state, having been systematically suppressed for centuries. English Canadians, he said, were the oppressors and should now accept their responsibilities. They must right the wrongs of the past. The French of Quebec were here first to challenge the wilderness and bring civilization to the New World.

At this point, Frank noticed out of the corner of his eye that the big Indian, who was sitting apart from the others at the side of the hall, also winced briefly. Then the Indian seemed to break into a subdued smile. The English came in as usurpers, Treadwell continued, to steal lands, businesses, birthrights. Before he could say more, however, he was interrupted by a large man in a peaked cap and heavy work shirt, whom Bill identified to Frank as a local farmer called Aubry Wells.

"That's bullshit!" said the farmer in a loud voice, rising to his feet.

"I beg your pardon, sir," said Treadwell.

"I said you're giving us a pile of bullshit."

"Then you refuse to accept the facts of history."

"I don't know who the hell you are, mister, but you're the one that don't know nothing about the facts of history."

"Perhaps, then, you will be gracious enough to enlighten me," said Treadwell with an air of condescension, straightening his tie.

"You said that the French were here first," said Wells, "and that we came along and stole their lands. Well I got news for you, mister. My family, like a lot of others in these here Eastern Townships, have been around for five generations. We were the pioneers in this region of the country, which was never part of New France. My great-great grandfather, Orville Wells, along with his three sons, came up from the States and cleared every inch of the land that's now my farm. There weren't nobody there before him."

As the farmer spoke, once again Frank noticed the Indian showing a hint of a smile.

"The French came later, a lot later, and took over some of the farms," Aubry Wells continued. "They had run out of land up around the St. Lawrence River, which is where they had settled in the first place. They were hard-working, good people, and we have always got along together and helped one another. The land don't speak neither English nor French, and neither do the cows and chickens. The language difference didn't bother us none. We understood each other, and we still do."

"What you don't seem to understand, sir," responded Treadwell, "is that the French are a suppressed people in their own province."

"Suppressed by who?"

"By English Canadians, of course. By the group you represent, sir, whether you are ready to admit it or not."

"I don't represent no group. And I ain't never suppressed nobody."

"Nevertheless, like many of the English in Quebec and the rest of Canada, you stood by and let it happen because it was to your advantage, so you share the guilt, sir. You are a cog in the wheel of oppression."

Treadwell was now pointing his finger at Aubry Wells, who responded by advancing toward him.

"Listen, mister," said the farmer, "I came here to see if I could do anything to help sort out this mess, because me and the other farmers around here, English and French both, don't want it. But you ain't telling me nothing. Who are you, anyway?"

"I'm a simple citizen concerned to see justice done,"

replied Treadwell, defiantly holding his ground against the much bigger man.

"You seem to me more like a weasel in a henhouse."

"And I think, sir, that you are a typical English-Canadian bigot."

"You limey bastard!" shouted Wells as he grabbed Treadwell by the lapels of his jacket. Bill Martin immediately jumped up to intervene, followed by Frank, who precluded further hostilities by inserting his huge frame between the cocky little man from Yorkshire and the Townships farmer. Wells then left the meeting, and Marcel Tremblay, pleading another pressing engagement, followed suit. The Indian also got up and left. Treadwell then tidied his jacket and asked if there were any questions. The room was silent for a few moments, then Bill Martin spoke up.

"All right, I have a question. Why are you so anxious to destroy Canada?"

"I beg your pardon, sir," said Treadwell, raising his eyebrows.

"I'm asking you what you are doing over here trying to destroy a good country."

"But I've said nothing about destroying Canada. When Quebec gains its sovereignty, the rest of Canada can continue as it always has."

"Have you ever looked at a map of North America?"

"Of course I have, sir. In fact, I've studied cartography."

"Then you should realize that to separate Quebec from Canada, to consider only the most basic problem, would mean slicing the country right down the middle, leaving two chunks of territory hundreds of miles apart. It simply wouldn't work."

"That's only a technicality," said Treadwell.

"A technicality? I'm talking about the basic logistics of operating a country— communications, transport, services."

"Listen, Bill," Gordon Jackson broke in, "there are always ways. Look at Martinique and Guadaloupe— they're hundreds of miles away and they're still part of France. So are St-Pierre and Miquelon for that matter. And what about Hawaii, Alaska, Greenland?"

"Those are all islands or territories which were never joined to the mother country geographically," said Bill. "What we're talking about here is severing long-established and essential lines of communication, the nation's arteries—railways, roads, the Seaway, telephone and mail. It can't be done without total chaos."

"Gentlemen," said Treadwell, "secondary technicalities. The issue here is the destiny of the French-Canadian people. We have a duty to assist in the birth of a nation, to redress the abuses of the past. . . ."

"Listen, Treadwell," said Bill, "we Canadians, English and French and Italian and Greek and Ukrainian and whatever, we already have a nation, a model for the world. Our duty is to make it even better, not to tear it apart."

"A typical attitude," said the Englishman. "You're comfortable in your position of privilege, therefore you refuse to recognize that there can be anything wrong with Canada."

Bill now rose, and Frank squirmed in his seat, thinking that the man from Yorkshire was determined to become a martyr one way or another.

"Let me tell you something, Mr. Treadwell," said Martin in his booming voice. "We don't need you to tell us what is wrong with Canada. I am perfectly aware of the faults. But I am also aware that there is only one way to judge a country—are people trying to get into it, or are people trying to get out of it?"

"Precisely, sir," Treadwell retorted. "French Canadians want out."

"You're wrong. Even the most fanatical Separatists wouldn't dream of leaving Quebec. The FLQ terrorists exiled to Cuba threw themselves on the mercy of the courts to come back here. And you, Treadwell, you don't really give a damn about French Canadians."

"I beg your pardon, sir."

"I said you don't really give a damn about French Canadians."

"That's not true. I most certainly care. My record speaks for itself. Before I came to this country, I was involved with both the Scottish and Welsh nationalist movements. Had I not decided to come over here, I would be in Spain helping the Basques, with whom I was also involved."

"Then why the hell don't you go back and get involved with them again? They need your help more than French Canadians do."

Looking around the room, Frank could see that the president of CAPIQ was not endearing himself to anyone, let alone Bill Martin. The two other men still in the hall besides Jackson and himself had bored expressions on their faces.

"Come on, Bill," said Gord Jackson, "you're being unfair. This man has a right to express his opinions."

"Certainly. Let him spout all the garbage he likes. But he'll have to take the consequences when he insults people like Aubry Wells. And I don't have to listen to him either."

Frank was relieved when Bill Martin grabbed his coat and left the room. The meeting then drew quickly to a close. Treadwell took the names of the three remaining participants and also tried to enlist Frank, who declined with the explanation that he was a neutral observer.

Gord Jackson and Frank walked back from the town hall together as far as the Inn, and Frank discovered that Martin's colleague and neighbour was hardly as dedicated a Separatist as he might have imagined from the heated arguments between the two professors. Jackson allowed to Frank that he thought Treadwell was a meddling ass, the type of loser who attempts to offset a sense of his own deficiencies by running around supporting all the causes he can dig up. It was only a matter of time until the man from Yorkshire discovered that the baby seals being clubbed and skinned by Newfie fishermen on ice floes in the Gulf of St. Lawrence were a much sexier cause than Quebec independence, Jackson remarked. So far as he was himself concerned, he had been listening to the lamentations of nationalists, notably a number of fellow poets, ever since he first came to Quebec, and he had decided that it was about time to get it all over with. If Quebec wanted to separate, then let it separate and see what would happen. Canada was probably too vast and too much of a hodgepodge to be properly governable in any case. Bill Martin, according to Jackson, was a sentimental idealist with a vision of Canada as a model for the world, a perfect pluralist nation where all the diverse ethnic groups co-existed in harmony, living and letting live, enriching one another, and all that sort of rot. Jackson, on the other hand, claimed to be a realist, perhaps even a bit of a cynic. To his mind, nations were like marriages—if things weren't working out, if there was constant bickering and mutual misery, then why be damned masochistic fools? Call it quits and pick up the pieces. When the two men arrived at the Inn, Frank invited Jackson in for a beer, but the latter declined, saying that he had classes to prepare.

In the bar salon, Frank was greeted cheerfully by Wilt Wadleigh, who, without asking, reached into the refrigerator and handed him a Labatt 50 beer.

"And where's your charming wife tonight?" asked Frank, feeling genuinely deprived.

"Oh she's off delivering a pizza to my cousin Morton," said Wilt. "Crazy bastard would starve to death if we didn't feed him once in a while. He's one of those mad scientists, you know. Only things he thinks about are his screwball inventions."

Frank mulled over Wadleigh's words, recalling what the cleaning lady Marge Miller had told him about Lisette and cousin Morton, and at the same time triggering the now-familiar spicy images of Lisette to flit across the video screen of his mind. He was beginning to feel slightly sorry for the tyrannical but probably naive innkeeper, and perhaps also for himself and for males in general, who could all be so easily reduced to whimpering mush by a female *ben stackée*. Men were more pitiful than dogs, he told himself, because dogs only went out of their skulls when a female was in heat. Women could turn on the heat any time they took the notion, and a normal man was at their mercy. Was it possible that Walt Wadleigh did not realize . . . Frank's meditation was interrupted by the arrival in the bar of a man with flowing white hair who was carrying three cartons of eggs under his arm. The man turned out to be Joe Larose, who, as Frank had been told, was operating a delivery service for fresh eggs from the farm of one of his cousins. Frank introduced himself and invited Joe to join him for a beer. They sat down at one of the tables while Wadleigh went into the kitchen.

"*Ben oui,*" said Joe, raising his glass, "I'm hear all about you from Jeannie. She tell me you a big shot from de State."

"Well, I'm no big shot," Frank replied. "I'm just a student trying to write a doctoral dissertation."

"Hey, *mon garçon,* me I got trouble just for write my name. So how you like dis place?"

"I find it quite intriguing. Although I must say that I'm a bit concerned about all the bitterness over the Referendum."

"Hey, *Chrisse, ça fait rien.* It doan mean nothing. A few guy make a lot of noise, *c'est tout.*"

"You really think so?"

"*Ben oui.* We got some English and we got some Québécois dat like to make noise and trouble all de time. Dey doan got enough in life to be happy, so dey want everybody else to be unhappy too. You got de same ting in de State, *n'est-ce pas?*"

"Yeah, that's for sure. We have our share."

"*Voilà. C'est pas grande chose.*"

"So you're not worried then?"

"Jeannie, she worree all de time. Me, I got too much work to do."

"And how do you really feel about the Referendum, Joe? Do you think Quebec should separate from Canada?"

"*Mais non.* All we gonna have left is Québec *tout foké* and Canada *tout foké. Ça ne fait pas de bon sens.*"

"You mean you like things the way they are?"

"No, I doan like. But now we change a few thing, and pretty soon we change a few more. Dat's good. But you doan burn *toute la forêt* for chop a dead tree. Like

Jeannie say all de time, you doan cut your nose for spit on your face."

"What changes would you like to see, Joe?"

"De big one I'm see already. Québec is get to be *vraiment français asteure.* People now dey can work *en français. C'est normal ça.* Not like when I was a kid."

"And you see that really happening?"

"*Ben oui, partout.* Some English doan like. But for me, if dey doan like, dey go someplace else. Jeannie, she say *exactement la même chose que moi.* She doan mind to speak French."

"Oh, I didn't realize that she spoke French."

"She say all she want to say. She get pretty good when she lose de goddamn temper. She speak French like hell."

As Joe lifted his glass to finish his beer, Frank noticed that Lisette was back and that the black-bearded man who had been with Michel Bertrand and the OUI committee at the Café Québec Libre had just come into the bar salon. The man glowered at Wilt Wadleigh, gave Lisette a longer, seemingly pained look, then headed straight for the table where Joe and Frank were sitting. Addressing the older man as *"mon oncle,"* he explained that he had seen Joe's truck parked outside. Frank immediately noted the resemblance between uncle and nephew, whose name was Paul Larose—they were both built like lumberjacks, heavy-shouldered and barrel-chested. They had the same masses of curly hair, except that Joe's was now frosty white. It occurred to Frank that the two men, if slightly smaller versions, were physically much like himself, which was not surprising in view of the fact that his grandfather had come from Quebec to Michigan to work as a lumberjack. He had read in a book on the fur trade that the French-Canadian *voyageurs*, the men who paddled the boats in the early days of the trade, were exceptionally sturdy and powerful, capable of portaging heavy canoes over rough, hilly trails with 200-pound packs strapped to their backs besides. Something of the old *voyageur* had come down to himself and to both Laroses at the table with him, he mused, as Lisette strutted over. But before she could take an order, Wilt Wadleigh called out from behind the bar.

"Listen, Paul, if you've come here to make trouble, you bastard, I'll get the provincial police right away. After the last time, they'd love to get another crack at you."

"*Mange d'la marde, maudzitte tête carrée!*" Paul shouted back, causing his uncle Joe to wince and Wilt to narrow his icy blue eyes and reach for the telephone. Lisette simply stood by the table, contemplating the three burly men with a Mona Lisa smile. Then Frank spoke up.

"It's okay, Wilt. I'm conducting an interview with Paul and Joe. We'll have three more quarts, please."

Wilt Wadleigh's face remained contorted in a snarl, but he replaced the telephone receiver and opened the refrigerator. Lisette fetched the three bottles and gave Paul an exaggerated, pointedly phoney smile as she placed a glass in front of him and poured the customary couple of inches of beer. The black-bearded man snatched the bottle from her hand and filled the glass until the foam erupted over the rim.

Frank soon learned that Joe Larose and his nephew did not always see eye to eye, which he hardly found surprising. Paul's mind seemed to be poisoned by a potent bitterness toward the "*maudzits Anglais*," whom he blamed for the high rate of unemployment, acid rain, the abominable music on jukeboxes, fashions in women's clothes, air pollution, the exorbitant cost of living, the government deficit, the weather and the lousy, tasteless beer everyone was forced to drink because the big, English-owned breweries had a secret pact to sell only lousy, tasteless beer in Quebec. Even the famous American brand, Budweiser, was somehow changed into a lousy, tasteless beer when it was distributed in Quebec, Paul claimed. The reason it was so popular was that it made the *Québécois* think that they were on vacation, since vacation for the entire population of Quebec meant Florida or Old Orchard Beach.

Paul and Joe conversed in rapid, colloquial French, and Frank had some trouble following at first, but with each successive beer, however tasteless, communication, like a mountain climber or a treacherous bluff, seemed to clutch and crawl its way to a higher level. Either that, Frank speculated, or else he was experiencing the phenomenon of biological memory.

Joe shook his head vigorously as his nephew banged the table and proclaimed that all the *"maudzits Anglais,"* starting with that son-of-a-bitch Wilt Wadleigh, should be kicked out of Quebec, should be plunked down on the 401 Trans-Canada highway and pointed toward Toronto, or piled into leaky canoes without paddles and shoved into the current of the St. Lawrence River, which would carry them into the North Atlantic and maybe back to England, where they could drink tea and eat goddamn crumpets. When, however, his uncle mentioned Jeannie McVicar, Paul referred to her as *"ma tante Jeannie"* and assured Joe that she was an exception and therefore exempt from his population-redistribution proposals. It turned out, in fact, that there were many exceptions, including arch-Federalist Bill Martin, whose heart was in the right place, Paul admitted, and who would eventually realize the error of his ways.

On the other hand, contended Paul, there were many Québécois who were traitorous *"vendus"* and should be sent packing the moment the trumpets sounded and *L'État du Québec* was declared sovereign over loudspeakers attached to the stone walls of the National Assembly Building. As he uttered the last statement, Paul Larose glanced over at Lisette, who was half-sitting on one of the high stools in front of the bar. In her tight, slit skirt, with one foot perched on an upper rung of the stool and the other on the floor, she was providing an excellent view of shapely leg. As Paul's glance lingered, Joe asked him where he intended to send all the so-called *"vendus."* Nodding toward Lisette, who obligingly accentuated her display by reversing the position of her legs, or who was perhaps simply trying to give each foot a rest from her high-heeled shoes, Paul remarked that Quebec girls who sold themselves to the *"maudzits Anglais"* could all be shipped off to sleazy Ontario strip joints, for all he cared. He claimed that in places like Sarnia and Windsor, which he knew well from his truck-driving days, and even in once-upon-a-time Toronto the Good, Quebec strippers were in great demand and were hauling in huge salaries, supplemented by mittfuls of extra cash for doing expository acrobatics at individual tables. They were all, according to Paul, wearing mink stoles, driving red Thunderbirds and on a diet of *"mer et terre,"* which Frank took to mean surf and turf. Paul couldn't explain why they were so popular, because after all, a naked woman was a naked woman, and certainly some of the big blondes and red-headed

Anglaises could knock a man's eyes out, but somehow the Quebec strippers seemed to be able to exhibit their bodies more enticingly than other women who danced in the nude.

As Frank's beer-befuddled brain wrestled with this enigma, Lisette stood up and glided her sheathed *Québécoise* body over to the table to collect the empty bottles on her tray and to inquire if the three customers wished to order another round. Once again, Frank could not keep himself from visualizing how Lisette would look if she were working in Windsor, Ontario, but his revery was abruptly shattered by a loud voice. He had vaguely noticed the four men come into the bar earlier, but between contemplating Paul's remarks about Quebec strippers and monitoring the peregrinations of Lisette's skirt as she lolled on the bar stool, he had had no heed left over to pay to the newcomers.

"Hey, Joe," one of the men shouted, "tell that Separatist nephew of yours to guzzle his brew at the mad woman's place next door with the rest of his hairy buddies."

"Yeah, we don't want him oui-oui-ing all over the floor in here," added another of the men. "It stinks the place up."

Frank had seen the four men, who had obviously had quite a few drinks before they arrived, around town before. Two of them worked at the local garage with Ed Wilson, another in the grocery store, and the fourth was a truck driver. Paul Larose was now standing up with his fists clenched. His black beard and bushy eyebrows bristled, giving him the appearance of an enraged bear. As he slowly advanced toward the four men, who were now also on their feet, he swept aside a table and a couple of chairs as if they were falling leaves. The largest of the opposing four, who was taller than Paul but not nearly as thick and broad, raised his fists in anticipation. Frank noticed one of the men grab a quart beer bottle, while the other two gripped the backs of chairs. He also noticed that Wilt Wadleigh had emerged from behind the bar with a baseball bat and that old Joe had gotten to his feet and was shuffling over to back up his nephew. There was an ominous silence in the bar salon, like the calm of a sub-zero winter night.

Frank Collins was bewildered. The last thing he wanted was to become involved in a brawl between English and French Canadians. Since the moment he had arrived in St-Alphonse de Chadley Nord he had carefully avoided taking sides, which was the only way he could get on with his research. Why the hell did he have to get caught in the middle of a mess like this one? he asked himself. Perhaps he was being punished for looking at the innkeeper's wife with too much lust in his eye. But even born-again Christian President Jimmy Carter had confessed to looking at women with lust in his eye once in a while.

Whatever, Frank told himself, he had to do something. He couldn't just sit and let his drinking companions of a few moments earlier, one of them a man in his seventies, take on five opponents, because there was no doubt which side Wilt Wadleigh would be on. With the chairs, beer bottles and baseball bat as weapons, there was also no doubt that somebody was going to get hurt, if not worse. Frank rose to his feet, thinking that if he moved quickly he might be able to neutralize the two men with the chairs. Paul, snorting like a bull about to charge, and the tall man were now standing face to face, each waiting for the other to make the first move. Old Joe, the man with the beer bottle and Wilt with the baseball bat held in front of him were edging closer to the main ring. Any second now, Frank sensed, all hell was going to break loose.

Then suddenly, as if she had vanished from one spot in the room and reconstituted herself in another spot, Lisette was standing between Paul and his adversary. She was dwarfed by the two men, but with her head tossed back, highlighting the delicate features of her pixy face and her long, ebony hair, she seemed to exude an aura of inviolable femininity.

"Sit down in that chair, you silly arse!" she commanded the tall man, slapping down his raised fists.

"*Paul, ça suffit! Assieds-toué!*" she continued, swinging around to Larose.

Frank could hardly believe his eyes when the two men, who only a moment ago were about to hurl themselves at each other like a pair of crazed tom cats, did exactly what they were told. Joe Larose then moved the table which Paul had swept aside back to where it was supposed to be and righted the tipped chairs. Still standing, he drained his glass of beer and signalled his nephew to follow suit. Then the Laroses both shook hands with Frank and left the bar salon.

After a few moments had elapsed, one of the men from the garage invited Frank to join him and his friends at their table. The four men were in high spirits and seemed not the least bit shaken by the fact that they had narrowly escaped a brawl with a furious and patently dangerous colossus. They actually seemed disappointed that Lisette had intervened to protect, as they put it, "one of her own." Frank could not help marvelling that these English Canadians, reduced now to a minority even smaller than the white remnant of the inner city of Detroit, who lived in a constant state of fear, did not show any signs of apprehension. Perhaps, he speculated, it had simply not dawned on them that they were a minority. In any case, they were certainly not a visible minority. The tensions between the English and French in Canada, therefore, could hardly be considered as complicated as the black-white situation in the United States. Nevertheless, Frank concluded, some Canadians seemed damned determined to make the most of them.

After one more beer and a last admiring look at Lisette, who was again a composite of exquisite legs and Mona Lisa smile perched atop a bar stool, Frank said good night to all and stumbled off to his room and his obese black cat. Mirabel went out when Frank came in, but within minutes she was scratching at the door.

Chapter Eleven

Nobody actually saw the car sink below the surface of the thawing Lake Missawappi. It happened not at high noon, when the rays of the sun were presumably at their mush-producing peak, but in the dark of a moonless night, either late on April 28th or in the early hours of April 29th, unobserved by human eye, as if the old Ford, like a dying animal in the bush, had opted for privacy to begin the ultimate stages of the process of being reduced back to the elements from which it had been created.

Since the exact time of the sinking was not known, the winner of the lottery was not announced immediately, causing as much consternation in Chadley North as when the residents woke up to discover that a mysterious Arab was trying to buy most of the town's prime real estate. Clémentine held the ticket for 4:00 p.m. on April 28th, Mrs. Edna Richmond had one for noon on April 29th, and the latter let it be known around the village that she would not be surprised if the café owner, a woman of doubtful character at best and a raving Separatist to boot, had sneaked out during the night on snowshoes to sprinkle rock salt around the wrecked car. Clémentine's response was that *"la vieille Anglaise"* had been seen marching along the lake road on the afternoon before the night the car sank, and that her very presence was enough to freeze hell over, let alone prevent the lake ice from melting.

Naturally the English-speaking townsfolk for the most part took the side of Mrs. Richmond, while the

French lined up behind Clémentine, and for a while it seemed to Frank that open warfare in the streets was imminent. Two eggs and a tomato were hurled against the front window of the Café Québec Libre, and the mail-box post by the driveway to the Richmond house was knocked down. Crowds gathered ominously in front of the snack bar and the café, shaking fists, muttering threats, and voicing fulsome obscenities in the two tongues.

Ed Wilson resolved the dispute between the two women, to his satisfaction if not entirely to theirs, by officially declaring that the car must have gone down at or about 2:00 a.m. on April 29th, because Phil Peters, one of the garage mechanics who had been quaffing a few ales with friends at the Inn on the night in question, in front of witnesses of both persuasions and a neutral Yank besides, had staggered home at about 1:30 and had noticed that at that time the car was still on the lake. Then Henry Ralston, who gets up at the ungodly hour of 2:30 in the morning to attend to his milk route in Brooke, had looked out his window while he was drinking his coffee and noticed that the car wasn't there. Clémentine protested that Phil Peters, even when he wasn't blind drunk, couldn't tell the difference between his arse and an automobile, and that the *maudzits Anglais* were in cahoots again to cheat and oppress the *Québécois* and to screw them out of what was rightfully theirs. But Ed Wilson holding the prize money—some $463 after his twenty percent cut and towing charges— in his possession, it was finally split between Mrs. Richmond and Clémentine, each being presumably an equal ten hours off the mark.

Meanwhile, as Frank learned from the headlines and reports in the morning newspapers, thousands of other

Quebec women were bringing the Referendum campaign to new and astonishing heights. They called themselves the "Yvettes," and the previous night more than 14,000 of them had held a mass rally in the hallowed hockey shrine of the Montreal Forum. Nothing like it had been seen since the notorious "Rocket Richard Riot" of 1956, following the suspension of the idolized Canadiens' star by the then National Hockey League president, Clarence Campbell. For many Quebec hockey fans, Frank knew as a hockey fan himself, the suspension of Richard was a clear case of a French hero being slapped down by the English boss, who furthermore had the arrogance to show up at a game between the Rocketless Canadiens and Frank's hometown and favourite team, the Detroit Red Wings. The face-off occurred when somebody at the game threw a stink bomb at Campbell. He had to be escorted out of the arena by a cordon of police, then pandemonium erupted. The Montreal team was obliged to forfeit the game, and suspended Maurice Richard was denied the scoring championship, callously bypassed in the last few games by his own teammate "Boom Boom" Geoffrion, who was never forgiven by the Rocket's more ardent fans.

Frank gathered from the newspapers that the Quebec Government's *Ministre d'État à la Condition féminine,* Madame Lise Payette, would likewise never be forgiven by ardent Separatists for the monumental gaffe which unleashed the "Yvette" fury. It appeared that while she had started off a major address with the noble intention of simultaneously liberating the massses of *Québécoises* and *la patrie* itself, she had somehow managed to lose her way, and *Madame la Ministre* had ended up inadvertently scaling the cliffs on the shore of the St. Lawrence

River and single-handedly reenacting the Battle of the Plains of Abraham, with the same outcome as the first time.

While following the various newspaper reports and commentaries on the Referendum, Frank had recalled various anthropological studies on the use of symbols in politics. Even the most radical political movements, he had read, would platform the symbolic order of a former, idyllically perceived regime, for the simple reason, however ironic, that change could most easily be achieved if the illusion of continuity were nurtured in the minds of the people. To Frank's mind, that was exactly what the Separatist group, the Parti Québécois, were trying to do, were in fact accomplishing quite well. The OUI committees were evoking glorified images of a rural, egalitarian, garden-of-Eden, pre-British-Conquest French Canada to get through to the people. They had the enthusiastic support of popular chansonniers such as Gilles Vigneault, Pauline Julien, and Félix Leclerc. Frank had heard one of Julien's songs—a tearful, heart-rending piece called "Mommy, Mommy," which presented the scenario of a small child no longer able to communicate with her own *Québécoise* mother in the mother tongue, the implication being that if the people did not vote OUI, that was what the future would be. One of Leclerc's verses, which Frank had seen on a wall of the Café Québec Libre, projected how the morning after everyone had voted OUI, there would be no more bosses, no more landlords, no more troubles, just perfect peace. By some miracle presumably. The OUI option, thus, was associated with paradise regained, pride in the French cultural heritage and solidarity with one's *Québécois* brothers and sisters.

NON, on the other hand, as interpreted to the people by the independentists, meant denial of all these wonderful things, betrayal of the collectivity, cowardice, and treachery. The NON committees, besides outlining the economic pitfalls of separation, were desperately trying to counter emotional nationalism by the campaign slogan *"Mon NON est Québécois,"* playing on the identical pronunciation of *non* and *nom,* the French for name, and thereby proclaiming that both one's name and one's *non* could be a positive affirmation of Quebec identity. It was a cunning bit of word play, Frank thought, but nevertheless, so far as he could tell, the OUI people had a monopoly on all the effective ethnic symbols.

One problem he did note—although he suspected that extremists would not see it as a problem—was that the nationalism of the Separatists was strictly tribal. The term *Québécois* as they generally used it had come to signify only francophone descendants of the settlers of New France, people for whom the provincial motto, *Je me souviens,* meant remembering a pioneering past and a heroic survival. Thus the solidarity theme being used to consolidate and mobilize the *Québécois* community had the side-effect of generally alienating everyone else in the province, all those who were outside that particular community, notably the English, the native peoples and the various other ethnic minorities such as Italians, Portuguese, Greeks, Haitians, Poles, Latin Americans, and Ukrainians.

Frank had also noted that the OUI committees were apparently much more concerned about another group than about the minorities. That group was the women of Quebec, who according to various polls were not responding to the OUI stimuli as wholeheartedly as they ought to be. Frank had been intrigued by this curious phenomenon. He knew that like hand grenades, political symbols could sometimes be caught in the air and flung back at the people who threw them in the first place, or they might even swing around all by themselves and return to smack you on the snozzle, like a boomerang. The Parti Québécois had quite naturally called upon the Minister of State on the Status of Women, Madame Lise Payette, to politicize the women of the province. Before entering politics, she had been a popular talk-show hostess, a kind of female francophone Johnny Carson, and now she was the champion of women's rights. And she had certainly done a job of politicizing Quebec women, but as Frank was discovering in the morning papers, not quite in the way intended. The working of women's minds, he mused, was still one of the mysteries of the world, even to other women evidently.

According to the various accounts, Madame Payette, addressing a gathering of 750 women in Quebec City, had referred to a well-known Grade Two school reader which depicts a supposedly typical family with two children, Yvette and Guy. Guy takes part in sports, helps his father with repairs around the house and all that manly sort of thing, while his sister, the gentle and obedient Yvette, learns to cook, wash the dishes and sweep the floor in imitation of her mother. Madame Payette promised her audience that the stereotype of the submissive, servile woman would soon be forever banished from the textbooks used in Quebec schools. She then lamented that for the present generation the damage had already been done. Like herself, they had all been conditioned to accept that a woman's role was to serve, to give pleasure, to submit, to bear children, to stay home and look after house and family. As she continued her address, Madame Payette identified herself with Yvette, but she also explained that it was possible for contemporary Quebec women to break away from their role conditioning, to act independently, to vote OUI in the Referendum. Her speech, reported the newspapers, was received with a loud and long ovation. It was only when *Madame la Ministre* decided to add a few additional, spontaneous remarks that her foot got *tout jammé* in her mouth.

The leader of the opposition Liberal Party in Quebec was Claude Ryan, who was also acting as chairman of the NON committees. He had formerly been the highly respected editor of the influential daily *Le Devoir,* and Frank had gathered that he was a somewhat rigid, intellectual, devoutly religious man, who used to be referred to as "The Pope of St-Sacrament," the name of the street where the editorial offices of *Le Devoir* were located. His wife, Madeleine, a low-keyed, reserved lady, quite the opposite of the flamboyant Lise Payette, was helping him in the Referendum campaign, occasionally giving short speeches here and there. Claude Ryan, Frank had observed, had a way of infuriating his opponents, probably because he could not help exuding an aura of moral superiority.

Whatever, Madame Payette began her post-speech remarks by stating that Mr. Ryan was "just the sort of man I hate." Her audience was hardly surprised by the statement, nor by the next statement that to Mr. Ryan, all women were Yvettes. Then came the monumental ministerial gaffe. "He's married to an Yvette," added Madame Payette. "With that one remark," Frank read in an editorial, "she took careless aim at Claude Ryan and hit instead his wife and with her the sensitivities of thousands of housewives."

Many commentators were astonished by the immediate reaction of Quebec women, the bitter protests and the massive rallies which were bursting forth throughout the province. Reflecting on the phenomenon with professional interest, Frank concluded that it was a dramatic example of the perils of playing with symbols in the arena of social realities. Madame Payette was doing just fine so long as she sustained the pretense of identifying with the mythical Yvette. But the moment she stepped away, letting the image drop like a discarded night gown, then pointed an accusing finger at the innocent and unassuming Madeleine Ryan, the roof caved in. It appeared, speculated Frank, that a lot of Quebec women were content with, indeed were proud of their roles as dutiful housewives and mothers. Moreover, a hell of a lot of them could identify with "Yvette" Ryan more readily than they could with "Liberated Lise."

Frank noted in the newspaper reports of the Forum rally that the speakers had lost no time exploiting the possibilities for word play. One woman had apparently struck an especially vibrant chord when she stated, "My mother, like all good Quebec mothers, taught me that there are times when a girl must say NON." Thousands of women in the audience had responded instantly with a thunderous chant of NON! NON! NON! NON! . . . which lasted for several minutes. Absolutely ingenious, Frank thought, associating the OUI group with the image of the ruthless seducer, or perhaps the unfeeling husband. The NON had thus been converted into an expression of protest for every woman who had ever been pressured into doing something that she hadn't wanted to do, or whose dreams had been frustrated one way or another by a dominating male. And in a society governed by civil law based on the old Napoleonic

Code, where only a few years back a woman could not go to a hospital to have a wart removed or open an account in a department store without the endorsing signature of a father or husband, there were multitudes of such women.

As Frank sat at a table in the bar salon sipping a coffee, reading the papers and reflecting, he noticed the stone-faced Indian, whom he had last seen at the abbreviated CAPIQ meeting, come down the stairs and sit at another table. He was carrying an old leather briefcase, which he probably used, thought Frank, for his tooth brush and shaving gear. He placed the briefcase on the chair beside him at the table and gave Lisette his order of black coffee, sausages and porridge. Frank continued leafing through the newspapers until the man had finished his breakfast, then his anthropological curiosity got the best of him. He stood up and walked over to the other table, taking his cup of coffee with him.

"Good morning," said Frank. "Mind if I join you?"

The Indian looked up at him, but he did not reply and his expression did not change. Frank hesitated for a moment, then he placed his coffee cup on the table and sat down opposite the other man.

"I guess it's all over for the ice fishing this year," said Frank.

The other man simply nodded his head.

"By the way," Frank went on, "my name is Collins. I'm an anthropology student. Last summer I worked with an Amerindian band in North Dakota, helping them sort out their hunting and fishing rights."

"Is that so," responded the other man, showing a flicker of interest which Frank regarded as a breakthrough.

"Yes," Frank continued, "a lot of graduate students get involved in summer projects like that. We can learn a lot, and sometimes we can be of help to the native peoples."

"How?"

"We do research. Dig up the old treaties and maps. Go through the records. Check what's happened in similar situations. That's the sort of thing we're trained to do as anthropologists."

"I see. Is that what you're doing here?"

"No, not exactly," Frank replied, thinking that he was now making real progress. "I'm studying the evolution of institutions in the town for a Ph.D. dissertation. What are you here for this time?"

The Indian took a swig of his coffee before replying.

"I have business," he said.

This time Frank simply nodded and waited.

"I'll rent a boat and do a little spring fishing perhaps."

"Hey, that's right. The fishing's always good right after the ice breaks up, isn't it?"

"So I've heard."

"By the way," said Frank, holding out his hand, "I'm Frank Collins. What's your name?"

The man reached over slowly and shook hands with Frank.

"Billy Carcajou," he said.

"Carcajou? Doesn't that mean wolverine in French?"

"The word comes from the Algonquin language."

"What tribe do you belong to, Billy?"

"Missawappi."

"Missawappi? I thought all the Missawappis were ... were ...."

"Dead?"

"No. I mean assimilated into the various other tribes and the population in general."

"Not all," replied Billy Carcajou.

"No, obviously not."

"This used to be our land, the entire area around Lake Missawappi."

"Yes, I know. I've read some histories of the region."

"What histories?"

"Well, you know, various accounts of how the area was settled and that sort of thing."

Billy nodded his head, and his features hardened again, persuading Frank to get back to the neutral subject of fishing.

"Say, when you rent that boat and hit the lake, would you like some company? I wouldn't mind trying my luck."

"I fish alone," replied Carcajou. Then he stood up, reached for his brief-case and turned toward the door. Before leaving, he looked back at Frank with what might have been a hint of a smile.

"Maybe some other time," he said.

Frank took a sip of his coffee. Billy Carcajou was a strange character, he told himself. He was not overly talkative, but when he did talk, it was not in the monosyllables of a Hollywood redskin. His diction, in fact, seemed quite polished, as if he were a man of some education. Frank resolved that he would try to get to know Carcajou better. Maybe he was the last of the Missawappis.

Chapter Twelve

Frank Collins was not sure what he was letting himself in for when he volunteered to help rebuild the Murphy house, which had burned down shortly before he arrived in St-Alphonse de Chadley Nord. He had already contributed some money toward the purchase of materials, because the Inn, the Snack Bar, the Café Québec Libre, the grocery store, and the hardware store all had donation tins by their cash registers. Despite their Irish name, the Murphys, Frank learned, were French-speaking, like hundreds of thousands of others with Irish names in Quebec. Being for the most part of the Roman Catholic religion, Irish men who immigrated to Quebec had intermarried with Catholic Quebec girls more readily than did the Protestant immigrants, and their children had generally adopted their mother's tongue. Frank knew from his reading of Quebec history books, as well as from talking with Jeannie McVicar, that while the Church was all-powerful in the province, which was the case until just a few years ago, religion was a much more formidable barrier to intermarriage than was language.

The father of the North Chadley Murphy family, a fairly tall man with a hook nose and curly black hair, had been crippled while working as a labourer on the construction of the Olympic Stadium in Montreal. Because of some error in calculation, or because the project was being rushed too frantically in order to be completed in time for the games, or perhaps a combination of the two, a huge concrete cantilever had slipped its moorings and crashed down on several workers. André Murphy's left leg, Frank was told, had been mangled beyond repair. He was now limping around with a cane and collecting workman's compensation to support his wife and seven children.

To save money when fuel oil prices began to skyrocket, Murphy had shifted from an oil furnace to a potbellied stove called a "Quebec heater" to keep his little wood-frame house warm in the winter. But the wood he burned, not all of it dry, had caused a build-up of creosote in the old brick chimney. When the chimney caught fire, Frank learned from Wilt Wadleigh and other people in town, the flames shot fifteen or twenty feet in the air. The volunteer fire brigade arrived in time to see Murphy limp out of the house with the baby in his arms and the house burn to the ground in a matter of minutes. Murphy and his wife and the three youngest of their children had been living at Joe Larose's place since then, while the other children were with various relatives.

The May sunshine was conducting a clean-up operation on the remaining patches of dirty snow along the sides of the road as Frank walked over to the construction site at the edge of town near the river. He was startled to see about twenty people already there at 7:00 a.m., and it was not long before they were all hard at work. The two local carpenters, Geoff Taylor and Jacques Richard, each formed crews of six and began to lay out the walls of the new house. Frank gathered that these wall frames would be put together on the ground then raised as complete units. The carpentry crews, which included Gord Jackson and one of Bill Martin's daughters, would get them ready and pre-cut the various beams and joists during this first Saturday, while the remaining volunteers poured the cement foundation.

Two bench saws, presumably belonging to Taylor and Richard, were already hooked up to a jerry-rigged electricity box connected to a hydro pole, as was a concrete mixer, which stood between a pyramid of sand and stacked bags of Portland cement. Frank saw that the excavation of the basement had already been finished, probably with a backhoe, and that plywood forms and metal reinforcing rods were piled nearby. He also saw that his job, no doubt because of his size, would be to transport the cement by wheelbarrow, or a *"barouette"* as Jacques Richard called it, from the mixer to the foundation site, along with Bill Martin, Paul Larose and the same big garage mechanic who had almost gotten into a brawl with Paul a few nights earlier. The other garage man would be loading the mixer with Joe Larose and André Murphy himself, who could still handle a shovel well enough.

By noon the footings for the foundation had been poured, and Joe explained that they would let the cement set while they had lunch, then put up the forms and pour the basement walls in the afternoon. He had no sooner finished talking when a van pulled up, followed by a car. In the next few moments, Frank was somewhat surprised to see Clémentine, Lisette Wadleigh, another one of the Martin girls, Jeannie McVicar, Margery Miller, and of all people, old Edna Richmond, set up picnic tables and begin serving a meal of thick, steaming clam chowder, ham, mashed potatoes, vegetables, and all the trimmings. They also had several cases of cold beer and soft drinks.

Every muscle in his body was aching as Frank lowered himself into a folding chair. His three wheelbarrow mates, including 50-year-old Bill Martin, seemed none the worse for wear, or perhaps they were better at hiding their discomfort.

"How you like dis research, *monsieur l'étudiant universitaire?*" asked Joe Larose, handing Frank a beer from one of the cases.

"I'm certainly getting right down to the concrete facts," replied Frank, gratefully accepting the bottle of beer and taking a long draught.

"Joe is our expert on concrete," remarked Bill Martin, also wetting his whistle. "He has all the facts about cement in his head. His head is full of it, you might say."

"*Ben oui,*" Joe retorted. "Dat is how come me I got de hard head, and Bill he got de soft head."

"*Hein, Joe, sais-tu que l'Arabe, Monsieur Gabib, a acheté La Presse de Montréal?*" Paul Larose asked his uncle.

"*Non, c'est pas vrai?*" responded Joe.

"You're kidding. You mean that Gabib has bought the Montreal *La Presse?* When did he do that?" asked the tall garage man, whose name, Frank had learned, was George Carson.

"*Ce matin,*" said Paul.

"You know, it doesn't surprise me," said Bill Martin. "He's been trying to get control of everything and to influence people. Just think of what he can do with his own newspaper."

"*La Presse* is the biggest daily in Quebec, isn't it? asked Frank.

"It sure is," said Bill, looking genuinely concerned. "You know, Frank, controlling the media is a serious business. I can't understand how the owners would sell to outside interests. *Sais-tu combien Gabib a payé, Paul?*" asked Bill, turning to the black-bearded man, who, for the first time since Frank had met him, had a smile on his face.

"*Quarante sous comme tout le monde,*" replied Paul, "Forty cent like hall the rest." And the whole assembly broke into howling laughter.

As soon as the laughter began to subside, Bill Martin took aim at Paul.

"Hey, Paul," he shouted, "you hear about the three cats named *Un, Deux,* and *Trois* that went out on the ice? *Les trois chattons qui sont allés sur la glace du lac?*"

"*Non, pas encore,*" said Paul.

"The ice broke and *Un, Deux, Trois* cat sank."

The good-natured bantering back and forth continued through the lunch, shifting from one language to the other depending on the speaker and subject. Frank noted that some of the people, like Lisette, Bill, Richard and Taylor, were totally bilingual, while others like Paul Larose and Edna Richmond were almost unilingual, or at least used mainly one language to express themselves. But obviously there was no problem of communication, even when puns and jokes were being tossed among the picnic tables along with Clémentine's hot rolls. There were enough fluently bilingual people to assure that any linguistic log-jam would be broken up before it interfered with the flow of conversation. Besides, thought Frank, everyone was in a good mood, building something together, working as a team. With three beers and a lot of good food now under his belt, the complaints from his muscles were becoming increasingly muffled. He was not exactly enthusiastic about getting up and going back to work, but he followed the others when Jeannie McVicar gave the signal by beginning to clear off the tables.

"Don't make poor old Joe work too hard," she said.

"Poor ole Joe!" responded Larose. "I show you poor ole Joe!"

He gestured as if to slap Jeannie on the rump, and she reacted with an exaggerated contortion as if desperately trying to escape the imaginary slap.

"Hey! Hey! None of that stuff in the noonday sun," shouted Taylor, as Jeannie stepped back and blew Joe a kiss, and everyone cheered.

By five o'clock the basement walls had been poured, and Frank could see that the frames for the walls and roof had also been completed. Spreading out the blueprints on a work bench, Taylor and Richard explained that the following Saturday, when the foundation was ready, the frame of the house would be assembled and the roof built. If he were willing to volunteer another day's work, Frank was told, he could be used to carry and place the heavy joists for the floors and roof. Once the pipes for the plumbing were installed, the cement floor for the basement would have to be poured. Paul, George, Bill, and Frank all nodded their heads. André Murphy, whose wife was now by his side with a baby in her arms, was beaming as he surveyed the elements of his house-to-be.

"*Merci, merci, mes chers amis,*" he kept repeating.

When Joe Larose came over to him and extended an invitation from Jeannie McVicar to have dinner at her place, Frank accepted immediately. He told Joe that he would go back to the Inn to shower and change then head right up the hill. He was tired, but nevertheless, he decided, he felt good. In fact, when he gazed at the plywood forms with pieces of wire sticking out every couple of feet and reflected that they contained many wheelbarrowfuls of cement which was now hardening and would soon be the solid basement walls of the

Murphy's new house, he had an exhilarating sense of satisfaction and pride. He had not had such a feeling since the time when, as a strapping teenager, he had helped his grandfather build an outhouse behind his summer camp in the woods of northern Michigan. He remembered now that his grandfather called it a *"becosse,"* which was probably, Frank speculated, simply a French adaptation of back house.

Chapter Thirteen

The long, hot shower having considerably eased his muscle aches, Frank decided to walk up the hill to the McVicar house. Water was still cascading down the ditches at the sides of the road, the run-off from the last patches of snow in the hollows of the forest which covered the summit of the hill like a head of unruly hair. The trees seemed to be quivering with their heavy loads of pregnant buds, as if at any moment they might explode into a blizzard of green leaves. And only a few days ago, Frank mused, the same trees were bending in the icy blasts of real winter blizzards. The maples, oaks and birches gave off a rich musk which heightened the atmosphere of expectancy. As he walked under a towering pine the branches of which formed an umbrella over the entire roadway, Frank slowed his pace and took deep breaths of pure oxygen. He felt his lungs swell as if in appreciation.

When he had settled himself on the sofa in the large parlour of the McVicar house, Jeannie offered Frank a cocktail, but he opted to follow Joe's example and have a cold beer. After a long day of toil and sweat, he knew from summer jobs digging ditches, there was nothing on earth so restorative as a cold beer. Casting a glance around the room, Frank's eyes focussed on the framed photograph on the mantelpiece of Jeannie and Joe when they won the Ballroom Dancing Championship. They had been a remarkably handsome couple, he could see, Jeannie statuesque in her long gown and flowing light hair, Joe with his broad shoulders and mass of black curls. Frank would have loved to be able to turn back the hands of time and watch them gliding across a dance floor.

"It's kind of you to help out on the Murphy house, Mr. Collins," said Jeannie. "When enough people pitch in, the job soon gets done."

"I can see that," said Frank, "and I'm happy to help. But I had a hard time keeping up with guys like Joe here. I've let myself get out of shape."

"For a scholar, you seem to be in very good shape, Mr. Collins. By the way, we'll be having dinner quite early. Joe likes to watch his wretched hockey games on Saturday night. Do you follow the hockey too?"

"Not much lately. I used to go to all the Detroit games at the Olympia Stadium when I was younger, but the Red Wings aren't what they used to be, I'm sorry to say."

"*Détroit, tabarnac!*" pronounced Joe. "Dat was one good team. Howe and goddamn Lindsay. Sawchuk in de goal. We see good game in dose day."

"I don't know why Joe keeps watching," said Jeannie. "It just isn't the same since they had the expansion. Now he doesn't know who half the players are. They keep changing. Although I'm glad there isn't all that nastiness between Montreal and Toronto any more. Joe used to get so upset. He'd smash his fist on the arm of that sofa you're sitting on, Mr. Collins, and I don't know how many times we've had to repair it."

"I'm tell you all de time," said Joe, "get a good sofa, and it doan break."

"Joe, for heaven's sake, it's a valuable antique. My parents brought it over from Scotland. And you used to treat it like a park bench. You wouldn't believe how furious he used to get, Mr. Collins, especially when he thought someone was picking on poor Rocket Richard. Who was that Toronto player you hated so much, Joe?"

"I hate *toute la gang* of Toronto."

"But there was one in particular who used to hound Richard. Bill something or other, I think."

"Yeah. Bill Ezinicki. One bad *enfant de chienne.*"

"You see, Mr. Collins, all the English were for the Toronto Maple Leafs, and the French were for the Montreal Canadians, and that's why there was so much bitterness."

"Yes, but wasn't that all hype to sell tickets, Miss McVicar?" asked Frank.

"You're right, I suppose. And it certainly worked. I understand that there wasn't an unsold ticket at the Forum or the Maple Leaf Gardens for years."

"I'm afraid it always works. Simply a matter of playing on peoples' fears and prejudices. Politicians do it, entrepreneurs do it, even real-estate agents do it."

"Me, I doan got no fear and prejudice," said Joe.

"Come on, Joe," said Jeannie, "you wouldn't believe it when you saw how when they weren't playing hockey against each other, the players were all as chummy as could be. Playing golf together and running summer hockey schools and all the rest. Even your Rocket Richard and that Bill fellow."

"It's amazing what people can be conditioned to believe, Miss McVicar. At least the great majority of people," said Frank.

"I often despair for the great majority, Mr. Collins."

Frank could not resist pumping Jeannie for bits of information about North Chadley and its residents, which he knew would be forthcoming if he provided the appropriate cues. He mentioned that he would soon have to arrange an interview with Morton Wadleigh, the eccentric inventor, and that remark triggered a flood of reminiscences on Jeannie's part. Morton, she said, had been madly in love with Madeleine, the mother of Lisette, who was now his cousin Wilton's wife. The woman had indeed been a strip-tease performer and a lady of pleasure. She made no secret of it. In fact, she seemed proud of it. She had definitely been a chorus girl in Las Vegas for a while, and her son, Jeannie assured Frank, confirming what he had already heard, had been fathered by none other than Elvis Presley. The boy looked so much like his father that he now made his living doing imitations of the legendary American singer. He had even appeared in a movie on Presley's life, playing the role of his father as a young man. Madeleine, commented Jeannie, was really no more attractive than a lot of other women. She had a good figure perhaps, but her facial features were far from handsome. Her nose was too small and slightly cock-eyed, and her mouth was too big. Nevertheless, she was one of those women who, no matter how much they cheapened themselves, no matter how many times they demonstrated that they were tramps, could still attract any number of adoring men.

"She was amazing really," Jeannie concluded. "For the life of me I don't understand what it was she had that fascinated men so much."

"Me, I know," remarked Joe, with the hint of a twinkle in his eye.

"Oh? And just how did you get to know?" Jeannie snapped back.

"What you tink? I see wit de eye."

"And what exactly did you see, Joe?"

"*Elle était très belle, ça c'est certain.* She dance good too."

"Oh really?" said Jeannie. "From what I've been told, Madeleine's stage performances involved more removing of her clothes than dancing."

"Sure she dance."

"Is that so? Then maybe you should have had her as your dancing partner instead of me."

"*Voyons,* Jeannie, it's not de same ting. Madeleine dance all by herself alone. She doan need no partner."

Obviously a bit peeved, Jeannie got up and headed briskly for the kitchen, while Joe turned to Frank and held up his hands in a gesture of incomprehension. Frank would have liked to pursue the subject of the notorious Madeleine, but he did not want to generate friction between his hostess and her fiancé of fifty years. He was amused that after such a long time a woman of Jeannie's age could still harbour petty jealousies.

"*La petite Lisette,* she look a lot like Madeleine," volunteered Joe when Jeannie was out of the room, "but Madeleine, when she do a strip-tease, she could make all de men *totalement fou.*"

"I think I know what you mean," Frank replied, for a wistful moment regretting that the progression of time had denied him the chance to put his own sanity to the test. He had also missed Helen of Troy, Cleopatra, Marie Antoinette, Lily St. Cyr, and a lot of other legendary menaces to rational behaviour in the normal male. Visualizing Lisette strutting across the floor of the bar-salon with a tray held high, Frank decided that he had a good idea of what Joe was talking about. When Jeannie came back into the room, seemingly recovered from her huff, Frank resolved to steer the conversation into less treacherous waters.

"I hear," he remarked, "that Mr. Richmond has a sister who doesn't exactly share his political convictions"

"I'll say she doesn't," Jeannie replied. "She's a ridiculous woman, that Phyllis. The whole province is talking about her. Poor Reggie must be frantic with embarrassment. She's been widowed three times, you know, and she lives in one of those posh houses in Westmount. Have you ever seen Westmount, Mr. Collins?"

"No, not yet."

"It's probably the wealthiest area in the whole of Canada. More money per square inch than your Fort Knox. On the east side of Mount Royal, along the river, you have the working-class districts of Montreal, rows and rows of tenement flats with outside metal staircases twisting down in front of them like scraggly beards, and the people are packed in like sardines. But on the west side, where the rich fur merchants first built their mansions, you'll see estates with servants' quarters that make my place look like an outhouse. One street near the top of the mountain actually has its own private fire department and police force. Westmount has the world's only five-storey bungalow."

"Did you say five-storey bungalow?"

"That's what I said. If you come up to the front door, it's a bungalow, but the back section of the house goes five storeys down the slope of the mountain, each level with a spectacular view of the city. But to get back to Reggie's sister, she's suddenly decided that she supports the OUI side in the Referendum, and she's been running all over the place raving that Quebec has to separate. The OUI people are delighted of course. It's quite a coup to have a rich Westmount matron espousing their cause. She was on television the other night, and it was so pitiful that I had to turn it off. And you can imagine how her antics are going over with her neighbours.

Good Lord! Half of them already have their houses up for sale and have lit out for Toronto. Apparently, Mr. Collins, you can pick up a mansion in Westmount for a song these days."

"And how is Mr. Richmond taking all this, Miss McVicar?"

"I'm sure that he'd like to strangle her."

"Same ting *avec les frères Tremblay,*" remarked Joe.

"You mean Marcel Tremblay, the chairman of the local OUI committee?" asked Frank.

"C'est ça. Marcel et son frère Robert."

"That's true," added Jeannie. "The two of them are at each other's throats. Robert is as strong a Federalist as Marcel is a Separatist. Can you imagine? Two brothers in the same family."

"It looks to me," said Frank, "that quite a few families are divided over the issue. Brothers and sisters against brothers and sisters, husbands against wives, parents against children."

"I'm afraid so, Mr. Collins. I don't know how it's all going to turn out. People are getting so bitter, you know. They're being egged on by the extremists on both sides. To tell you the truth, I'm becoming a bit frightened. We may never be able to put this country together again."

"Doan worry, Jeannie," said Joe. "We be all right. You see."

"But I do worry, Joe. You crazy French Canadians are just about as bad as the Scots."

"How is that, Miss McVicar?" inquired Frank.

"Too easily bamboozled into supporting foolish, lost causes. Like Bonnie Prince Charlie and the Jacobite Rebellion and all that nonsense in Scotland. Charles Stuart was a useless reprobate, and he didn't give a hoot for the people of Scotland. He only wanted them to risk their necks to make him the King of England. And like idiots, a lot of them did, and were slaughtered, and Scotland was devastated because of misguided, romantic loyalty. Then Charlie hightailed it back to France, and all that the people of Scotland were left with was a bunch of sentimental ballads."

"So you think Quebec Separatism is a lost cause, Miss McVicar?"

"Of course it is. The English and French have to work together, not fight against each other. In many ways, you know, they actually complement each other, and when they work together they can accomplish all kinds of things. Take my father and Louis Morin, for instance. They built Morin and McVicar Machinery Incorporated together, and it's been one of the most successful companies in Brooke. They were as different as night and day, Daddy and Mr. Morin, but they were a great team."

"That's one thing I have noticed in this part of Quebec," said Frank. "A lot of businesses have names that are a combination of English and French. That jewellery store, Skinner and Nadeau. There's a television place called O'Boyle and Duplessis. I've noticed Parizeau and Downey, Rouillard and Bean, and a bunch of others."

"Exactly, Mr. Collins. Just as I was saying, when the English and French work together, they generally do well. That's why it's so tragic that all these misguided, self-styled messiahs are trying to set them against each other, digging up all the old prejudices and frictions, reopening all the old wounds. We're going backwards instead of forwards. But I guess I'd better stop talking and get dinner on the table."

The dining room of the McVicar house was on a

scale with the living room, spacious with oak wainscotting, upper walls and ceiling in white plaster, and an elegant crystal chandelier. Joe seated himself at the head of the large oak table, seeming to Frank to be much like a Scottish laird in his manor, until he opened his mouth.

"*Tabarnac!* Me, I can eat two horse all dress."

Frank, too, needed no encouragement to load his plate with lamb chops, roasted potatoes, peas, carrots, and pickled beets. Shifting a few tons of cement in a wheelbarrow, he now knew, gave the appetite a sharp edge. He also indulged himself in a second helping of home-made apple pie and ice cream without the usual pangs of guilt. As he ate to his stomach's content and watched Joe do the same, it occurred to Frank with a measure of anxiety that his hulking frame was not ideally suited to an academic career behind a desk. Perhaps he could find some way to mix cement with anthropology.

During the meal, Jeannie commented on the upcoming debates which were scheduled to take place at Clémentine's Café Québec Libre on the few Sundays left before the Referendum. Apparently the various television and radio stations would be covering the so-called debates, but they were bound to be totally one-sided, because the café would be packed with fanatics from the OUI side. There would be no point in the English who were not completely fluent in French, people such as Jeannie herself, going, because they would not be able to get a word in edgewise. And the French supporters of the NON would certainly stay away, because they knew all too well that they would be ridiculed and shouted down as traitors and "*vendus*," and they didn't have to put up with that.

Very likely, Jeannie speculated, poor Bill Martin would have to hold up the NON side all by himself, one against the mob, so that there would be some semblance of an actual debate. But at least Bill would be in no physical danger, because no matter how much she disagreed with his political opinions, Clémentine thought the world of Bill Martin. They had been brought up together in the East End of Montreal, and something about the district, maybe the foul-smelling air from the oil refineries, had fixed an indelible bond between them. Whenever she found herself with an unexpectedly large crowd in her café, according to Jeannie, Clémentine was in the habit of calling the Martin girls to help her out, which had caused her a highly embarrassing incident last week.

A cabinet minister and his entourage had turned up at the Québec Libre, and one member of the group, a deputy minister apparently, taking her allegiance for granted in view of the locale, had asked the oldest Martin girl what she was doing to support the OUI campaign. The girl's reply, delivered with a stinging defiance honed by regular sisterly confrontations, had driven the man into a rage. He had shouted for Clémentine and demanded that the girl be fired immediately. Clémentine's reaction, Jeannie had been told, was to tell the government man to mind his own damned business and not try to advise her on how to run her own café, which was not called Québec Libre for nothing. The man then made the mistake of slapping Clémentine on the face. Martin's daughter, a sturdily built young woman, came immediately to her employer's defence with a haymaker to the deputy minister's eye. Recoiling sideways from the blow, the man was soon straightened up again by a punch in his other eye, this time delivered by Clémentine herself. The minister and his gang had then quickly departed, and the deputy minister had been wearing dark glasses for the last few days.

Frank and Joe offered to help Jeannie clean up after the meal, but she insisted that they had done enough work for the day and shooed them into the living room to watch the hockey game. Frank watched a few minutes of the first period as he settled himself comfortably into an easy chair. The next thing he knew the score was eight to six for Montreal over Hartford, Jeannie was knitting and Joe was still sound asleep at the other end of the sofa. Shaking the cobwebs out of his head, Frank apologized to his hostess for being such bad company, but she simply laughed.

"I'm used to it," she said. "Joe's been having his after-dinner nap right there on the sofa for years. My father and my uncle used to do the same thing. Although Uncle Bob, who was a minister, you know, would never admit that he had fallen asleep. He used to call it meditation. And often it was pretty noisy meditation, I can tell you."

Deciding that he had better get back to his room before he fell asleep again, Frank thanked Jeannie and took his leave without disturbing Joe. The rich, almost spicy aroma of buds about to burst filled the air as he made his way down the road toward the centre of town. He walked slowly, still feeling pleasantly sated from the big dinner, reflecting that the quiet serenity of a small town at night was a wonderful contrast to the rumbles, sirens, and screeching of brakes in Detroit. Then suddenly he heard two sharp, metallic bangs. Moving gingerly now, Frank edged toward the source of the noise. A few feet from the side of the road, by the driveway leading to a house, he discovered a huge raccoon wrestling with a garbage can. The owner of the can had secured the top with two springs, presumably to thwart raccoons, but the creature was certainly giving the challenge its best shot. Frank watched as the raccoon pried the lid open from one side and then the other only to have it clang back shut. After a few more attempts, the raccoon tipped the can over and began rolling it against a tree. It was so absorbed in the effort that it did not seem to notice that Frank was there. And finally the animal actually succeeded—banging against the tree somehow dislodged one of the springs and the lid fell open. When Frank applauded, the raccoon turned toward him, but it was not about to abandon its booty. Musing that man's ingenuity is not always what it's cracked up to be, Frank moved along down the road.

Just before he reached the intersection with the lake road, a camper passed by. In the light of the streetlamp, Frank could see that it was grey with red fenders. It had to be the same vehicle which had cut him off and caused him to go into the ditch when he first arrived at the outskirts of St-Alphonse de Chadley Nord. Feeling swells of anger, Frank ran down to the lake road, but the pickup-truck-camper had already disappeared around a bend. Frank shook his head in resignation and continued walking back to the Inn.

Chapter Fourteen

Frank Collins walked through a verdant world of translucent new leaves as he headed for the site of the Murphy house on Saturday morning. Along the sides of the road, a few spring flowers were already in bloom, and he saw beds of yellow and blue crocuses near several of the village houses.

As on the previous Saturday, the carpenters Jacques Richard and Geoff Taylor took charge. Bill Martin, the garage mechanic George, Paul Larose, and Frank were enlisted to remove the plywood forms from the cement walls of the basement, while various other volunteers readied the joists, window frames and door frames, including metal-tubing structures which Frank took to be scaffolding. Once the cement forms were loaded on a truck to be taken away, the actual erection of the Murphy house began. Joe Larose and André Murphy himself lined up the heavy joists hauled by Paul and George and Bill and Frank working in pairs, then the carpentry teams were nailing down the tongue-and-groove underflooring as fast as the boards could be delivered.

The crews all worked together to raise the pre-constructed wall frames. The scaffolding was set up, then the roof frames, which had also been assembled the previous Saturday, were lifted on high and set into place. By noon, to Frank's amazement, the complete skeleton of the house was standing, and the carpenters had already started to nail down the roof boards.

When the women arrived with lunch, they set up the

picnic tables on the wall-less new ground floor of the house, and everyone ate a first meal at the Murphy place, surrounded by bare upright two-by-fours and empty window and door frames.

"*Hein, André—chauffer cette maison, ça va coûter ben cher,*" shouted Paul Larose.

"Don't worry," said Bill Martin's oldest daughter, "all he has to do is go to the big Referendum debate tomorrow and can all the hot air."

Before the end of the afternoon, the first floor of the new house had been enclosed with sheets of plywood, and one team of carpenters was working on the second floor. Meanwhile, the other team had finished shingling the roof. When the day's work was over, Taylor and Richard explained what the subsequent steps in the construction would be. Plumbers and electricians would do the plumbing and wiring during the week, while Murphy and a couple of other men with free time would be insulating, hanging the windows and doors, and working on the interior. Frank volunteered to return the following Saturday to help pour the cement floor for the basement. Totally engrossed in the house-building project now, he was determined to see it through to the end. And had he had the least hesitation, it would certainly have been dispelled by Murphy's six-year-old daughter, a tiny delight with a yellow ribbon in her jet-black hair, who jumped into his arms, hugged him and said, "*Merci, Monsieur Frank, tank you for help us.*"

This beats union rates any time, Frank told himself, wrapping the child in his arms. He had gotten to know the little girl called Christine during his wanderings around town, and concerned that she looked so thin and fragile, he had bought her ice cream on a few occasions, after checking with her mother the first time to make sure that she approved.

That night Frank ate dinner with the Martins. He learned that Bill was indeed preparing to do battle in the Referendum debate scheduled for the next day, but none of his daughters indicated any interest whatsoever in the event. They seemed to think that it had nothing to do with young people. When Frank suggested that the outcome of the Referendum could have a profound effect on their futures, that they and their friends and the young in general would be the ones most affected by whatever decision was taken, they remained cavalierly unmoved, telling him that most of their francophone friends, the majority of whom were more or less unilingual, felt exactly the same way they did. The Referendum was for old fogies with old axes to grind, so far as they were concerned. Get it over with, then get down to important issues, such as making sure there would be decent jobs available for the new generation, cleaning up the awful pollution everywhere, making travel easier for young people, particularly to Fort Lauderdale during spring break in schools, banning the bomb and zapping the proliferation of nuclear arms.

Frank was surprised to hear that the young, French-speaking Québécois shared the Referendum indifference of the Martin girls, because he had read many times that the OUI pushers despaired of converting the older, more conservative segment of the Quebec population to their cause but were confident that the young, notably college and university students, would provide the massive and wholehearted support needed for victory.

"Are you sure the French students are not interested?" he asked.

"Well, there are a few foaming-at-the-mouth types," the oldest girl replied, "but discos and taking off to

Florida on spring break—that's what most are interested in."

When Frank inquired how the Martin girls could be so definite about the attitudes of their counterparts in French-language schools, he found out that three of the girls were in fact attending French junior colleges called CEGEPs. He also learned that the young francophones generally did not give a damn about language issues, did not have the same anxieties about the threatened status of their mother tongue as some of their elders seemed to have. They had lived and learned securely in French all their lives and therefore could not understand what all the fuss was about.

"Most of them want us to talk to them in English," remarked the second eldest Martin girl. "They want to practise so they can travel out west and to the States."

"And understand the big rock stars," said one of her sisters.

"And don't forget Country and Western," added another of Martin's daughters. "Québécois are crazy about schmaltzy Country and Western. That and McDonald's hamburgers."

When Frank arrived back at the Inn, there were several people in the bar-salon. Deciding that he needed a nightcap to help his digestive system cope with the unconscionable quantity of Mrs. Martin's fried chicken and cornbread he had consumed at dinner, he sat down at a table with the cleaning lady Marge Miller and, to Frank's surprise and pleasure, Norma Duffin, Mr. Gabib's strawberry blond private secretary. He had never seen Norma in the bar-salon before, but it turned out that she had been working late because her boss had some business dealings with three men from Saudi Arabia, and she had decided to grab a sandwich before going home, where her children were being looked after by her regular and reliable baby-sitter. Norma had no sooner explained her presence when the three men arrived in the room. They nodded to her and sat down at a free table.

"Brace yourself, Frank," remarked Marge, indicating the three men with a movement of her eyes.

"Brace myself for what, Marge?" asked Frank.

"For an eyeful of Lisette. You'll see what I mean in a minute. She does it every time those A-rabs come in here."

Frank looked over at the other table, and sure enough the three men, all in regular business suits, were casting expectant glances at Lisette, who was at the bar picking up a beer for Frank. She and her husband were talking in low voices, obviously in some kind of disagreement. Frank noticed Wilt clench his fist and glare at his wife menacingly. Marge also noticed.

"That poor man," she said. "I can't understand why he puts up with it. But he won't be able to stop her, you'll see."

Mrs. Wadleigh did in fact head up the staircase as soon as she had served Frank, and Marge nodded her head knowingly. Frank looked over at Norma, wondering if there was any chance of striking up a conversation. She was not wearing her glasses, and as Frank looked at her he perceived to his slight discomfort that her light blue eyes were focussed on him. As if divining what was on his mind, she smiled and said, "I'm sorry if I was a bit short with you the other day at the office, Mr. Collins. My boss, Mr. Gabib, tends to be quite demanding, and somewhat less than . . . accommodating on occasion. I was simply trying to . . ."

"Oh, I quite understand, Mrs. Duffin."

"Thank you," she replied, warming her smile.

"To be perfectly honest, Mrs. Duffin, I would prefer to talk to you."

"About what?"

"Well . . . about the general implications of Mr. Gabib's presence in North Chadley."

"I see," Norma replied, casting a glance at the three Arab businessmen, then lowering her eyes reflectively. "And do you think there is something wrong with businessmen from Saudi Arabia and other countries in the Middle East wanting to come here?"

"No, of course not. I take this to be a free country."

"Then why are you concerned?"

"I'm not really concerned, Mrs. Duffin, I'm simply curious. As I mentioned to you the other day, since I'm trying to write a doctoral dissertation on the evolution of institutions in North Chadley, I have to find out what effects Mr. Gabib's operations are having and are likely to have in the future."

"She'll be down in a minute, you'll see," remarked Marge Miller.

"And why do you think Mr. Gabib's operations, as you put it, should have any effect at all on the village, Mr. Collins?" asked Norma.

"Pretty soon he'll own most of the downtown."

"Possibly."

"Well that's bound to have an effect, depending on what your boss intends to do with all that property."

"You wanna see an effect?" said Marge. "Wait till you see the effect she has on them A-rabs. It's a scandal, it is."

"What do you think he intends to do, Mr. Collins?" asked Norma.

"I have no idea. That's why I'd like to talk to you,

Mrs. Duffin. I would be grateful if you could give me a few minutes of your time."

Norma was looking directly at Frank, again causing him slight discomfort. She seemed to be analyzing him, making an assessment, and he was uneasy about the conclusions she might be formulating. "What do you think?" he asked.

"I'm not sure, Mr. Collins. Perhaps we could have a little talk. There are some things I'd like to . . ."

"You know," interrupted Marge, rolling her eyes toward the staircase, "it's not that I don't like the girl. She's a good kid really. She'd give you the shirt off her back, as the saying goes. But I guess that's the problem. When there's men around, she just can't seem to keep her shirt on, or much else for that matter. Here she comes. See what I mean?"

Frank instantly appreciated that Wilt Wadleigh had hardly been exaggerating about the scantiness of the waitress costume he had bought for his wife in California. The fledgling anthropologist found his eyes being irresistibly drawn to Lisette's torso in expectation. The tight, low-cut blouse was a display case rather than a cover for her prominent bust, which was threatening at any moment to burst its meagre bonds. Then as soon as she leaned over to wipe the table where the three Arabian men of affairs were seated, it became evident that the minuscule skirt could not meet the challenge of the bouncy Lisette's black-nylon-sheathed rump. Frank also observed that when she turned her back to the three men, retrieving her tray from the next table, she seemed deliberately to bend low from the waist, holding the pose for a few moments while she looked pointedly over at Wilt with an exaggerated grin. Her husband simply smiled smugly.

"Would you believe it?" said Marge. "She does it for the tips, you know. Totally shameless, she is. That's why them A-rabs come in here. They don't see that sort of thing to home, you know."

"Keep their own women all bundled up in Mother Hubbards and veils, I've been told. She'd sure enough be out here stark naked if it weren't for Wilt. The man is a saint to put up with the way she carries on."

"I think maybe you've got it all wrong, Marge," Frank commented quietly.

"What's that?" Marge responded. "Look for yourself. Now if that isn't making a vulgar exhibition of herself, then I don't . . . Just look at that, will you."

Frank did turn his head to look. No, it was not really a vulgar exhibition, he judged, as Lisette leaned over a bar stool waiting for Wilt to place drinks on her tray.

No doubt there was a hormonal bias involved, Frank mused, but undeniably he was gazing upon an esthetically pleasing composition—the perfect symmetry of the parts, the blending shades of nylon, the harmony of the curves, the way they guided the eye, concentrated the mind. . . . He intended to place his beer mug back on the table, but somehow he missed the edge, and the mug went crashing to the floor. Frank sat there flushed with embarrassment as Wilt Wadleigh came out from behind the bar with a mop and the cause of his discomfort served him another beer.

"What did you mean about me having it all wrong?" asked Marge when order was restored and Frank was staring into his beer to keep his eyes from straying.

"It's not Lisette's idea to dress like that. Wilt puts her up to it," Frank replied.

"I wouldn't be surprised," Norma commented.

"Don't be crazy," said Marge. "Why would a man

have his own wife showing herself off in a sleazy outfit like that?"

"He probably bought it for her," said Norma.

"As a matter of fact, he did buy it for her," said Frank. "He told me himself that he picked it up in California."

"Go on. You've got to be kidding," said Marge, shaking her head.

"And he insists that she wear it, I imagine," said Norma.

"Yes, I believe that he does put a little pressure on her," said Frank.

"Listen, I know that girl," protested Marge. "She's just like her mother. You know, when her mother was just a little nymphet, eleven or twelve years old, she used to go behind the marina with a bunch of the young boys and charge them each a dime to watch her take her clothes off. Everybody in town knew about it. Well Lisette enjoys showing herself off to men the same way. She's got a good figure, I admit, but she knows it, and she likes to take full advantage of it. I tell you, she likes to show herself off."

"I think, Marge," said Norma, in her quiet voice, "that Wilt's the one who likes to show off his wife. The same way he likes to show off that big car of his. That's the way some men are."

"But you can't compare a woman and a car," said Marge.

"Oh no?" replied Norma.

"But that makes Wilt seem like one of them pimps almost, and with his own wife. It just doesn't make sense."

"A little rough on the beer mugs too," commented Norma, smiling at Frank, who lowered his eyes sheepishly.

"It's all right, Mr. Collins," she added softly. "You needn't be embarrassed for having normal reactions."

"No, I suppose you're right. But I wish I wasn't so clumsy."

"I find it rather pleasant," said Norma, "to meet a man who can still blush."

Frank could not decide whether Norma Duffin was being ironic or not, but he knew that he definitely had to arrange an interview with this bright, sophisticated, attractive blonde as soon as possible. She was an astute observer, and undoubtedly she could provide the kind of information which would put his dissertation research on the right track again. Her ladylike reserve, moreover, might be a healthy antidote to the blatant sensuality of the innkeeper's wife, who, however inadvertently, never failed to derail his thought processes from the narrow track of scholarly pursuits. He might even have started asking Norma serious questions that very night, had it not been for Lisette's costume and Marge's constant mutterings.

"Tell me the truth, Norma," the cleaning lady spoke up again, "would you ever be seen in public in something as skimpy as that? Just so's damn fool men like them A-rabs would slip you a few bucks."

"I don't know," replied Norma.

"What do you mean, you don't know?" asked Marge.

"It would depend on circumstances, I suppose. I do have a problem about being shy, and that might keep me from doing it. But I don't feel that I'm in any position to judge other women who are more outgoing and less self-conscious than I am."

"Really?" responded Marge.

"If I had to do it to feed my kids, I imagine that I'd get over my shyness. But fortunately, I don't have to."

"Neither does Lisette."

Norma finished the last bite of her sandwich, wiped her mouth with a napkin, then got up to leave. Good God, thought Frank, having a close look at all of her for the first time, she's every bit as *ben stackée* as the other one. Norma had gone before he was able to gather his thoughts enough to arrange a date and time for a talk with her. But at least he had made a little progress. She had actually acted quite friendly with him. Feeling profoundly weary from a long day, he bid good night to Marge, made a final, lingering observation of Lisette, then headed for his room and his black-cat roommate.

Chapter Fifteen

Fifty or more people were already gathered in the Café Québec Libre when Frank arrived. The cameras from a television station were set up around the room like Cyclopes sentinels, and Clémentine was seating the principal debate participants at the head table, which was set with glasses, jugs of water and trays of hors d'oeuvres, including smoked oysters, small rolls of ham, pickles, and cheese. Michel Bertrand and Marcel Tremblay were there on each side of a man Frank recognized from newspaper photographs as Bernard Provencher, the Parti-Québécois member of the National Assembly for Brooke. Marie-Ange Monet, the French teacher, was sitting next to Paul Larose, but there were conspicuously few other women in the crowd. On the opposite side of the table, Bill Martin sat alone, and Frank had the urge to go over and sit beside him. But knowing that it was essential for him to remain neutral in this Canadian family affair, he sidled over to the far wall and took a seat.

The debate was conducted entirely in French, but the presence of the television cameras seemed to foster precision in diction, perhaps even to slow down the usual rapid pace of Quebec French, and Frank had no trouble providing himself with almost simultaneous interpretation. The lead-off speaker was Michel Bertrand.

"My friends," he began, "we are approaching the most historic occasion in the history of Quebec. Our ancestors, who came from France more than 300 years ago to pioneer this land, will be watching what we do now, and future generations will remember the day when we had the courage to take our destiny into our own hands."

Loud applause at this point confirmed to Frank that Jeannie McVicar had called it correctly. Apart from Bill Martin, the room was packed with the converted. It was a rally rather than a debate. Frank noticed that the Indian, Billy Carcajou, had slipped into the back of the room and found a seat near the door.

"Our intentions are honourable and positive," continued Bertrand, who was obviously in the tradition of the Quebec orators who, Frank had heard it said, could charm the birds out of the trees. "We have nothing against English Canada. It is for that reason, my friends, that we are proposing sovereignty-association. We firmly intend to continue our association with the rest of Canada. In the future, however, we will do so not as craven sheep, not as a crushed minority, not as mendicants in tattered rags begging for crusts of bread, but with our heads held high, as a proud, independent people, as a true nation. There can be no turning back, my friends. We have come this far, we have survived three centuries of subjugation, and now we must move forward. It is the will of the people. It is the national ethos of Quebec, which was repressed for so long but which has now begun to swell within our breasts. Do you feel it, my friends? Do you feel in your hearts that the time has come, that the moment has finally arrived?"

Bertrand was interrupted by a chant of OUI, OUI, OUI . . . which lasted several seconds. He went on.

"Then I say to you, my friends, we must do what our hearts and our minds tell us to do. Our pioneer forefathers looked to France for salvation, but as we all know too well, they were cruelly abandoned. The French were not interested in 'a few arpents of snow.' Succeeding generations turned to the English conquerors for justice, appealed to the so-called 'fair play' of the British. But the English could not be expected to be concerned for the welfare of a pitiful handful of Habitants. Hewers of wood and drawers of water—that's what we were, and that's what they wanted us to continue to be. It was a mistake to hope for anything from the English, just as it had been a mistake to hope for anything from the French of France. It is upon ourselves, and ourselves alone, that we must depend. But I am perhaps going on too long. We are here to debate, to hear arguments from both sides."

The cameramen seemed confused about where to point their cameras until Clémentine indicated Bill Martin. Frank noticed that sitting next to Bill was a man about 30 years old with hair down to his shoulders and a wild, glassy look in his eyes. He had arrived late, and Clémentine being occupied in another part of the room, he had simply seated himself in an empty chair. From where he was sitting by the wall, Frank had a clear view of the door into the back kitchen, and as the cameras zoomed in on Bill, Frank noticed the door open slightly. Clémentine's man, Giovanni, must be listening in, thought Frank, but looking more closely, he spotted a black cat slinking through the door. Now how in hell did Mirabel get in here? he immediately asked himself. Then he saw that the cat was not Mirabel — with a huge head and great, drooping jowls, it was obviously a tom-cat. Bill and the long-haired man next to him exchanged a few words before the former realized that he was being called upon to speak.

"Ladies and gentlemen," said Bill, "I agree with

Monsieur Bertrand that we will soon be participating in a momentous occasion. There are some who have waited a long time and who have struggled hard for this occasion."

Has he decided to capitulate right from the start? Frank asked himself, as Bill turned to the long-haired man next to him.

"For example," Bill continued, "Monsieur Gaston Bourgault sitting right here by my side. How long have you struggled for the separation of Quebec, Monsieur Bourgault?"

The cameras swung slightly as the man replied in a loud voice, "Since I was a small boy in school. Since I learned to think."

"And how strongly do you feel about separating Quebec from Canada?" Bill asked. Frank was not sure what Bill was trying to do, but he took note that Provencher, the member of the National Assembly, had a frown on his face.

"May I intervene a moment to point out," said Provencher, "that we are not talking about separation but of sovereignty-association, as Monsieur Bertrand has clearly explained."

"Of course," said Bill, "but we cannot deny Monsieur Bourgault here the right to answer my question. How strongly do you feel about separating Quebec, Monsieur Bourgault?"

"I am ready to give my life for it," the man replied solemnly.

"You are a dedicated Separatist then, is that correct?" asked Bill.

"Absolutely!" was the loud reply. "And I am proud to say so."

"Ladies and gentlemen," Bill went on immediately,

"I believe that in order to conduct this debate intelligently and honestly, we must first have a clear definition of terms. I maintain that sovereignty-association is a misleading term, which will cause us to lose sight of the realities. What we are really concerned about here is the separation of Quebec from the Dominion of Canada ..."

"No! No! Not at all!" exclaimed Bernard Provencher. "Sovereignty-association is not the same thing as separation."

"Is it not? asked Bill, turning to the politician. "Then I think that you should make that clear to Monsieur Bourgault here, and to all the other patriots like him who believe that by supporting you and your party they are working for separation. After all, Monsieur Bourgault tells us that he is ready to give his life for the cause of separation. The separation of Quebec from Canada. Is that not so, my friend?"

"Yes! Yes!" shouted the long-haired man, getting to his feet and waving a fist in the air. "I am ready to fight and die for the cause of separation!"

"And did you realize, Monsieur Bourgault," Bill continued, "that the OUI officials, the Parti-Québécois government you voted into power, are not interested in separating Quebec from Canada? That is what Monsieur Provencher seems to be telling us."

Bourgault glared at the obviously disconcerted Bernard Provencher.

"Is that true?" he demanded. "You don't want to separate Quebec?"

"Well ... uh ... actually we do believe that Quebec should separate," said Provencher.

"Good. That's what I want to hear," said Bourgault, sitting down.

"And that's what I wanted to hear," said Bill Martin.

"From now on we will call a spade a spade. The debate today, therefore, ladies and gentlemen, as Monsieur Provencher has just been good enough to clarify for us, is about the possible advantages and disadvantages of separating Quebec from Canada. We are talking about the consequences of separation pure and simple."

Frank realized from the expressions on the faces of Provencher, Bertrand, and Tremblay that Bill had just pulled off a coup. The OUI officials, he knew, were desperately trying to avoid any mention of the word separation, because all the polls had indicated that the masses of people in Quebec were frightened by the idea. The term "sovereignty-association" had been invented expressly to calm these fears, to give the illusion of a quiet, calm transition rather than an abrupt, disruptive split. Now, by using a long-haired desperado as a lever, Bill had cunningly forced the OUI side to play the game according to his rules. Truly a brilliant maneuver, thought Frank. Provencher and the others would never have admitted to Separation, especially in front of the television cameras. They would have talked around it. But by setting up the confrontation between Bourgault and Provencher, the former representing a group of devotees which the OUI people could not afford to alienate, Bill had trapped them into admitting publicly that they were Separatists. Provencher, who had no doubt received strict directives and warnings from party strategists, seemed particularly upset.

When, however, he jerked back in his seat and let out a yelp, it had nothing to do with his state of mind. Out of the corner of his eye, Frank had been watching the big tomcat creep under the head table, and he knew exactly what was happening when a black paw reached up over the edge of the table and toward a plate of hors d'oeuvres in front of the member of the National Assemby. But the latter was taken by surprise, and the crowd watched in bemusement as he swatted at the table wildly, as if he were suffering an attack of epilepsy.

"*Va-t-en, minou!*" Clémentine yelled, shooing the cat away and at the same time providing the crowd with something of an explanation for Bernard Provencher's peculiar behaviour. No doubt the cat made a habit of scavenging around the tables when people were in the café, thought Frank. The bigger the crowd, the better its chances.

"*C'est un maudzit chat fédéraliste,*" someone called out.

"*Ben non! Il est encore tout équippé,*" Clémentine quickly retorted, and the gathering burst into laughter mixed with shouts of OUI, OUI, OUI. The cameramen, unable to locate the fully equipped cat, which had slipped under the chairs along the wall, swung their cameras back to Bill Martin. Frank resumed interpreting for himself.

"We have heard from Monsieur Bertrand that the advantage of separating Quebec would be the creation of a great deal of pride in the Québécois people," Bill continued.

"Our ancestors, he tells us, will be witnessing this phenomenon—presumably from on high, although I imagine that a fair number of them, especially those with an eye for the pretty Indian maid or the good-looking Irishman in the woodpile, might be peeking in from down below. . . ."

There was another roar of laughter in the room. Bill too, mused Frank, knew something about charming the birds out of the trees. Certainly he understood how to tap the vein of anti-clericalism which ran deep in the psyches of the Québécois.

"Now I might well ask you all why you don't have any pride at the moment. I mean, are you ashamed to be Québécois?"

Shouts of NON, NON, NON came from throughout the room, and Frank noted the pained expressions on the faces of Provencher and Bertrand.

"But I won't ask you that. I am more interested in the future generations also mentioned by Monsieur Bertrand. By breaking Quebec away from Canada, what will we be leaving our children, our grandchildren and our great-grandchildren? Let us, ladies and gentlemen, look objectively at a few of the facts. First of all, it is a fact that the economy of Quebec depends upon the Canadian market. Our farmers, for instance, sell a large percentage of their milk production in the other provinces because of the Canadian quota system, which allows our people to produce more than half the milk drunk in Canada. Without that quota system, farmers, many of whom you know right here in the Townships, would have to pour their milk down the drain or slaughter their cattle. Some 25 percent of the working people in this province are in the textile industry. The entire population of the town of Magog, only a few miles from here, is dependent on the textile industry, as you all well know. Now as you also know, this industry cannot compete with imports from Taiwan, Korea, and various other Asian countries. The only reason the textile industry continues to exist in Quebec, ladies and gentlemen, is because of the Canadian Government's protective tariffs and the fact that the market for Quebec textiles extends across the whole of Canada. Separate Quebec, and a quarter of the jobs here will disappear. Whoosh! Just like that."

"Just a moment, Monsieur Martin," interjected Marcel Tremblay. "You are beginning to sound like a typical English Canadian. All you can think about are dollars and cents. But there is a great deal more at stake here than money. So far as the textile industry is concerned, there is no reason why we cannot negotiate a solution. That is precisely what we mean by sovereignty-association. We are six million people in Quebec. We too constitute a significant market—for Western beef, for fish from the Maritimes, for grain from the Prairie provinces. When we become a sovereign nation, then we will do exactly the same as other sovereign nations, nations much the same size as Quebec, such as Norway and Denmark. We will negotiate trading deals to protect our workers. Are we not capable of looking after ourselves?"

The audience now responded with a chorus of OUIs, and Bernard Provencher finally managed a faint smile. Tremblay then answered his own query.

"Of course we can look after ourselves. We have the expertise—economists, engineers, agronomes, specialists in every domain. Our experts are now in demand throughout the world, and particularly in the French-speaking areas, in the Caribbean, in the South Pacific, in North Africa, even in France itself. At the moment, I must tell you, our development is being slowed down, held back, hampered by the Federal Government of Canada, which naturally favours the English provinces. Just look at the statistics on the funding for research. Per capita the nine other provinces get twice as much as Quebec. But what do you expect? So long as we remain part of Canada, we will be the weak sister, the Cinderella, the one who must be contented with left-overs. My dear friends, we now have the means to change all this. . . ."

Again the room resounded with shouted OUIs, and Frank wondered what Bill could say to regain the advantage. The black tomcat was now slinking along the wall under the chairs toward where Frank was seated. Every so often it emerged to sniff, and he imagined that it was puzzled and angry that in such a large gathering no scraps were falling off the tables. Almost to Frank's chair, it surveyed the room with a silent snarl, and he saw that it had only one fang. Both of its ears were tattered and torn like the sails of a ship caught in a hurricane. The cameras were now swinging in Bill's direction.

"I must take issue with several of the remarks my respected opponents have made," he began. "First, however, let me tell you that I agree that Quebec has rich resources of expertise. Our universities, I am proud to say as a veteran professor in one of them, are now turning out highly skilled graduates in a variety of fields, and it is true that these people are in demand around the world. Now in view of this indisputable fact, I would like to ask a simple question—if Quebec has been as crushed and hampered by Confederation as the other speakers have implied, how is it that so much has been accomplished? How is it, I ask you, that even a highly developed nation such as France sends students over here to be trained?"

"We did it in spite of Confederation," stated Michel Bertrand.

"Nonsense!" replied Bill. "Confederation is the reason that the French fact has survived in North America."

This remark was greeted by a loud chorus of booing, causing the tomcat to pull back under the chairs along the wall, and before Bill could explain himself further, the cameras zoomed in on Gordon Jackson, who had been sitting at a table near Frank and who had gotten to his feet. Jackson spoke in halting French, but it was appropriate for his comments, thought Frank.

"I simply wish to point out," he said, "and this is something I know about because I come from English Canada, that French Canadians have had to endure many abuses as a result of Confederation . . ."

Jackson was interrupted by enthusiastic applause and cries of OUI from throughout the room. Bill Martin was now glowering, Frank noted. He also noted that Bernard Provencher, no doubt still upset about being railroaded into admitting on television that separation was the issue in the debate, was eyeing the door, obviously anxious to leave the gathering.

"English Canadians," Jackson continued, "were influenced by anti-French and anti-Catholic sentiments. At one time the Orangemen, those infamous Protestant fanatics originally from Northern Ireland, pretty much controlled the governments of Ontario and Manitoba. That is why French schools were actually abolished for a time in both provinces. The rights of francophone Canadians have never been respected in English Canada. Nor is the situation likely to change, so far as I can see. The old-time bigots of the Orange Lodge have perhaps died off, but now the prejudices have simply been replaced by indifference. Nobody cares what happens in Quebec. On many occasions, even among my own relatives, I've heard people say, 'If they want to go, then let them go, and good riddance.'"

"So much for your marvellous Confederation," announced Michel Bertrand, looking pointedly at Bill as the applause died down. With friends like Gordon Jackson, Frank told himself, Bill Martin must be recalling the old saying that he didn't need any enemies. Given the predisposition of the crowd, Bill might not now even get a chance to reply. Several people were waving their hands to get the floor, undoubtedly to elaborate on the anti-French prejudices, the Orangemen, rednecks and black Protestants who had mired the pages of Canadian history. Clémentine indicated a scholarly-looking man with horn-rimmed glasses, and the cameras swung toward him.

"My name is Rudolphe Dubé," said the man, "and I was born and raised in the aluminum-mining town of Sudbury, Ontario. I can tell you that I went through hell as a child. My mother insisted that we speak French at home—there were twelve of us in the family—but as soon as we stepped out the door, we were terrified to speak French even to each other. We hated the place, and we begged our parents to leave. But my father was a miner, and the only way he could support our large family was to go down into that dreadful pit day after day..."

"To make big profits for the *maudzits Anglais!*" someone shouted, and the crowd responded with the chant of OUI, OUI, OUI.... Bill Martin now raised both hands in the air. Clémentine moved over to him and took one of his hands.

"Bill," she said, "I know that deep down you are on our side. Why don't you just say so. Tell us that you are for the OUI."

OUI, OUI, OUI chanted the crowd again. He must be sorely tempted to go along, thought Frank. He could be an instant hero. Despite his opposition to the will of the gathering, Bill was obviously held in high esteem by many. He had succeeded, with an assist from the paw of a black tomcat, in putting *hors de combat* the politician

Bernard Provencher, who, Frank saw, had whispered some excuse to Clémentine and was now hastily slipping out the café door. Given the circumstances, perhaps Bill might decide to content himself with that accomplishment.

"My dear Clémentine," he replied, the cameras having now zoomed in on him again, "Quebec is my birthplace and my homeland. I love Quebec and the people of Quebec. But it is for that very reason that I must say NON to something that will destroy the things I love. My friends, I admit that Confederation has been far from perfect. I know all about Mr. Jackson's rednecks and Orangemen. Ancestors of mine fought William of Orange on his white horse at the Battle of Boyne in Ireland. The history of every nation, my dear friends, is the sad tale of man's inhumanity to man. The English killed and oppressed the Irish, the French slaughtered the Huguenots, the Spanish crushed the Moors, the Turks tried genocide on the Armenians, the white Americans abused the Blacks, both French and English Canadians murdered and exploited the Indians. But we simply cannot dwell on the injustices of the past. They cannot be undone, and we cannot allow them to poison the present and cancel the future. Despite all its weaknesses, despite its imperfections, the Canadian Confederation, as I said a moment ago, has preserved the French fact in North America. Look around you, listen to one another. You, ladies and gentlemen, are the proof. In New England today, not to mention the rest of the United States, there are literally more than ten million descendants of Québécois, people with exactly the same roots as most of us in this room. And I ask you, what has happened to them? Do they live in French? Can they shop in French? Do they watch television in

French? As you all know perfectly well, they do not. These people, who are our cousins, have been assimilated. They have been boiled down in the famous American melting pot. Is that what you want? Is it?"

Once again Bill succeeded in evoking a chorus of NONs. He waited for the shouts to die down.

"Of course you don't want to be assimilated like the Franco-Americans," he went on. "By contrast, within the imperfect Canadian Confederation, the French language and culture have been protected and have prevailed. Sure it was a struggle, but it nevertheless worked. Separated, a tiny nation surrounded by 230 million anglophones, economically weak, increasingly dependent on the United States, the people of Quebec today could not hope to survive as they are, to preserve their identity. They wouldn't stand a chance. They would go the way of the descendants of Québécois in New England. The Boisverts would become Greenwoods, the Boulangers would become Bakers, the Leblancs would become Whites, the Bertrands, namesakes of our esteemed Michel across the table from me, would perhaps call themselves Burtons and spend a lot of time chasing future Elizabeth Taylors, whose family name used to be Tellier . . ."

A ripple of laughter spread among the crowd. By God, thought Frank, he may be swinging it around again. Frank noticed that the tomcat, not more than three or four feet from him now, had suddenly reared and was glaring fiercely at something across the room near the café door, which Provencher had neglected to close after beating his hasty retreat.

"On the other hand, ladies and gentlemen," Bill continued, "we can keep the Canadian shield against assimilation. In Quebec today, the French language is flourishing. Anglo-Quebeckers have learned French, have accepted to work in French. Many of the English-speaking people I grew up with in the East End of Montreal are still here and function entirely in French. My friends Hugh Mariano, John "Ti-Mac" MacDonald, Alec Morrison all teach in French CEGEPS. We are now in a position to make Canada into a model for the world, a nation where different and distinctive ethnic groups live and let live in harmony with each other, a nation enriched by diversity, a nation which is going forward rather than backward."

There was a moment of hesitation when Bill stopped talking. No hands had been raised, and the cameramen did not know where to point their cameras. Then Frank heard a low-pitched growl coming from the big black tomcat. Its single fang, now bared, gave it a grotesque appearance more ferocious than if it still had two fangs, and in the next instant Frank spied the cause of its rage. A second tomcat, long-haired, yellow and almost as big as the first one, had come through the door left ajar by Provencher. Clémentine or Giovanni had probably been feeding the creatures with café leftovers, thought Frank. Then the yellow tom spotted the black one, and the two started stalking each other, advancing a few inches at a time, lurking behind human and chair legs. Meanwhile Marcel Tremblay had spoken up.

"What Monsieur Martin says sounds wonderful, I admit. Like Shangri-la, like Disneyland, like the Garden of Eden before the first Elizabeth Taylor started fooling around with snakes and apples. But it is equally illusory. It has never been, it does not exist now, and it will never be. I know that millions of Québécois have been assimilated into the American melting pot, and I can tell you why. Because in the United States they had no choice.

They had no control over their lives. They had to live the same way as the Americans live, speak the same language, fit into American society, adjust to and eventually be overwhelmed by the powerful American culture. The only reason the same thing did not happen in Canada, my friends, is because English Canadians have never had any culture of their own to speak of. Their culture is like an inert gas—colourless, odourless and tasteless . . ."

"Now just a minute," protested Bill. "The gas in here at the moment is coming entirely from you, Monsieur Tremblay, and although it may be colourless and tasteless, it is certainly not odourless. In fact, it stinks. English Canada has a distinctive and rich culture. You simply have never taken the time to find out anything about it. I can recall your reaction when I mentioned an excellent Canadian novel to you a few years ago, *The Watch That Ends the Night,* by Hugh MacLennan, which he wrote while spending the summers right here in St-Alphonse de Chadley Nord. Your reaction—I remember your exact words—was, 'Why should I waste my time on English-Canadian books when I have all the great French, British, and American authors to read?'"

"It is true, isn't it?" Tremblay retorted. "Are you trying to tell us that your Hugo MacLelland, or whatever his name is, is as important an author as Jean-Paul Sartre, Albert Camus, Ernest Hemingway, George Bernard Shaw?"

"So far as the culture of English Canada is concerned, Monsieur Tremblay, MacLennan is more important, because he is telling us about ourselves. Just as for the Québécois, Gabrielle Roy, or Ringuet are important."

"I still say that English-Canadian culture is nothing but a pale imitation of the American."

"We are all influenced by American culture. As a matter of fact, the Québécois are probably much more influenced than English Canadians. What do the masses here like to eat? McDonald's hamburgers, hotdogs, *poulet frit à la Kentucky*. What music do they listen to? Country and Western. What group of people bought more Elvis Presley records per capita than any other population group on the face of the earth? The people of *la belle province,* Monsieur Tremblay. I could go on and on, but you all know what I'm talking about. Quebec is at least as Americanized as the rest of Canada, and the rest of the Western World for that matter. . . ."

"But don't you see?" interrupted Michel Bertrand. "That is precisely why we must have sovereignty. So that we can purge our society of all that alien mediocrity, so that we can go back to a culture that is purely Québécois, which is truly our own. And we have no time to waste. Soon it will be too late."

While he listened, Frank was still watching the two tomcats approach each other in cautious spurts among the legs, like Indian braves in a forest, and he wondered if they would actually come to grips. From his seat against the wall toward the back of the room, he had a good view of the floor. One of the cats would no doubt back off when they got within clawing distance, he speculated. After all, they had nothing to fight over.

"It is already too late," said Bill. "Do you think for a moment that you can stop people eating hamburgers, or going to discos, or listening to Dolly Parton, or watching 'Dallas' on television? Unless, of course, what you have in mind is a police state. Unless you intend to conduct, to use your own word, Monsieur Bertrand, great purges in the footsteps of dictators like Joseph Stalin, or the Ayatollah Khomeini."

"When we have sovereignty, we can start re-educating the people. We can teach them to discriminate."

"Absolute nonsense! If you separate Quebec, then in order to maintain anything approaching the current standard of living, you will have to become more economically dependent on the United States than ever before, and that will mean cultural submersion, the end of the French fact in North America. Once and for all. What I've been trying to tell you and everybody else here today is that the political independence of a small country is meaningless in the contemporary world. It is a symbolic gesture in exchange for which you will lose your soul. Under the Canadian umbrella, we have maintained strong regional cultures—in Lac St-Jean, the Gaspé, here in the Townships—and if we all work together, if we begin to take an interest in what we've got, then we can maintain and strengthen what is distinctive in our cultures."

"You take care of yours, whatever it is," said Marcel Tremblay, "and let us take care of ours."

"Goddamnit, Marcel!" said Bill, raising his voice. "That's exactly the attitude that will destroy Quebec, and Canada along with it."

"We are not concerned about Canada," said Tremblay.

"Then you're a bigger fool than I thought, because whether you like it or not, Quebec is a part of Canada, and it is going to stay a part of Canada."

"NON! NON! NON!" shouted the man with the long hair next to Bill. "We will fight. We will take up arms to liberate our nation."

"And you're another goddamned fool," said Bill. "Do you want to bring in the Canadian Army? Do you want all your counterparts, all the patriotic redneck idiots of English Canada, lining up at military recruiting centres in Halifax and Winnipeg and Calgary and Vancouver to enlist for the Quebec campaign?"

Bertrand then rose to his feet. Frank felt decidedly uncomfortable about the turn the debate had taken. In fact, he concluded, there hadn't been a debate at all on the pros and cons of separation, or sovereignty-association, or whatever they wanted to call it. Minds were already made up and were not about to change. The issues were clearly emotional, and they were becoming increasingly emotional. Just before Bertrand opened his mouth, Frank saw the yellow tomcat begin to back up. But it was too late. The black tom darted out to the open space and sprang four or five feet through the air.

"Good God!" Frank exclaimed out loud. Heads immediately turned toward him, and to his consternation the cameras began to point in his direction.

"No, no, not me! The cats! The cats!" he called out, trying to wave the cameras away. At the same moment, accompanied by ear-piercing howls, growls and screeches, the yellow and black fur began to fly. Clémentine rushed forward with a broom, and several others jumped to their feet. But the yellow cat was already hurtling toward the door with one-fang in hot pursuit, and the cameramen were trying to capture some of the action through a maze of bodies, tables and chairs. Clémentine then closed the door, and Michel Bertrand beckoned to the cameramen, much to Frank's relief.

"My friends," announced Bertrand, "Professor Martin has just confirmed what we have been asserting all along. What future is there for us in Canada, in a country where volunteers, like those two vicious beasts you just saw trying to tear each other to pieces, are ready to line up at Army recruiting centers to fight

Quebec, to come here with the purpose of crushing our legitimate aspirations? But I must also point out that although I quite understand and admire the zeal of our friend Gaston Bourgault here, we do not intend to resort to violent means. There are other, more effective ways. Once we have indisputably established the will of the people, and I trust that a massive OUI in the Referendum will leave no doubt in that regard, then we can appeal to the United Nations in the event of the Federal Government refusing to negotiate."

"Monsieur Bertrand," said Bill, "you know perfectly well that the United Nations will never interfere in the internal affairs of a member nation. What has the U.N. done for the Basques? Or the Bretons? Or the Latvians? Or the Palestinians? This matter must be settled by Canadians, by us."

"That presumes a level of intelligence," interjected Marcel Tremblay, "among English Canadians which is not readily apparent."

"I can see that I've wasted my time. You are not interested in listening to the opinions of others."

"We are fed up with listening. We don't want to hear any more of your distorted ideas, Monsieur Martin. We know what we have to do."

Once again the chant of OUI, OUI, OUI reverberated in the room, but before Bill could say anything more, the producer of the television program signalled that the allotted time had expired, and the cameramen immediately stopped filming. At that point, Gaston Bourgault jumped to his feet.

"So I am a goddamned fool?" he shouted at Bill and took a swing with his fist. The latter was quick enough to fend off the punch and was about to retaliate with one of his own when Clémentine grabbed him from behind.

Meanwhile Paul Larose had wrapped his arms around Bourgault. The television people paid less attention to the commotion than they had to the cat fight and continued to move their equipment.

Well, so much for the debate, mused Frank. These Canadians, people and cats both, are a pretty perverse bunch. He could not imagine how the Referendum issue was going to be resolved without violent confrontation of some kind sooner or later, eventually leading to the disintegration of the country. After all, there didn't seem to be much holding it together in the first place. Frank recalled the wry comment he had heard someplace that the Canadian Confederation was like a mail-order brassiere—it was intended to uplift and support, but instead it simply showed off the cleavage.

Chapter Sixteen

Frank Collins finally found his way to the North Chadley Legion Hall a little while after the so-called debate. Remnants of the OUI crowd were lingering at the Québec Libre, talking politics and cultural purity and the irrepressible despicability of the *maudzits Anglais,* with a few rare exceptions. Meanwhile, as Frank discovered when he went back to the Inn next door, after devouring six slices of Clémentine's delicious quiche Lorraine, a number of their NON counterparts had gathered in the bar salon, and from the tone of conversations littered with "separatist bastards" and "sons-of-bitches in the P.Q.," Frank grew apprehensive that the venom might overflow the confines of the two neighbouring public houses and fuel a full-scale town riot.

Curiously, the people at the Inn, none of whom had actually been to the afternoon debate, seemed unwilling to believe Frank's account of Bill Martin's one-man, Horatio-at-the-Bridge performance. It was a matter of guilt by association, Frank concluded. Bill worked at the francophone Université de Brooke, functioned a good bit of the time in the French language, had once fought for the right of French-speaking villagers to deal with the municipality in their mother tongue and therefore had to be "another damn Separatist." The gang at the Inn, increasing in number and imbibing quart bottles of bravado as quickly as the innkeeper's wife could deliver them on her tray, were obviously spoiling for a fight. It might be an opportune time, Frank speculated, for the lithesome Lisette to present her credentials in the California non-costume, which if it didn't exactly elevate her customers' preoccupations would certainly divert them for a while. But whatever, he was determined to avoid the threatening confrontation. The last thing he wanted was to get involved, especially in physical violence, whether to help one side or the other. He had come close the night the Laroses were in the bar, and he didn't want to risk a similar situation. When his two telephone calls did not get through to Norma Duffin and he overheard someone say, "Let's go over there and straighten out those buggers," he left the Inn and headed for the Legion Hall.

The atmosphere at the hall, which had a bar on one side, tables and chairs set around the room, a pool table at the far end, a dart board alongside it and gambling machines along the wall opposite the bar, was relatively serene. Having not seen him there before, the bartender first told Frank that he would have to be signed in by one of the regular members, and Margery Miller hastened over to do so, but upon learning that Frank had served two years in the U.S. Marine Corps, the bartender explained that as a veteran, whether of the Canadian or American armed forces, Frank was automatically a welcome guest.

Marge then invited Frank to a table where she was sitting with two men in their sixties or seventies, introducing them as Colin Bradford and Bill Bilodeau. In the course of the ensuing conversation, he found out that the two local men had spent most of the Second World War together in a Japanese prison camp. When Marge got up to play one of the gambling machines standing against the wall, thus creating a vacuum in the conversation, Frank could not resist asking Bradford and Bilodeau for details of their war experiences. Neither man was overly talkative, but each was willing to respond to genuine interest, particularly after they learned that Frank had been a U.S. Marine. At the end of the War in the Pacific, the slave-labour camp where they were interned had been liberated by a unit of American Marines. Some of the battle-hardened Yanks had actually wept when they saw the sunken-eyed, walking skeletons of the surviving Canadian prisoners of war, according to Bradford.

"One of them took off his combat jacket and wrapped it around me," Bradford went on. "I still have that jacket, and it's one of my treasured possessions."

As the conversation continued, Frank found out that a regiment called the Royal Rifles of Canada had been recruited in the Eastern Townships and Gaspé regions of Quebec. After a brief period of training in Newfoundland, they were suddenly ordered to the West Coast to join the Winnipeg Grenadiers in an expedition ostensibly to defend the British colony of Hong Kong. What the raw recruits did not know at the time, Bradford pointed out, was that Winston Churchill and the British War Office had already decided that Hong Kong was indefensible against the massive Japanese Imperial Army, which by then had devastated the surrounding areas of the Chinese mainland, cruelly slaughtering hundreds of thousands of men, women, children and even tiny babies.

It was also apparently decided, although neither Bradford nor Bilodeau could say precisely by whom, that a few hundred Canadian troops were expendable in the greater scheme of military affairs. Many of the troops had yet to fire a gun, and much of their basic equipment somehow never arrived at the port of embarkation, but off they went nevertheless, cheerfully innocent of any idea of what was in store for them. Nor did the mothers, wives and sweethearts who waved goodbye at the railway stations and dockside have any idea.

"When we arrived in Hong Kong," said Bill Bilodeau, "we were given a briefing by a British officer, and it still amazes me to think about it. Never in the history of human warfare—and that's a pretty long and rich history, mind you—have soldiers been given such a pile of bullshit. The guy stood there twisting his moustache and telling us that the Japanese victories in China should not be taken seriously because of the poor quality of Chinese resistance. We would have to deal with only about 5,000 badly equipped troops who couldn't fight worth a damn. They would haul arse and flee in terror when they came face to face with a real British soldier, by which he meant to include all the worthy colonials, he said, sweeping the air with his swagger stick. The Japanese had no artillery, and they were all short-sighted because of their slanted little hooded eyes. Their pilots had to be led by the hand to their obsolete planes, which were useless for dive-bombing in any case. By the time the briefing was over, we were all wondering what the hell we were doing there at all. This British officer could obviously handle the Japs all by himself."

Frank learned from Bilodeau and Bradford that the siege of Hong Kong began on December 8th, 1941, one day after Pearl Harbor. The defenders were pounded with shells from the non-existent Japanese artillery, and the short-sighted pilots managed to drop tons of bombs on military installations with astonishing accuracy. When the Imperial Army eventually moved forward toward the major line of defence on the mainland, which had been dubbed the "Gin Drinkers' Line" and which was guaranteed to prevent the invaders from ever coming within striking distance of the island colony itself, the line did not hold much longer than it would take to drink a gin and tonic, according to Colin Bradford. In five days the Japanese had total control of the adjacent mainland, and the impregnable fortress of Hong Kong was a sitting duck.

"Mind you, Frank," Bradford went on, "as we found out later, the British War Office had not expected us to hold out for more than a few hours, although they hadn't told that to any of their own officers. We were placed under the command of a British Brigadier, who had spent his whole career in India and had no notion of how to handle Canadians, and that sure didn't help much. The Japs kept up a heavy bombardment with their artillery from the mainland and their planes, and we had absolutely no defence against either. Refugees were all over the place, and some of the local Chinese were collaborating with the enemy and sniping at us from buildings. Twice the Japanese commander, a General Sakai, I remember well, sent over a demand for surrender, and twice the governor of the colony, Sir Mark Young, refused. Of course, he had no idea that Sakai had about 60,000 troops."

"Including goddamned pearl divers," added Bilodeau. "We had anti-invasion nets and mines along the shore to keep the Jap troops from landing. But they sent over these pearl divers. Sons-of-bitches can stay under water longer than a porpoise. Or maybe they got gills like fish, I don't know. But they cut the nets and got rid of most of the mines, so the bastards were home free."

On December 18th, Frank learned from the two veterans, the Japanese invaded Hong Kong, with an order from a Colonel Tanka to take no prisoners while the battle lasted. Miraculously, fighting hand to hand and inch by inch, the defenders held out for eight more days, but when it was all over, the Royal Rifles of Canada had suffered nearly forty percent casualties. Of the 832 survivors who became prisoners of war, 129 more died in the prison camps. Neither Bilodeau nor Bradford would say much about the camps, and Frank gathered that conditions had been horrendous. They did mention, however, a certain Corporal Innouye, a prison camp guard.

"He was a Canadian, born and raised in Kamloops, B.C., *tabarnac!*" said Bilodeau. "Spoke better English than me."

"When he arrived, we all breathed a sigh of relief," added Bradford, "but he turned out to be the cruellest bastard of the lot. Beat us all mercilessly. Killed at least a half a dozen prisoners in cold blood with his sword. We could never understand it, him being a Canadian and all."

The conversation was interrupted by a shout of glee from Marge Miller, who had just won the jackpot on the gambling machine. She insisted that Frank and the two other men get up and see for themselves the winning poker hand—four aces—which had registered on the machine with coloured lights flashing. Several others and the bartender also came over, the latter to verify the amount of money Marge would be paid. Frank gathered that it was more than $200, and Marge ordered a round of drinks for the table as she came back to sit down with the three men.

Before the evening was over, Frank decided that the Legion Hall was much like a British pub. Although officially restricted to veterans and members of the Women's Auxiliary, since any member could sign for any number of guests, anyone in the village could come for a drink or to play darts, pool or the electronic one-armed bandits. The older people seemed mostly English-speaking or fluent in English, like Bill Bilodeau, but Frank heard many of the younger ones speaking French. The Legion, he concluded, appeared to be serving the whole community well, at least in North Chadley, although the national organization, according to both Bilodeau and Bradford, had often tended to be ultra-conservative, conducting a bitter fight against the adoption of a proper Canadian flag to replace the old Red Ensign with its British Union Jack, for example.

"You know," said Colin Bradford, "it's no damned wonder the French get upset with this country sometimes."

"That's true," said Bilodeau, "but still, you can't judge a country by the people who happen to be in power at any particular time."

"Bill," responded Bradford, "you know as well as I do that a few rotten officers can mess up a whole army. I'm thinking of some of those towns in Ontario where the population is majority French, and the officials still refuse to allow bilingual services. That certainly is not doing the country any good."

"I couldn't agree with you more," said Bill, "but it's slowly changing, even in those towns. People are afraid of change, so it has to come slowly."

"What about right here in North Chadley?" asked Frank. "What's happened here?"

"This is one town that has certainly changed," said Colin Bradford. "Used to be totally English, but now it's completely bilingual. But Bill is right. It took time. A lot of people here in town were dead set against using French in the municipal council and bilingual services and all that sort of thing. It took time."

"But what about now?" asked Frank.

"Now it's the reverse. Some people would like to see English banned altogether. That's what the Referendum is all about, the way I see it."

"Not really," said Bilodeau. "To get rid of English here is the same thing as refusing to allow French in those Ontario towns you were talking about. It means going backwards instead of forwards. But I know a few people in the P.Q., and that's not what they have in mind."

"Oh yeah?" said Bradford. "Well it's pretty damned clear that's what some of them have in mind."

"You better believe it," added Marge. "Some of that bunch would like nothing better than to get rid of us completely. They want the English out of Quebec, and that's all there is to it."

"Come on now," replied Bill Bilodeau, "the great majority simply want Quebec to have the right to decide its own future. And that's exactly the way it should be. There's nothing wrong with that."

"There's nothing wrong so long as the decision is really made by the great majority and not by a small gang of fanatics," said Bradford.

"Listen, Colin," said Bilodeau, "the P.Q. is in power, right? They could push something through the National Assembly if they wanted. Instead they're going to the people with a Referendum. So in effect they are letting the people have a voice in the affair. The majority will decide."

"And how do you intend to vote, Bill?" asked Bradford.

"I don't know yet."

"There you are. What if the majority don't know?

What if the majority are taken in by all the propaganda and emotional blackmail and vote the wrong way?"

"That's democracy, *mon vieux*," said Bilodeau. "That's what we fought the war for, remember."

"Yeah, I remember," responded Colin Bradford reflectively. "To keep the world free for democracy—the right to be governed by any parcel of silly arses or power-hungry crazies who can manage to hoodwink the unwashed masses. Sometimes I wonder if it was worth it, Bill."

"You had no doubts in the old days, Colin, back there in the camp. Dreaming about getting home to Canada was what kept us going all those years. *Sacrament*, how we used to dream. We saw this country as paradise on earth, including the ice and the snow and the potholes in the roads."

"That's true. But that's exactly why I can't understand why anybody would want to break up this country. They don't seem to realize what a good thing we've got. And now even you, Bill. I thought that you at least would know better."

"Don't worry about me. I know what I'm doing."

"The hell you do—not if you're going to vote for the goddamned Separatists who want to tear apart everything we fought for."

"I fought for a free country, which means that I can vote any bloody way I like. And it's nobody's business but my own."

"Christ! I don't believe this."

"Believe what you like, Colin. Anyway, I'm getting out of here before we get into an argument. Besides, I'm tired."

"Yeah, me too."

"Did you know," said Marge, addressing Frank,

"that these two old farts can sleep standing up?"

"What?" Frank responded.

"They can sleep standing up, both of them, just like horses. In the prison camps they were forced to stay on their feet for hours on end, and anyone who fell down, the Jap guards would shoot him. So they learned to sleep standing up. I saw it with my own eyes when they had a big do at the armoury in Brooke. Some blimp of a general gave a long, boring speech, then when the Vets' unit turned and marched off, both Bill and Colin were still standing there. Isn't that right, boys?"

Both men nodded and looked at each other.

"The general just stared at them in disbelief," Marge went on. "He was one of them military college tin soldiers that didn't know nothing about the real thing. 'What's the matter with those two men?' he shouted finally. Then one of the other vets came back and woke them up. 'Just catching a little nap, sir,' he said. Right, boys?"

Bilodeau and Bradford nodded and looked at each other again. Then Marge offered to buy a last round with her winnings, and the two men smiled at each other and accepted the offer.

Back in his room, Frank noticed that Mirabel was acting strangely. She kept meowing raucously, but when he opened the door to let her out, she stayed in. When he poured milk in her saucer, she showed no interest. Finally he went to bed, and the combined effect of the beer and scotch he had drunk at the Legion soon put him into a deep sleep. He was awakened by Mirabel scratching at his arm. Through half-shut eyes he could see that it was morning and that the black cat was in a state of great agitation. She had jumped back down off the bed, and she was meowing frantically.

Frank rolled over and looked down just in time to see a kitten deposited in his shoe. Then he noticed another black creature in his other shoe and still another on one of his socks. Mirabel was now circling, no doubt ready to give birth to a fourth kitten. Frank jumped out of bed, grabbed the cat with both hands and placed her gently in the suitcase she had appropriated a few weeks earlier. How in hell didn't I realize? he asked himself. That's why she got so fat. He gingerly picked up each of the three new-born kittens and placed it in the suitcase beside the mother. By the time he was finished, she was biting the umbilical cord of her fourth kitten. Then she seemed to relax, and she began to clean the offspring now snuggling up to her in the suitcase.

Frank waited and watched for a few moments, anxiously at first, not knowing what to do. Mirabel lay on her side, and eventually all four of the minuscule bundles of fur were latched onto her, feeding vigorously. Feeling that the situation was now under control and as proud as a new father, Frank decided to go to the Café Québec Libre for coffee and breakfast. He knew that Clémentine opened early for people who had to go to work. He was nevertheless the first customer, and Clémentine was still in her night dress when she unlocked the door.

"*Qu'avez-vous, François?* What's the matter with you?" she asked.

"I just had kittens," he replied.

"*Comment?*" she responded, stepping back and holding up her hands.

"I mean the black cat that moved in with me, she's just had four kittens."

"*Aha. Ça c'est plus catholique,*" replied Clémentine. When one of the Murphy children, a boy about ten years old, came to the door of the café to deliver the morning paper, Frank told him to go to his room behind the Inn—he had left the door unlocked—and he would see something special. The small boy put down his paper-route bag and ran off. In five minutes or so he was back, his eyes glittering with excitement.

"*Six tits chatons, tous noirs—qu'ils sont tellement beaux!*" exclaimed the child.

Six, thought Frank. It must be true what they say about the schools these days. They don't even teach kids how to count any more.

"*Viens avec moi,*" he said to the young Murphy, and the two of them returned to the room now become a feline maternity ward. Then Frank pointed down at the suitcase to provide the boy with a lesson in basic arithmetic.

"*Regard,*" he said, "*un, deux, trois, quatre . . . Cinq? Mon Dieu! Six! Sept! Huit!* Good God! She's had eight of them!"

Frank and the Murphy boy recounted twice. There was no doubt about it. Eight tiny black creatures, their eyes still unopened, were squirming for the eight available feeding stations. Frank noticed that two of the kittens had not yet succeeded in plugging themselves in, and he reached down to steer them toward Mirabel's last two nipples. As he was doing so, young Murphy slipped out of the room. Frank was staring transfixed at the mother cat now lying on her side contentedly with the eight kittens neatly packed alongside her, speculating on the miracle of birth and the fact that Mirabel's maternal facilities were now operating at full capacity, when the boy returned. He had a sign from the Inn in his hand, and he placed it against the wall by the suitcase, causing Frank to nod his head and laugh. The sign read NO

VACANCY—NON VACANT.

Before leaving to finish his paper route, the boy asked if he could bring his sisters and brothers back later, and Frank agreed that they could all have a peek, provided that they didn't disturb the mother and her litter. At eight o'clock he went over to the general store to buy a pint of cream for Mirabel, reasoning that she was going to need all the help she could get. When he returned, he sat for several minutes contemplating the scene in wonder, asking himself how on earth he had not realized long ago that the damned cat was pregnant. It also occurred to him that he was now responsible for nine black cats. What the hell was he going to do with nine black cats?

Deciding that he needed some fresh air, Frank left Mirabel and her progeny sleeping, locked the door and went for a walk up the hill. The gardens were now ablaze with red and yellow tulips, and he passed by an entire field of daffodils. It would soon be the time of the lilacs, he noted as he walked along the road. When he came to the old McVicar house, he saw Jeannie outside inspecting her rose bushes, and he stopped to tell her about the proliferation of cats in his hotel room. When she invited him for a coffee on the large veranda, he accepted immediately, knowing that the coffee would be accompanied by a cornucopia of cakes, scones, muffins, and cookies as well as home-made jellies and jams. Older ladies, Frank had learned from experience, delighted in feeding big men with big appetites; whereas young women generally couldn't boil an egg, and pretty young women expected to be taken out to dinner. His hunch proved correct—there was even some of Jeannie's Scottish shortbread.

As usual, Jeannie brought Frank up to date on activities in town. He learned that the Referendum campaign was causing increasingly bitter divisions in the Richmond and Tremblay families. Apparently Phyllis, Reginald Richmond's sister who lived in Westmount and was a Separatist, came down to visit, got into a violent argument with her brother and his wife and was ordered out of the house. She then went over to Marcel Tremblay's place, expecting a more sympathetic reception, only to discover that he was locked in battle with his older brother Robert, who was a Liberal member of the National Assembly and an avowed Federalist. Marcel's wife, Anne-Marie, an old friend of Jeannie's, actually the daughter of her father's partner in the machinery business, had described to her what happened next. Phyllis entered the fray between the two Tremblay brothers, accusing Robert of disloyalty to his own people, cowardice and kowtowing to the English Establishment, the decadence and ruthless arrogance of which she felt uniquely qualified to comment upon, having been successively married to three prime representatives. Robert apparently retorted that he was under the impression that rather than a measly three, Phyllis had been married to, or at least had engaged in intimate relations with the entire male component of the English Establishment; whereupon Phyllis threw an antique porcelain figurine at him, one of the Tremblays' most treasured possessions, and it smashed to pieces against the stone fireplace. Then she slapped him across the face, and when Robert tried to retaliate, Marcel jumped between the two, and Robert hit his brother instead. Seeing Phyllis grope for another porcelain figurine, Anne-Marie finally intervened and ordered both Phyllis and her brother-in-law out of her house. The two of them went to the bar at the Missawappi Manor, presumably to continue their battle. But they both got drunk and ended up taking a room for the night at the Manor.

"A room together?" asked Frank.

"I gather they had no choice," replied Jeannie. "They're having some kind of convention of a group from Boston over there, and only one room was available."

"Two single beds, I trust."

"One double bed, I understand. The convention had booked all the singles."

"My God!" said Frank, bubbling with mirth. "You don't mean to tell me that a Canadian Federalist and a Quebec Separatist had to share the same bed?"

"I'm afraid so. And neither one of them exactly in the blush of youth."

"I wonder how it worked out."

"That I don't know," said Jeannie. "Joe was over there with his eggs this morning, and he says that Phyllis and Robert were having breakfast together and seemed to be getting along quite well."

"Aha! Then maybe that's the solution to Canada's problems. Get them all into the same bed together."

"What a lot of them don't seem to realize, Mr. Collins, is that they're already in the same bed together. Or at least in the same boat."

Jeannie also told Frank about the "Battle of the Generals." One renowned military man, who had a chestful of medals from both world wars, was suing a former comrade-in-arms, likewise a much decorated general, for half a million dollars in damages. The first general had been persuaded to make a statement in favour of the OUI side in the Referendum, and the second had commented in an interview that his old friend's war wounds had obviously caught up with him at last, bringing on complete senility."

"So far as I can tell, they're both senile old fools," said Jeannie.

"This Referendum business is certainly cutting a wide swath," Frank commented. "Families divided, and now generals."

"And don't forget the boxers."

"Boxers?"

"Oh yes. Two retired boxers, both of them pretty punch-drunk, I gather, are going to have a match at the big arena in Montreal. One of them will fight for the OUI and the other for the NON."

"For what purpose?"

"For their own satisfaction, I guess."

Frank ate one last piece of shortbread and left the McVicar house with an offer from Jeannie to take one of his black kittens. Now if I can get rid of the other seven, not to mention momma puss, then I might be able to get some work done on my dissertation, he told himself.

When he passed by the Café Québec Libre, Frank noticed the huge, one-fanged tomcat which had attended the Referendum debate lurking at the back door. Suddenly grasping that the black tom was without doubt the cause of his kitten complications, Frank instinctively clenched his fists and advanced toward it menacingly, and the big cat bared its solitary gleaming fang before slinking away among the garbage cans.

Now what on earth did sweet little Mirabel ever see in an ugly brute like that? Frank muttered to himself. Then it occurred to him that all creatures on the face of the earth were slaves to their basic urges, which was the reason why humanity was in such a mess. Civilization was a thin veneer indeed.

Chapter Seventeen

It seemed to Frank that the entire village of North Chadley was engulfed in the fragrance of lilacs when he walked over to the new Murphy house on Saturday morning to help pour cement for the basement floor. He discovered that the electrical wiring, the plumbing and the Murphys themselves had all been installed in the house during the previous week, and he was gratified to learn that the Murphy children had already conducted a successful campaign to increase the household by two black kittens. Counting the one going to Jeannie McVicar, that left him with a mere five, plus Mirabel of course.

Frank had resolved that he would pay the veterinary fees to have the mother cat spayed. There was nothing else for it. A female cat capable of such epic reproduction, presuming that the trait was passed on to her offspring, could conceivably inundate the entire continent with black cats. Civilization as it was known would be threatened, he told himself. The cats would wipe out all the smaller animals—birds, chipmunks, squirrels, mice, moles, snakes, and frogs—then they would form packs, as alley cats have been known to do in New York City and Montreal, to hunt sewer rats, then probably dogs, and who knew what else.

That afternoon, after completing the cement floor, taking a long shower, eating lunch at the Inn and napping for an hour to restore his strength, Frank was sitting at the table in his room, ostensibly checking his notes but really spending more time staring at the lively kittens, when there was a knock on his door. He was surprised, but pleasantly surprised to see Norma Duffin. Her long blond hair was not wound up in a tidy bun as it had been on the previous occasions he had seen her. It flowed down to her shoulders, at once accentuating and softening the strong features of her face, her nose, cheekbones and chin. She was wearing a light, summery blouse and skirt which contrasted with her usual trim, no-nonsense business suits. Frank stood in the doorway gazing at his visitor, simply enjoying the look of her.

"May I come in, Mr. Collins?" she asked with a smile.

"Yes, yes, please," Frank muttered, stumbling back from the doorway and almost stepping on one of the black kittens.

"My God!" Norma exclaimed. "Where did you get all those cats?"

"The big one moved in with me when I rented the room. The next thing I knew . . ."

Frank ushered Norma over to his chair, then he sat down on the edge of the bed, still gazing at the woman with undisguised admiration. She cast a quick glance over the assorted papers, cards, books, paper clips and ballpoint pens and crumbs cluttering the table.

"Looks as if you could use a good secretary, Mr. Collins."

"I . . . I sure could, Mrs. Duffin . . ." Frank noticed a large bandaid on Norma's hand. "What happened to your hand?"

"Oh, just a small cut. In too much of a hurry slicing the tomatoes for dinner last night."

"Perhaps you could use a cook."

"I sure could. I never know when my boss will want me. He doesn't work regular hours, you know. And he expects me to be on call all the time, night or day."

"I see," Frank replied, thinking I'll bet he wants you every night.

"Are you a good cook, Mr. Collins?"

"Some people like my cooking."

"Just looking at the size of you I'd imagine that you're an appreciator of food, and most people like that are usually also good chefs. But I didn't come here to talk about cooking, Mr. Collins . . ."

She obviously thinks I'm a big slob, thought Frank as Norma's face stiffened into a look of seriousness.

"I'm worried," she continued, "and I'm not sure quite what to do. If I go to the mayor or any of the town councillors, they probably wouldn't believe me. I'm also worried about losing my job, which pays well and which I need to support my three children. I'd have to go to Montreal or Toronto to get another job like the one I've got now, and the kids love it here."

"What is it, Mrs. Duffin? What's the problem?"

"The other night you asked me about the implications of Mr. Gabib's presence in town. Well, finally I've managed to get a pretty good idea . . ."

"Yes, go on," Frank urged, intrigued by the unexpected turn of events.

"I've seen the plans, Mr. Collins. The whole town will be torn down, totally demolished, erased like yesterday's lessons on a blackboard."

"That doesn't surprise me."

"It doesn't?"

"No. Why else would your boss be buying up everything unless he had a specific project in mind?"

"Well he certainly has a project. Hotels, condominiums, exclusive boutiques, theme parks . . . everything ultra-modern, concrete and steel . . . just dreadful. I have to try to do something to keep it from happening, Mr. Collins."

"And why are you telling me all this, Mrs. Duffin?"

"Because you asked me . . . and I think you care. Everyone else in town is obsessed with the cursed Referendum. The damned fools—while they're at each other's throats, the whole town is being yanked from under their feet."

"Can't you simply make public what you know? I imagine there are ways Gabib's plans could be curtailed, at least to some extent, if the people of the town pull together to stop him."

"Do you think that's possible?"

"I'm not sure. The present political climate is not exactly conducive to cooperation, I must admit. But I'm a stranger here, remember. You know a lot more about the town than I do."

"Yes, I know that we have our share of perverse fools who won't look beyond their noses."

"Every town has a share of those."

"Will you help me do something, Mr. Collins?"

"It's really none of my business, Mrs. Duffin. I shouldn't get involved."

Frank shuddered to see the look of disappointment which suffused Norma's face as soon as he had spoken. He should have put it differently, he told himself. But he was still determined not to become entangled in the internal problems of Québec in general and North Chadley in particular. He was here simply to observe, then to organize his observations into some kind of acceptable PhD dissertation. Besides, he had personal problems to deal with, and gazing at the statuesque blonde sitting right in front of him on his chair was hardly doing anything to alleviate those problems. Was she really a playmate as well as a secretary for her boss? What exactly did she mean by saying that she was on call night and day?

"Perhaps you should talk to Mr. Gabib himself," Frank ventured. "As his private secretary, working all hours of the night and day as you say, you must have a close personal relationship, I would imagine. You must be . . ."

"No, I am not, Mr. Collins. Our relationship is strictly professional. And that's the way I intend it to remain, especially . . . especially after something that happened last week. In any event, Mr. Gabib would not pay the least attention to my, or to any other woman's, concerns about how he conducts his business affairs. He receives his instructions directly from his father, who is a powerful sheikh in Saudi Arabia."

Frank was relieved to hear Norma's words. Although he hadn't said as much, she had divined what was lurking in his mind. He was curious to know what had happened to her last week.

"Have you ever met his father?" he asked on a hunch.

"Yes, once."

"When was that?"

"Last week."

Frank's hunch seemed on the mark. "How did you meet him?" he asked.

"He was visiting the United Nations in New York, and I flew down there with Mr. Gabib. That's how I found out about the plans for North Chadley . . . among other things . . ."

"You stayed over in New York?"

"Yes. They had a large suite in one of the hotels."

"And something happened to upset you. Besides the

plans for the town, that is."

Norma nodded her head.

"What was it?" asked Frank.

"Nothing really. I shouldn't even mention it."

"I'm intrigued to know, Mrs. Duffin."

"Simply a few remarks I overheard . . . comparing me to a blonde mistress the sheikh happened to have in his entourage."

"And what about her?"

"Well it seems that the old sheik has a rather limited view of the roles of women. He presumed that I was also a mistress. No arrangements had been made for me to have a separate room of my own."

"I see."

"Anyway, the bottom line is that he seemed to think that any Western woman could be bought. It was only a question of price."

"And what about the son, your boss? What does he think?"

"I don't know what he thinks."

"You mean he's not interested in you . . . uh . . . as a woman?"

"I can't answer that, Mr. Collins."

"Did you get a separate room?"

"Yes, eventually I did. In another hotel. But that has nothing to do with the threat to North Chadley, Mr. Collins. Do you mind if I call you Frank?"

"Not at all. Can I call you Norma?"

"I wish you would."

Frank suddenly had an inspiration. To avoid problems with the Customs, he had shipped his bicycle to Newport, Vermont, the closest American town to North Chadley, and he therefore had to drive down to the bus station there some time or other to pick it up. He knew that visiting the United States was a frequent and popular activity of the people in and around North Chadley, mainly because the American liquor stores sold half-gallon bottles of booze for about the same price as twelve-ounce mickeys cost in Quebec. New Hampshire was even more popular than Vermont, having no sales tax whatever. Customs regulations, Frank found out, officially permitted Canadians to bring back only one forty-ounce bottle after a visit of at least forty-eight hours, but in the Eastern Townships of Quebec, smuggling had long been a favourite local sport.

Regional folklore was replete with stories of legendary exploits, from vast caravans of trucks loaded with whiskey crossing the border southward during American Prohibition to a fake ladies' string quartet heading down one road and returning north by another a couple of hours later, their instrument cases jam-packed with bottles of liquor and cigarettes. Frank had concluded that everyone in the Townships was addicted to smuggling. They saw it as their inalienable right—elderly ladies and young children, businessmen and bums, priests, nuns, ministers, and gangsters. The most bizarre story he had heard was about a funeral director in Brooke who regularly crossed the border to pick up bodies of French Canadians for burial back home in Quebec. Two trips out of three, however, the coffin lying gravely in the back of the hearse was filled with contraband rather than anyone's remains, and not once did a Customs' official request that the lid be opened. More often than not the officer would remove his cap in respect for the dead, and the grim-faced mortician would nod in solemn acknowledgement as he drove over the line with enough smuggled goods to pay for a half-dozen funerals.

"Say, I have to go to Newport to pick up my bicycle," Frank said to Norma, chancing the idea would appeal to her. "Would you like to come with me this evening? You could show me the way, and we could have dinner together and talk about what's happening in North Chadley."

"Yes, I'd like to do that," Norma replied immediately. "What time would you like to leave?"

Frank couldn't believe that it had been so easy. He was actually going to go out for dinner with the woman who had been floating in and out of his reveries for the past several days.

"Any time, any time you like," he replied.

"How about if I'm ready for six o'clock?"

"I'll be at your door at six o'clock sharp."

Norma was already in the doorway, smiling at the kittens. Then she smiled at Frank, said goodbye and was on her way.

Frank spent more time than usual tidying himself up in the late afternoon. He shaved slowly and carefully, making sure not to miss a whisker, then he took several minutes to comb and brush his straight, brown hair. He tried on all four of his shirts before deciding which one to wear, and he cleaned his jacket with a wet cloth. Then he even took some toilet paper and shined his shoes as best he could. He couldn't remember ever having shined them before.

In a demure, light-blue dress, blonde hair cascading over her shoulders, Norma inspired Frank with a feeling of pride as he escorted her on his arm into a restaurant overlooking Lake Memphremagog. He glanced quickly from side to side, certain that other customers were taking notice. She seemed pleased to be with him, although he soon realized that she was genuinely and unusually shy. She seemed, for instance, to be embarrassed by her own proportions, keeping on the loose, buttoned sweater she was wearing as if to camouflage the ampleness of her bust. Frank ordered aperitifs, a martini, and a Dubonnet, while they pondered the menu.

Frank was naturally eager to find out more about her personal life, his knowledge so far being limited to the facts that she was a stenographer who worked for an Arab businessman and was divorced with three children. But she told him little more about herself. Her marriage had broken up by mutual consent. Her former husband was a school teacher, a good man, but they had simply not been able to make it work. She was the oldest girl in a family of seven children, and she had started working at the age of fourteen to help support the others because her father, an immigrant from Belfast, was regularly being laid off from his job in the shipyards of Montreal's East End. She loved to read and do crossword puzzles, and apart from that, she said, there was nothing else to tell about herself.

"And what about Gabib?" Frank asked. "What exactly is he up to anyway?"

"He's in the bolthole business, Frank."

"The what?"

"You know how rabbits and other little animals that live in the ground make an extra hole to use as an escape route, in case they have to bolt away. Well that's called a bolthole."

Frank took a sip of his martini and smiled.

"Now it all begins to fit together. The top dogs in Saudi Arabia want to make sure that they have a variety of options in the event that things fall apart at home."

Norma nodded her head, tugged at her sweater, then

took another sip of her Dubonnet.

"And the situation in Saudi Arabia," Frank continued, "is probably a bit shaky at best, with all the money in the hands of the royal family and the majority of workers imported from other countries and that sort of thing. So that's the way it is, is it? Gabib is simply a front man setting up a possible haven in case of a storm, and the town is to be redesigned to suit the new owners. Makes sense. The Saudis must have learned something from what happened to the Shah of Iran."

"Yes, maybe they did. He ended up with no place to go, didn't he?"

"That's pretty much the case. But do you think St-Alphonse de Chadley Nord would be a suitable place for *la crème de la crème* of the Arabian kingdom?"

"No, I don't."

"Why not?"

"Because it's a small community, and the people are set in their ways."

"Ways can change, Norma, especially when they're caught in a significant cash flow."

"True. In fact a lot of things are changing quite drastically now. But for a harmonious mixing of any sort, the Arabs would also have to change, and I have the impression that they're either unable or unwilling to adapt to the slightest degree. That's the whole point, I suppose. They want to create a totally isolated community of their own, like a colony on Mars enclosed in a glass capsule."

"I see."

"And just as I told you, Frank, as soon as Mr. Gabib completes the purchase deals for the Inn and Café Québec Libre, he intends to raze the entire downtown area. The new complex will be a kind of combination of

Place Ville Marie, Miami Beach, and Disneyland—highrise condominiums, exclusive boutiques, a hotel with a drive-in marina, for God's sake! With docking facilities for those monster cabin cruisers you see on the ocean. And Lake Missawappi is only eleven miles long and a mile wide."

Frank took notes as Norma provided additional details. Then he rapidly drew up a sample list of zoning and building restrictions which could be adopted by the town council to preserve the quaint, country-town beauty of North Chadley. The problem, of course, as he and Norma fully realized, was to generate a collective will among the townspeople. Being an outsider, Frank could do little except offer advice. It would be up to Norma to get the ball rolling. First of all, the English and French would have to put aside their differences and work together. For a while at least. Frank was happy to agree to work with Norma, to help her in any way possible.

The waitress arrived again at the table, and both Norma and Frank opted for the lobster special. They also agreed on a bottle of white wine for the meal and another cocktail each before eating.

"Incidentally," said Frank, after the waitress had left with the orders, "you mentioned drastic changes in Quebec. What changes?"

"The big one is that the basic working language has changed from English to French."

"Has it really?"

"Oh yes. I couldn't do my job now if I didn't know French. When I first started working, I didn't need a word."

"But aren't the English resisting?"

"Some of them are, sure. But the majority of those

who are still here have adapted. And we're making sure that our kids learn a lot more French than we ever learned in school. My three have all been in immersion courses and are already pretty much bilingual."

"So you go along with what's happening?"

"Sure I do. I don't blame the French for trying to provide themselves with a little linguistic security. That's the way it was supposed to be from the beginning of this country."

"And why wasn't it?"

"Because the English didn't make the effort. They didn't have to in the old days. People just don't do what they don't have to do."

"And now they have to?"

"Yes, now they have to."

"So you think everything will work out all right? So far as the English and French in the province are concerned, I mean."

"No, I'm not sure about that. We still have to get by the Referendum."

"Are you worried about it?"

"Sure I'm worried. Things could fall apart. And June 24th is coming up soon, you know."

"June 24th?"

"St-Jean Baptiste Day, Quebec's national holiday. We're bound to have trouble then."

"Ah yes, I remember now. That's when the parade in Montreal turned into a big riot, wasn't it? When the mayor and the premier of province ran for their lives, and Pierre Trudeau stayed on the platform and defied the whole mob."

Norma nodded her head as the waitress arrived with second cocktails. Frank asked her a few more questions while they sipped their drinks, but as soon as the lobster appeared the conversation was interrupted. Picking the meat out of the shell, dipping it in garlic butter and trying to keep his chin clean, Frank decided, required his undivided concentration. He definitely did not want this attractive and intriguing woman to think that he was a slob. She was about his own age, he estimated, or maybe a little older, around thirty or thirty-one. No doubt she had married young to have three children. She had been working since she was fourteen, she had said, taking time off only to have her babies. Frank couldn't help wondering again what sort of romantic life she led. Was she really able to keep her relationship with her boss and his associates strictly professional? And if so, then for how long? She had as much as stated that Gabib was after her body. He was probably just biding his time. Another trip someplace, just the two of them, another hotel, a romantic dinner . . . After all, Gabib and his associates were all normal, garden-variety males, judging from their reaction to little Lisette. Of course, Lisette was like a shot of electricity. But Norma was different. Certainly with her features and figure and long blond hair she could attract men whenever she took the notion, although she did not have Lisette's exuberant sexuality. She was like a mountain peak in the distance, inviting a climber, while Lisette was more like a lush, tropical garden on the other side of the street. Unfortunately, Frank speculated, he was not much of a mountain climber. The only time he had tried, on a boy-scout hike in Colorado, he had stumbled and sprained an ankle. Then limping back to camp he had almost been bitten by a rattlesnake.

"A penny for your thoughts," said Norma, having now finished her meal.

"Uh . . . they may be worth at least a buck and a

half," replied Frank, buying time to shift his mental gears.

"All right then. I'll take a dollar's worth."

"I was just wondering, Norma, how the English in North Chadley were reacting to the changes in various institutions. That's the basic subject of my dissertation, you know."

"What institutions are you referring to?"

"The town council, the school board, the social groups, and so on."

"Well the social groups—like the Legion, or the Village Improvement Society, or the Missawappi Club— haven't really changed that much. They always catered to select groups, and they still do. So far as the other institutions are concerned, the Government obliges them all now to operate in French. Even the Brooke Hospital, which was built and operated by the English in the Townships. There's even talk of it being closed altogether. Local people used to run the schools and hospitals, but now Quebec pulls all the strings."

"And what's the reaction?"

"Some people get upset, but most are adapting."

"You really think so?"

"They have no choice, if they don't want to leave. Actually what you have now is simply the reverse of what it used to be. Now the English have to be bilingual instead of the French. Which to my mind is only normal, considering that it's a French province."

When the waitress came over to clear away the dinner plates, both Norma and Frank passed on dessert and ordered coffee.

"And how do you see it all turning out, Norma?"

"Two possibilities, I imagine. As I was saying before. Either the Referendum pulls the plug out from under the country, or else Quebec evolves into a pluralist society."

"A pluralist society?"

"That's the way it looks to me, Frank. For centuries the French kept pretty much to themselves. A few Irish and Scotch Catholics intermarried with them, but they were soon assimilated. Religion, not language, was the real barrier."

"And now religion has lost its influence."

"It seems so. Which means that there's going to be a lot more intermarriage. And not just with the so-called English of Quebec. Also with the hundreds of thousands of Italians, Greeks, Haitians, Vietnamese, Cambodians, South Americans, and what have you. So if the nationalist fanatics can't fence in the place and create an exclusive little country and kick out all the foreigners who are already here and are multiplying at three times the birthrate of French Canadians, then Quebec, it seems to me, is bound to become a pluralist society. It'll be French-speaking all right. A lot of the new immigrants spoke French even before they came here, like the Haitians or the Vietnamese. But it'll definitely be pluralist, if that's the right word."

"It is. And so what you're saying is that the old tribal nationalism will be going the way of the horse and buggy."

"I think so. You know, Frank, I wouldn't be surprised if that's why the extremists on both sides, French and English, are doing their nuts these days—they both see themselves going down the drain."

"How's that?"

"Well the Separatists must realize that if they can't isolate French Canadians, keep them *pure laine*—pure wool—as they say, then their cause is lost. What does the old motto, the old rallying cry, *je me souviens,* mean to a Haitian, or a Vietnamese, or a South American? And the English Establishment types already know that they won't be calling the shots any longer."

"So the Referendum could be the last round-up, as it were?"

"Maybe. We'll see."

"And what would you do if worse comes to worse, Norma?"

"What do you mean?"

"If the situation deteriorates one way or another."

"I don't really know what I'd do. I love Quebec. I was born and raised here, and it's my place. I would hate to have to leave."

"I can understand that."

"You're lucky, Frank. You can just go back home."

"I'm beginning to feel very much at home here, believe it or not. Especially now that I've . . . I've . . ."

Frank almost said, now that I'm getting to know you. He found himself being strongly attracted to Norma Duffin, but he knew that he could not risk making a fool of himself. She was probably not the slightest bit interested in him as a man. Why should she be? She had a good job, her family, her home, her Arabian gentlemen, maybe a stable of lovers any one of whom she could call upon to be groomed, saddled and prancing the turf whenever she fancied going for a trot. He, on the other hand, was a penniless graduate student, still struggling to get a Ph.D. and with no prospects of a decent job even if he did complete the degree. And he was not exactly a ladies' man, except perhaps very old ladies. Thoughts of Terry Ellen crossed his mind. She had been his steady girlfriend for several years, his fiancée for all intents and purposes. Then just before he came to

Quebec, she dumped him for a lousy little computer specialist. They probably spent their evenings programming each other. Which was a damned shame, because in certain respects, however lacking in finesse he might have been, he had programmed Terry Ellen pretty well himself. Perhaps that was why he had come to Quebec, to get away from it all.

He was a reasonably good physical specimen, a big man. Awkward and clumsy once in a while, he admitted to himself. Still, he had made the university football team. He wasn't stupid—he had placed in the top five percentile in the Graduate Record Exam, which was administered to all graduate students in the United States. But with his mind burdened with the precepts of anthropological investigation and the cursed dissertation he was expected to produce, he was surely boring company. Especially for a bright, sophisticated career woman like Norma. Well, perhaps it wasn't entirely true that his mind was preoccupied with Anthropology, Frank mused. But when it wasn't, it took a nose-dive into the gutter, filling his head with fantasies about other men's wives in various states of undress, or else, as was happening that very instant, visions of how his modestly attired dinner companion would look in no clothes at all. She certainly had a full figure. That was plain to see. Norma's voice shattered his reveries.

"You'd be disappointed, Frank," she said in a low voice.

"Disappointed?" He was startled by the comment.

"Yes, I'm afraid so."

"Disappointed by what, Norma?"

"My figure isn't quite what it used to be. I look better when I'm dressed now."

"But . . . I . . . I don't . . ."

"You were trying to imagine how I'd look in the nude, weren't you?"

"Well . . ." Frank lowered his eyes sheepishly. Now how in hell did she know that? he asked himself. The woman must be psychic.

"If you were to see me naked, you'd beg me to get dressed."

"Oh no I wouldn't. I mean, I would . . . I would . . ."

Norma smiled and took a sip of her cognac.

"I'm afraid that I've been boring you. I'm sorry," she said.

"Good God, Norma, don't be ridiculous. I'm the one who's been boring *you*—talking shop all the time. That's exactly what was going through my mind a minute ago."

"You mean you weren't . . ."

"Well, yes, I suppose I was. That too. For a few moments."

On the drive back to North Chadley, Frank's disassembled bicycle stashed in the trunk of the old Buick, Norma snuggled up to Frank's side, and after several miles of hesitation, he put his arm around her and continued driving with one hand on the wheel. He felt himself being wondrously aroused by the innocent physical contact, a sensation he had not experienced since he was a young lad of thirteen or fourteen on a mixed hayride or holding hands at the back of a movie cinema. He could hardly believe that it was happening, given his advanced age and the jaded state of his romantic propensities. At the rate he was going, he told himself, he would soon be as disassembled as his bicycle in the trunk. After all, in recent weeks, his closest companion had been Mirabel, and now even she was totally occupied with her eight damned black kittens.

"Thank you for the lovely dinner, Frank," said Norma as they stood in front of the door to her house. Then she held out her hand.

Wanting desperately to be invited in, Frank pretended not to notice the proffered hand and simply stood there expectantly. Then for the second time that night Norma accurately divined his thoughts.

"I'd like to invite you in, Frank," she said, "but I'm afraid that it would disturb the kids. My oldest girl does the baby-sitting, and she's probably still up watching TV. You understand, don't you?"

"Yes, I suppose I do," he replied glumly.

"Then stop looking like a little boy who's just been refused a piece of apple pie."

"Apple pie! Good Lord! I like apple pie, but I . . ."

"Perhaps I'll invite you over for dinner some evening, Frank. When the kids are off at their father's place."

Frank nodded in resignation. Norma reached over and squeezed his hand. He noted what seemed almost an impish twinkle in her eye as she continued.

"And who knows? Perhaps we'll have apple pie for dessert eventually. With ice cream. I'm fond of it myself, you know. It's hard to beat."

"Yeah, that would be nice, Norma," Frank muttered, as she gave him a peck on the cheek and disappeared into the house.

She has a bolt-hole just like her boss, Gabib, he told himself as he drove slowly back to the Inn. Only in her case, it was her three children. She did mention that she might invite him over for dinner at her place. With apple pie for dessert. He wondered if she could possibly have meant what he thought she might have meant, or was he fantasizing again? It was an absurd state of affairs.

There he was, capable of deciphering the significance of various subtle gestures and signals exchanged between males and females in primitive tribes in Borneo, and he still was unsure about a woman essentially of his own cultural group and with whom he had spent the entire evening. Anyway, time would tell. And it would be more like dynamite than apple pie, of that he had no doubt, if ever it should come to pass. Beg her to put her clothes back on? She was more likely to see all 260 pounds of him hovering in the air like a hummingbird.

After parking the car at the back of the Inn and peeking into his room to see that the cats were all right, Frank wandered over to the bar-salon for a nightcap. He found Bill Martin and Gordon Jackson there, unwinding after a long meeting of the professors' union at l'Université de Brooke. Lisette, as bouncy and eye-catching as ever, was serving, but her husband did not appear to be around. After several minutes of listening to a catalogue of the deficiencies of the University administration, the major problem being that there was too much of it, what with a rector, five vice-rectors, coordinators, supervisors, executive secretaries, under-secretaries, assistants, aides to assistants and assistants to the aides, Frank finally got a chance to mention to Bill that he had interviewed Norma Duffin that night.

He then found out that Bill had known Norma since she was a small child, their two families having been closely connected back in the East End of Montreal. She had been an extraordinarily shy young girl, and her shyness had been aggravated by the ribbing she took because of the precocious development of her bust, according to Bill. No wonder she was so touchy about her anatomy, thought Frank. She had apparently not gone out much with boys. She had married her first steady boyfriend, but the two had simply drifted apart. She was still a somewhat insular lady, doing her job for the Arabs, taking care of her children, but otherwise keeping much to herself.

"Her place is full of crossword-puzzle collections, records and books," said Bill. "One time I went over there to find out if there was anything wrong. The kids were with their father, and we hadn't seen her around for three or four days. Well I knocked on the door, and there was no answer, so I began to get worried. I found a window open and I crawled in. And there she was, lying on the sofa with a big pillow over her head. God knows how long she'd been doing that. A strange woman sometimes, that Norma Duffin."

"Yeah, I think I know what you mean," Frank replied, although he really had not found Norma all that strange. Mysterious perhaps.

"But she certainly is capable at her work. Mainly self-taught," said Bill.

"Can she cook?"

"Excellent cook. We've been over there for meals many times. She makes an Irish stew which should be served with the sound of trumpets."

"What about desserts?"

"Desserts? Last time we were there I think we had chocolate cake."

"Ever have her apple pie?"

"No, not that I remember. Say, what the hell are you asking me all this for?"

"Just curious, Bill. She mentioned that she might have me over for dinner one of these days."

"Well go for it, man. You won't be disappointed."

"No, I don't think so," Frank replied.

Gord Jackson, who had been to the washroom and

on the way back had stopped to talk to Lisette, perched decoratively on her bar stool with one shapely leg stretched out and the other on a rung, called out to ask if Bill and Frank wanted another beer. Then he stayed at the bar with Lisette after she had served her three customers.

"He prefers her to us," commented Bill. "In fact, he seems to have a distinct tendency to drool every time he looks at her."

"Who doesn't?" said Frank, casting his eye toward the bar, thinking lemon, or possibly pecan pie.

"I'm going to have to get him out of here," said Bill, also glancing toward the bar. "She's a little too much for him in his current state. He's liable to go right off the deep end."

"What current state do you mean, Bill?"

"Gord's wife took off with a twenty-year old student and left him with their four kids."

"Good God! When did she do that?"

"A few months ago. The student had been boarding at Gord's place, but none of us had any idea what was going on. Then the next thing we knew she and the boy were gone."

"That must be hard on a guy."

"It's not easy, that's for sure. Although in the long run it may be just as well. Meanwhile, however, he's trying to pick up the pieces—taking care of the children, keeping the ship afloat. And he's doing a damned good job of it, although sometimes he gets pretty desperate."

"And you don't have to be desperate to appreciate Lisette."

"No. Just have half a hormone."

"That Norma Duffin is quite a doll too, don't you think?"

"She's beautiful. But I think she's probably leery about men. Whereas that Lisette is obviously a man's woman. She's perfectly at ease with men, and she knows how to handle them, except perhaps her husband Wilt."

"What makes you say that?"

"Because he uses her. Treats her like a slave. The man's money-crazy, you know. I really don't understand why she sticks around. In fact, one of these days maybe she'll do the same thing as Gord's wife. Well, not exactly the same, because she doesn't have four kids. It's ironic how a decent, good guy like Gord can get shafted, while a crude, abusive guy like Wilt gets away with doing what he likes. Women can be strange. But it seems to happen quite often that way."

"By the way, Bill, did I tell you that the black cat that moved into my room with me had eight kittens? I've been wondering . . ."

"You come to my place with any bloody black kittens and I'll write your department head and tell him you're making a menace of yourself in North Chadley and should be sent to Arctic Circle to study the effects of the skidoo on the mores of the Inuit."

"Maybe Gord Jackson might want one."

"Are you kidding? Look at the damned fool. He's totally mesmerized. Just standing there like a zombie, staring at her with his tongue hanging out. I guess it's time for us to get out of here. Hey, Gord, drink up."

After the two professors had left, Frank decided to have one more beer, telling himself that between Norma earlier in the evening and Lisette now, not to mention the prospect of being stuck with God-knows-how-many black kittens, he needed something to dull his senses. Lisette poured herself a Dubonnet and sat down with him.

"How's the research going, Frank?" she asked.

"So so. I've still got a few interviews to do."

"Who haven't you talked to yet?"

"Wilt's cousin Morton for one. I hear he's a bit strange."

"In some ways, yes."

Frank was curious to know the facts about Lisette and Morton. Marge had hardly convinced him that the two were having an affair, but there had to be something. Three beers had made him much bolder than he would normally have been.

"I understand that you and Morton . . . uh . . . are . . . quite close friends."

"Who told you that?"

"Well . . ."

"Never mind, I know. It was Marge Miller. That poor woman just can't keep her tongue from wagging. She's an alcoholic, only in her case it's rumours."

"Yes, I know."

"And what did she say?"

"Well . . . I really don't want to repeat idle gossip."

"She said that I was having an affair with Morton, a man old enough to be my father, didn't she?"

"Something along those lines."

"Then let me set the record straight, Frank. It's not true. Morton Wadleigh has never so much as laid a finger on me. And I'm certainly not having an affair with him."

"As I recall, Marge said that she thought he was paying you for . . . for something."

"In fact he does pay me, Frank, but not for what Marge thinks. He fancies himself something of a sculptor, and he pays me to pose for him every now and again."

"Pose? Pose how? I mean..."

"I know what you mean. Yes, I have posed for him in the nude. But generally he gives me costumes to wear, if you can call them that."

"Costumes?"

"All the things the girls used to use in the old strip-tease shows—pasties and G-strings and garter belts, a big feather and long white gloves. He's got a thing about the gloves."

"And does Wilt know that you do this ... uh ... posing?"

"Wilt? It's all because of Wilt. It was his idea in the first place."

"I don't get it."

"You see, Frank, Morton used to be in love with my mother. She's dead now, God rest her soul. She used to be a professional strip-tease dancer, and that's how come Morton has all that stuff. But she was a good woman, my mother."

"Yes. I've heard about her. Madeleine was her name, wasn't it?"

"Madeleine Marie-Anne. A lot of men were in love with her."

"So I've heard."

"So what if she made her living as a stripper? That's what men want, isn't it?"

"It is a pleasure to see a good-looking woman ... uh ... the way God intended her to look, that's true. I can't deny that."

"If it's a sleazy, degrading business, as some people seem to think, then it's the fault of men. They're the ones who push and force women to do it. I'm quite sure strip-tease was not invented by a woman."

"You're probably right. But what about Morton?"

"Well Wilt and I were over there for a few drinks one evening, and Morton started raving about what a superb figure my mother had. Then he dug out a couple of photographs from an old trunk he keeps in his bedroom. And he's quite right, Frank. My mother had a terrific figure."

"She must have had, from everything I've heard."

"And what exactly have you heard?"

"Simply that she was exceptionally beautiful... that just about every man around worshipped her. But go on with the story, Lisette."

"Anyway, Wilt looked at the old pictures and started arguing with Morton that in the same get-up, a G-string and a couple of those little stars you paste on, I would look better than my mother. Finally they bet fifty bucks. Nobody bothered to ask me, mind you. Mort had the stuff in his trunk, and Wilt told me to go put it on."

"You say they bet fifty dollars?"

"Right. Wilt said that if Mort wasn't convinced that I had at least as good a shape as my mother's, he'd pay him the money. And if he was convinced, then Wilt won the bet."

"And you went along with it?"

"I didn't have much choice. Wilt was insisting in his usual way, and then Mort started pleading with me to be a good sport, so eventually I decided what the hell, if that's what they want me to do. I must admit that I was also a bit curious. And I really wanted Wilt to lose the bet. I was sure that he would."

"Did he?"

"No. But I still think that he should have. My mother did have a better figure than mine."

"That's hard to believe, Lisette."

"It's true. She was perfectly proportioned. I'm not."

"I don't find anything wrong with your proportions. And apparently neither did Morton Wadleigh if he paid the fifty bucks."

"Mort paid because he got a good show, Frank. After all, I was just about naked. And he took his time to make up his mind, walking around staring at me from all angles, checking me against the photos. He even had me standing on the dining room table at one point, and I whacked my head against the chandelier."

"But you won."

"I didn't win. Wilt won. Isn't that the way it is, Frank? The women do the performing, whatever it might be, and the men make the money."

"You must have had a certain amount of satisfaction."

"None whatsoever. The only thing I got out of it was that Morton offered to pay me a hundred dollars a session to come over and pose for him, and again Wilt insisted. He greatly resents the fact that his cousin Morton collected more of the Wadleigh money than he did, you know."

"I see."

"And that's all there is to it so far as Morton and I are concerned. Nothing more. In fact, Frank, if you want to know the whole truth, the poor guy is still hopelessly in love with my mother. I'm just a prop to allow him to relive the past. And those long white gloves are something else. Would you believe that he actually gets me to throw them to him? If old Marge knew the whole story, she'd realize that what goes with Mort isn't an affair, it's a joke. The guy is only a hair this side of certifiable, you know."

"So I've been told."

"Would you like another beer?"

"No thanks, I'll just finish what I have. I'd better leave and let you close up."

"Don't rush. I'm all alone, you know."

"By the way, where is Wilt these days?"

"He's in Florida. Working on a deal to buy a restaurant down there. Probably working on a few other things too. Young things."

"I'm a bit surprised that he would leave you here all by yourself."

"I don't mind. I can look after myself."

"I'm sure you can. What I mean is . . . well, from what you've been telling me about that business at Morton's and all the rest . . . it seems to me that Wilt isn't very . . . uh . . . possessive about you."

"Oh he's possessive all right. That's the problem, Frank. He thinks of me as only one of his possessions, to do with just as he pleases. He also thinks that he did me a favour by marrying me."

Frank shook his head, wondering how a man with such an attractive wife, a woman he knew was lusted after by every male who caught a glimpse of her, could be so blasé about dangling her in front of other men. Perhaps he just didn't give a damn. Or perhaps it had something to do with the notoriety of Lisette's mother. Whatever, Frank mused, the whole thing was bound to backfire on Wilt one of these days. She was a warm-hearted person, and sooner or later she might take a notion to put some guy like Gord Jackson out of his misery. Frank was feeling a bit miserable himself, and an idea much more intoxicating than the beer he had drunk was now flitting through his mind, bumping against the sides of his skull like a bird trapped in a screened veranda.

"By the way, Frank," said Lisette, "I hope you won't be writing anything about Morton and my mother in that dissertation of yours. That's just between you and me. To make sure that Marge Miller didn't give you any wrong ideas."

"Don't worry. I'm writing strictly about institutions," Frank replied, at the same time thinking that in fact Madeleine the legendary stripper would qualify as a genuine institution. And at the rate she was going, little Lisette as well.

"Good. By the way, did you know that next Saturday is Quebec's national holiday, *la fête de la Saint-Jean Baptiste*? With the Referendum coming up, I'm afraid that we're going to have trouble around here."

"Oh?"

"Usually there's a big bonfire in the park. But the stupid municipal council has refused permission for one this year."

"Why's that?"

"Because they're afraid of the Separatists. As you know, except for Emile Brosseau, the council's all English."

"But how can they stop celebrating a national holiday?"

"Apparently they're going to have the volunteer fire department standing by, and if someone starts a fire, they'll put it out."

"That's crazy, Lisette. I presume it's like our Fourth of July. There should be a celebration."

"I know, but there won't be one if the council can help it. They're bringing in a band for July First, Canada Day, which is a week later."

"It seems to me they're just asking for trouble."

"I'm afraid you're right. Clémentine is determined to have a bonfire. That's why they're piling up that wood behind the café."

"I was wondering about that wood there."

"Something nasty is bound to happen. Anyway, I intend to stay out of it. I'm fed up with all the fighting and bickering."

"It's a pity, Lisette. But I guess feelings are high."

"They sure are. We're liable to have a full-scale brawl right here in town. Soon we're going to be like Northern Ireland, and Cyprus, and Lebanon, and all those places where they're at each other's throats all the time."

"I can't see it going that far, Lisette."

"Just wait."

"I imagine that's why Wilt is looking for a place in Florida. To avoid the trouble here."

"No, not at all. Wilt couldn't care less about political tensions and all that sort of thing. He's interested only in making money. He'd open a bar-salon in Hell if he thought it would rake in the cash, and he'd have me running around the tables in a halo and high-heeled shoes being chased by sixteen horny demons with long tails and pitchforks."

Frank choked on his beer, and Lisette handed him a napkin.

"Well I guess I'd better get back to my nine creatures with tails," he remarked once his throat was cleared.

"Would you like some more of those little containers of cream?"

"Yes. Mirabel would appreciate that."

Back in his room, Frank placed two saucers of cream on the floor, one for the mother cat and the other for all the kittens, which were gradually being weaned. In a few moments, Mirabel jumped onto the bed to purr her appreciation and be petted. Gazing over at the kittens before turning off the bed lamp, Frank saw an almost-perfect wheel-like configuration—a white hub and eight furry spokes extending to eight tiny black spikes. The image remained in his mind after he had put off the light. Then the wheel started to revolve slowly, intermeshing with other wheels of various sizes, forming an assembly-line panorama something like the Riviera mural on the wall of the Detroit Metropolitan Museum which had always fascinated Frank.

Then Frank himself became part of the scene. He is trudging along a moving walkway, which is being propelled in the opposite direction by the massive conglomeration of machinery operating now with a low rumbling sound. He sees a figure ahead of him at the end of the walkway. It is Lisette. She is wearing only shoes and long white gloves. Frank quickens his pace to get closer. Now he can make out that she has a halo over her head. She is beckoning him to come to her. As he sees her more clearly, he realizes that the woman is not Lisette. But the resemblance is so strong that she must be, she has to be Lisette's mother, Madeleine. Frank struggles frantically against the moving walkway. As he approaches to within a few feet of the woman, she pulls off one of her gloves and tosses it to him. He stoops to pick it up, and suddenly several demons with horns, barbed tails and pitchforks leap onto the walkway. Frank turns and runs away, chased by the demons. Assisted now by the movement of the walkway, he gains speed. Looking ahead, he sees another figure at the end. This time it is Norma Duffin, standing just inside the door of her house. Like Madeleine a moment earlier, she is beckoning him to come to her, offering him a refuge. He runs faster, as fast as he can, now lumbering down the walkway like a railroad locomotive at full throttle. But as soon as he reaches the door, Norma slams it shut, leaving Frank with the horde of onrushing demons. He turns to face them, and the closest one jabs a pitchfork into his right shoulder.

    Frank awoke in a sweat to find Mirabel clawing his shoulder affectionately while he was holding her tail in his hand. He let go of the tail, pulled the blanket up to discourage her attentions and closed his eyes again, thinking that it was bad enough being tormented by the real-life, flesh-and-blood figures of Lisette and Norma without having the spectre of the former's mother to deal with in his dreams. She should have the decency to restrict herself to her own demons, make their horns light up and their tails curl if she liked, but leave a poor aspiring anthropologist alone to finish his dissertation.

Chapter Eighteen

During the week before St-Jean Baptiste Day, Frank was initiated into the cocktail circuit of the American summer residents, who had now installed themselves in their chalets on Lake Missiwappi. Ironically, he discovered that by coming to a small town in Quebec he was able to learn something about his own countrymen, or at least about a segment of American society with which he had previously been totally unfamiliar. The American summer people all knew one another and were quite distinct from the Michiganders and Mid-Westerners Frank had grown up among. They spoke with a strong Eastern seaboard nasal accent and seemed to be acutely conscious of their social class, making them appear to Frank more British than American. Most of them were associated with the Ivy League universities or the elite of Washington, D.C. At the gathering Frank attended, organized on the spur of the moment by Mrs. Evelyn Millington Stanford to introduce him to the circle, names dropped like rain in a cloudburst.

"I was talking to Jackie the other day," remarked one woman. "She's looking dreadful, and she tells me Ted hasn't changed a bit."

"I know, I know, my dear," responded Mrs. Stanford. "He's just got to pull himself together. I've told him that. So has Charles."

Charles Stanford startled Frank somewhat when he remarked with obvious glee that "Evie's" principal claim to fame was having "committed deanery." He elaborated that his wife had had affairs with the deans of faculties at both Harvard and Princeton Universities, thereby establishing that she was supremely uncontaminated by middle-class American morality. The community, Frank also discovered, was likewise quite aloof from the internal rumblings in Quebec.

"I don't care what they do so long as they don't go Commie on us like the Cubans," said retired history professor Jonathan Weston, when Frank happened to mention the upcoming Referendum.

"In fact, the Separatists do lean quite definitely to the left," said Frank.

"Then if they take over, we may be obliged to do something about it," Weston replied.

"What could we do? It's really none of our business," ventured Frank.

"My dear boy," interjected Charles Stanford, offering Frank another martini from a tray, "the whole world is our business now. You don't imagine for a moment that we're going to put up with any more nonsense right on our doorstep, do you?"

"All this talk about separation and independence is utterly absurd," put in Weston. "There is no such thing as national independence any more. Canada is totally dependent on the United States. If we were to close our borders to Canadian imports—and mind you, people have been lobbying along those lines in a number of areas such as fish, lumber, pork, potatoes, auto parts, and so forth—the Canadian economy would collapse, because we take eighty percent or more of their exports. But we would hardly notice ourselves, because altogether it amounts to only a small percentage of what we import from foreign countries. Now if Canada is dependent on us, where does that leave Quebec?"

"Frankly," added Mrs. Stanford, "if they go ahead

with this separation bit, then I expect that Quebec will end up as a U.S. protectorate, like Puerto Rico, and that will probably mean the same kind of nastiness. So I'm against it. Things are fine just the way they are."

"But I must say," her husband continued, "that the French Canadians are becoming quite demanding these days, much like the Blacks and Hispanics at home. You wouldn't believe what that fellow Poulin charged me to trim the hedge and fix up the garden this week. Refused to do it for less. You'd think, with the unemployment rate so high, that they'd be glad to get work."

"It's the Canadian system of social welfare that's at the root of the problem," said Weston. "The people are coddled to the point that they've lost all initiative and pride. The government gives them huge unemployment benefits, free medical care, free colleges, family allowances, and God knows what else. So why should they move their butts?"

"Quite," added another man. "Did you know that with an unemployment rate of some fifteen percent or so in this area, they're still obliged to import workers from Jamaica to pick the apples up around Rougemont?"

Although he wasn't about to argue the point with Weston and the others, the weeks he had spent in North Chadley had brought Frank to the opposite point of view regarding the Canadian system of social welfare, especially universal medicare. He realized that there were flaws—the waiting periods, the abuses, even the smothering of self-reliance—but he had concluded that despite its disadvantages, the Canadian system prevented the awful destitution suffered by many in the U.S., especially in a big city like Detroit.

"By the way, Jonathan," said Evelyn Stanford, "you are aware that Teddy is pushing for a government-sponsored medical plan just like the one they have here."

"Just a sop to the Boston riff-raff," replied Weston.

"Or perhaps it's a form of biological memory," said Charles. "Remember that they came over from Ireland with not much more than the shirts on their backs. Like all the other Irish."

"Well, it's out of style to have had one's forebears come over on the Mayflower now," commented Weston's wife, a woman about half his age. No doubt a one-time student, Frank speculated.

"Why is that?" he asked.

"Haven't you heard about the Mayflower Madam in New York? Julia Dibble, a direct descendant of one of the original Pilgrim Fathers with all the documents and ribbons to prove it, and she's just been arrested for running a bordello."

"Yes, but what a bordello!" exclaimed Stanford. "Hardly your best little whorehouse in Texas sort of thing. Charged $1,200 a night. The girls were all models, dancers, beauty queens, and the like."

"And who were the customers?" asked Frank.

"Rich Arabs, business tycoons, judges, senators. That's why she'll never be convicted," answered Stanford.

"Nor should she be," said Weston chuckling. "An admirable piece of initiative, I should think. Obviously based on shrewd market research. Mind you, $1,200 is a considerable amount of money to pay for an evening of pleasure. I trust that they served good champagne."

"Women are what was served, Jonathan," said Evelyn drily. "Firm, young female flesh, perfumed and powdered, on silk sheets."

"Now, now, Evie," said her husband, "let's not get

into the Lib stuff again. You're hardly one to talk. Not when your c.v. includes multiple commissions of deanery."

By the time the party was breaking up, Frank had come to the conclusion that the American summer people of North Chadley constituted a tight, exclusive group with their own lifestyle, such as it was, and that apart from using the various services provided by the town, they had little to do with the local Canadians. In fact, the only two Canadians mentioned during the evening were F.R. Scott, poet and retired dean of the law school at McGill University, and Hugh MacLennan, the novelist. Like the Americans, both men had summer homes in North Chadley, and Frank had been waiting for a chance to interview them both.

Frank knew that F.R. Scott was an expert on the Canadian constitution and that his career had been closely associated with the evolution of institutions and human rights in Canada. He was one of the founding fathers of the socialist movement, which used to be called the C.C.F., for Cooperative Commonwealth Federation, but was now known as the N.D.P. or New Democratic Party. MacLennan's two novels *Two Solitudes* and *Return of the Sphinx* dealt with French-English relations, and Frank had read them with fascination.

Having eaten enough hors d'oeuvres to qualify as a dinner, after leaving the Stanford house, Frank decided to wander over to the home of F.R. Scott, which was on the road back to the Inn. He was a bit apprehensive about how he would be received by such a distinguished man, or indeed if he would be received at all, but there was only one way to find out. Hugh MacLennan was less of a challenge, because Bill Martin knew him well and had promised to introduce Frank to him.

Frank's apprehensions proved to be totally unjustified. When he arrived at the door of the Scotts' summer cottage and introduced himself, he was immediately invited in by a soft-spoken, beautiful older lady, who turned out to be Scott's wife, Marian, a reputed artist in her own right. Scott himself was a tall, vigorous man in his eighties. He was having an after-dinner digestif and invited Frank to join him.

"Thank you, Dean Scott," Frank replied.

"I think we ought to be frank with each other, don't you? My first name is Frank too, you know," said Scott.

"Okay, Frank," said Frank, smiling.

"In fact, to be perfectly frank, I'm actually F.R.S. F.R.S.C.—Frank Reginald Scott, Fellow of the Royal Society of Canada."

"Yes, I'm familiar with your reputation, sir... uh... Frank. You were dean of law at McGill for quite a long time."

"Afraid so. And it's quite sobering, you know, because old deans never die, they just lose their faculties."

Frank laughed, as he would many times before the highly informative interview was over. F.R. Scott, he soon found out, was a person of keen wit and good humour. His love of playing with words made him an inveterate punster. He was also a man of definite opinions, an avowed Federalist and a long-time human-rights activist. On two storied occasions, Frank knew from his readings about Quebec, Scott had descended from the ivory tower of the McGill Law School to take on actual cases and argue them in the Supreme Court of Canada. The first concerned the Padlock Act, a law passed in the provincial legislature empowering Premier Maurice Duplessis in his self-appointed other office as

Attorney General of Quebec to confiscate any library, private or public, suspected of containing "subversive" materials, notably Communist literature of any sort, and to prosecute the person or persons implicated. When Frank inquired about the Padlock Act, Scott explained that until his death in 1959, Duplessis had a strangle hold on the province, maintained over many years by carefully nurtured liaisons with the upper clergy and the most powerful English-Canadian and American financial interests, not to mention rigged elections orchestrated by goon squads, *pots de vin* or graft, and numerous other corrupt practices. Duplessis' party, called the *Union Nationale*, kowtowed to the farmers, banning for example the sale of margarine so that the market and price for butter would be maintained at an artificially high level, victimizing the urban working class. Despite drastic changes in the distribution of the population, according to Scott, Duplessis refused to modify the electoral districts, so that the City of Montreal, with more than one third of the actual population, had fewer than one sixth of the seats in the provincial parliament.

Duplessis ruled, F.R. Scott told Frank, in the conviction of divine right, like Henry the Eighth and Genghis Khan. Driving through the countryside along a primitive dirt road, one would suddenly come to an isolated stretch which was beautifully paved, either in front of the home of a *Union Nationale* organizer or a rural church and presbytery. Scott explained to Frank that Duplessis discouraged urbanization and industrialization in accordance with the desires of the Quebec Roman Catholic Church, which in turn supported his political party. His party was known as *les Bleus,* while the opposition Liberals were *les Rouges,* and although the clergy officially proclaimed a position of non-interference in politics, in the Sunday sermon before an election, the priests of Quebec could be counted on to remind their parishioners that *"Le ciel est bleu et l'enfer est rouge"*—Heaven is blue and Hell is red.

So far as the financiers were concerned, F.R. Scott told Frank, the Premier cum Attorney General scratched their backs by using his provincial police force to crush strikes and thereby suppress any attempt to raise wages. The police were on the take and thus were more-than-willing servants. Quebec women, unless they were nuns or else working the brothels of Montreal, or streetwalking on De Bullion Street or St-Laurent Boulevard, familiarly known as "The Dirty Main," were no more than child-bearing apparatuses. Young people were denied a modern education in the Church-controlled school system. Compared to the rest of North America, only one quarter of those otherwise eligible for higher education ever got into the elitist classical colleges. Workers were told that they were fortunate to have jobs at all, and the people in general were conditioned to believe that their lot in life, however miserable, was the will of God, dutifully administered by those whom God had chosen to occupy the office of the Premier, the Archbishop's palace and the executive suites of St. James Street.

"It was an incredible mess," said Scott. "There is no mystery about the reasons for the frustration and general discontent of the people of Quebec, and what we are witnessing now is an understandable aftermath."

The only politician who could occasionally stand up to Duplessis, Scott went on to say, was the flamboyant and eccentric Montreal Mayor Camillien Houde, who was a 300-pound blob of a man who lived in a suite in the Mount Royal Hotel and once in a while astounded guests from out of town by wandering around the mezzanine floor stark naked. At a meeting with Duplessis' cabinet once, Houde, according to reports Scott had heard, rose to his feet and announced, "Half the people in this room are crooks."

Duplessis reacted in fury. "Mr. Mayor," he stated, "I am the Attorney General of Quebec, and if you do not withdraw that remark immediately, I will begin slander proceedings which will bring you to your knees."

Mayor Houde then once again maneuvered his great bulk to a standing position. "Mr. Premier and Attorney General," he said, feigning submission, "I will correct my unfortunate statement. Half the people in this room are *not* crooks."

Houde's performance was hardly surprising, Scott explained. The Mayor was innocent of any capacity for efficient municipal administration, and of the social graces to the point of crudity, but he was an able man with words in either of the two tongues. He was definitely in the great Quebec tradition of the bird charmers. It was Houde, Frank learned from his host, who, after officiating at the ceremonial kick-off of the first Alouette football game in Montreal, picked up the microphone and announced in an exaggerated French-Canadian accent, "Gentlemen, I am appee to be in dis place today to kick off your ball, and I will be appee to come back again to kick all your balls off."

F.R. Scott described to Frank how in a test case he had defended a newspaper reporter who had been arrested and whose books and papers, including crumpled scraps in his wastepaper basket, had been confiscated by the police, and that was how he had succeeded in having the Padlock Act declared unconstitutional by the Supreme Court of Canada. He had also won the Roncarelli Case, concerning a restauranteur whose establishment was raided and whose liquor licence was cancelled after he put up bail for jailed Jehovah's Witnesses. The latter, of course, were despised by the Quebec clergy, and Duplessis had accordingly instructed his provincial troopers to round them up and burn the little booklets they handed out at street corners. Scott told Frank that he managed to sue Duplessis personally for $50,000.

"But what most people don't know," he added, "is that despite the Supreme Court victory for Roncarelli, Duplessis came out ahead in the end. He never married, had loads of money, so the $50,000 meant little to him. But by the time the case was over, Roncarelli was bankrupt. He left the country a broken man and never came back. That's one of the reasons I sometimes have doubts about the effectiveness of our system of justice."

"And what about the Canadian Confederation?" asked Frank. "A lot of people seem to have doubts about that these days."

"I've never had any doubts about it myself," replied Scott. "There are flaws, of course, items which have become outdated. Like any other system, it must be constantly examined and improved, brought into line with contemporary conditions."

"I presume, then, that you're not enthusiastic about the upcoming Referendum."

"Enthusiastic? I think it's a farce. French Canadians should be fighting for their constitutional rights rather than trying to destroy the country. The Referendum question is absurd—Do you want the Quebec Government to begin negotiations on the issue of Quebec sovereignty? Negotiate with whom? To do what exactly? In fact there are no provisions in the Constitution for opting out of Confederation."

"But couldn't provisions be adopted?"

"Yes, they could, by act of parliament, but why should they be? Quebeckers have the same rights as all other Canadians. There have been abuses in the past, that's true, such as the abolition of French schools in Manitoba and Ontario, but those abuses were shown to be unconstitutional, contrary to both the spirit and the letter of the British North America Act, and they were duly corrected, proving that the system works. French Canadians simply have to stand up for their guaranteed rights. Unfortunately, some of the extremists in the present Quebec Government seem to think that revenge is the only appropriate course. They want to make up for past mistreatment of the French in Canada."

"Some Francophones I've talked to believe that the situation is more complicated than what you've just described, sir."

"Nonsense. It's all perfectly simple. We have the law, and we have the courts to interpret the law, and we have courts of appeal when the lower courts get off the track."

Frank felt somewhat reassured after his long talk with F.R. Scott. Perhaps, he mused, the Canadian nation would last long enough for him to complete his dissertation after all. On the other hand, the former dean was a man of law, sweet reason and vast knowledge, which were not exactly the characteristics of the masses, either English or French. The North Chadley Town Council had just banned the traditional St-Jean bonfire out of pure spite. People like Paul Larose and other dedicated Independentists were too emotionally involved to be reasonable. They were certainly not disposed to engaging in long years of litigation through the various levels of the Canadian court system. They were probably not even concerned about their individual rights and whether or not those rights were adequately protected by the Constitution. What they wanted, it seemed to Frank, was a grand display of collective defiance, an explosion of self-assertion on the part of the entire Francophone population, which would erase once and for all the real and imagined humiliations of the past. Their need was psychological rather than rational or legal.

Hugh MacLennan, Frank decided, put his finger on it in his novel *Return of the Sphinx*. When he had first read the book, as part of his background preparation before coming to Quebec, Frank had found it pessimistic and depressing. At the end, the Federalist hero, whose own son has become a bomb-planting terrorist, seems to despair of any solution, saying that if that is the way it has to be, then let the French Canadians separate from Canada and be done with it. MacLennan seemed to be stating that no amount of consultation and accommodation would suffice. Some collective manifestation, however symbolic, was required, and the riddle was to figure out just what it might be. Frank resolved to arrange an interview with MacLennan as soon as he could to find out if the novelist had developed any new theories. It was a fortunate circumstance, he told himself, that both Scott and MacLennan were right in North Chadley. Another person who had a place in town was a young, curly-haired politician named Jean Charest, whom Frank had met at the Café Québec Libre. He had been impressed by the man's eloquence in defending federalism against a distinctly unsympathetic gathering, and he had a strong feeling that Charest would sooner or later be making a name for himself. Frank was hoping to get a chance to talk to him again.

Returning to the Inn, Frank noticed a boat trailer behind the Café Québec Libre next to a pile of scrap wood. A crude log structure resembling a raft was mounted on the trailer, and Frank concluded that the Town Council's prohibition of a bonfire was going to be circumvented by a floating fire on the lake, over which the town presumably had no jurisdiction. Frank smiled at the simplicity of the solution, but he wondered how the town officials would react. After checking on Mirabel and her kittens, then feeding the litter and letting the mother cat out for a nocturnal prowl, he wandered over to the Québec Libre for a coffee and doughnuts, but mainly to satisfy his curiosity.

Just as he had imagined it would be, the café was packed with people. Marie-Ange Monet, the plump French professor, spotted him immediately and insisted that he sit at her table. Before he could order a coffee, someone handed him a glass of red wine, several bottles of which were on the tables around the room. Frank soon learned that the plan for *"la St-Jean"* was to anchor the raft a few feet away from the shore of the town park and set it aflame. People would be dancing in the park, and they could also watch the fire from boats or from the wooden railway bridge over the river, which was right beside the park. And if *les Anglais* tried to interfere, it was made abundantly clear, then God help them, because besides cases of beer and jugs of *Caribou*, the trunks of the cars parked along the road by the park would be loaded with lead pipes and baseball bats. There might be no need for the Referendum coming up in three week's time. The issue might be settled right then and there.

Marie-Ange was in a state of great excitement, telling Frank that it was wonderful to see that *les Québécois* were finally going to take their destiny into their own hands. And although many of them did not realize the fact, or were unwilling to admit it, they might never have attained that level of resolve had they not been guided and egged on by sympathetic newcomers such as herself. Massaging his thigh to accentuate her message, she then suggested to Frank that perhaps it was time for him to place his own destiny in her capable hands. Everyone was now talking at once, and as he tried to grasp snippets of the animated conversation, Frank became embarrassingly aware that Marie-Ange was a woman of her word, and that if he stayed there much longer she would certainly have his destiny, for the immediate future in any case, in her hand. Why couldn't it have been Norma Duffin, or Lisette, or at least a woman ten or fifteen years closer to his own age? he asked himself.

Finally he made the excuse of having to go to the washroom and slipped out the back door of the café, reflecting that compared to so-called primitive societies, modern North American civilization was making an awful mess of the patterns of male-female relations. Older women such as Marie-Ange, divorced or separated, who now represented a significant and growing segment of the population, were frustrated. Most of the men in their own age group were either married or responding to the social dictate to latch onto pretty young women, and many young women were more than willing, because older men represented financial security, prestige, immediate access to the comforts of life, appreciation and tender loving care, especially when compared to a fumbling slob desperately struggling to get ahead such as Frank himself. The obvious solution was for the young slobs and the frustrated older women to get together, but contemporary mores still frowned upon such liaisons. The young man would be regarded as an Oedipal basket case, or an exploiter, or even a gigolo, and the woman undignified at best or a nymphomaniac at worst. Giovanni, Frank recalled, had once referred to Marie-Ange as a man-killer, yet the woman was simply trying to gratify perfectly normal physical desires. From his years of anthropology, however, Frank knew that all human communities had effective mechanisms to enforce their accepted customs, from raised eyebrows to raging lynch mobs.

On the other hand, he continued to speculate, Quebec society was currently in a state of general turmoil. Many of the erstwhile traditions had been blown away by the winds of change. Not long ago a divorce required an act of Parliament—now it was as common as a wave goodbye. During the age of the Revenge of the Cradle, families often achieved the epic proportions of one to two dozen children—now many of the young wives opted for one or two or perhaps, like Lisette presumably, no kids. It all fits together, Frank reflected—the Church's loss of domination, the break-up of the family, the political shambles. It was like Shakespeare's notion of the Great Chain of Being. When the established order and figures of authority tottered in one sphere, then all other spheres were similarly affected. The old rules no longer applied, so why the hell was he sneaking away from a warm-hearted lady who was merely doing her thing? Frank decided to stop in briefly at the bar-salon to check out what was happening there.

At two tables pushed together were the big garage

mechanic and the three other men who had almost gotten into a brawl with Paul Larose a few weeks earlier, and with them were four other men. At another table by himself was the Indian, Billy Carcajou, and Frank decided to join him. Apparently Wilt Wadleigh was still away in Florida, because Lisette was doing the bar-tending and waitressing by herself.

Billy was not in a very talkative mood, and during the long pauses in the conversation at his own table, Frank soon gathered that the gang at the other table were making plans for the St-Jean Baptiste celebrations the next night. The volunteer fire department, most of whom were apparently still English, would be on standby in the event that the French tried to have a bonfire anywhere in town, but the eight men were not sure what to do if the fire was on a raft in the lake.

"Fire or no fire, the bastards are spoiling for a fight tomorrow, and we'll be goddamned ready to give it to them," remarked one of the men.

"We should keep a few baseball bats handy just in case," added another man, "and make sure all the guys in the area are here, because they'll be sure as hell bringing in a mob from Brooke, maybe even Montreal and Quebec City."

"Don't worry, all the English know what to expect," said George Carson, the mechanic. "This time we'll teach them a real lesson."

Billy Carcajou seemed mystified by the overheard indications that a violent confrontation was being planned, and Frank, recalling what he had heard at the Québec Libre only a few minutes earlier, became alarmed. They're actually going to do it this time, he thought, spark a civil war. Each side was determined not to give an inch, and the people who hadn't taken sides would either be forced to do so or else be caught in the middle.

"But tomorrow is the day of the Ceremony of the Sun," commented Billy.

"Yes, the summer solstice, I believe. Celebrated by northern peoples since as far back as we know," said Frank sombrely.

"What are they talking about?" Billy asked, nodding toward the other table. "Tomorrow is a day of harmony and love, when we celebrate fertility, the union of earth, and sun to bring the harvests."

"Yes, I know, but harmony and love are in short supply around here these days, I'm afraid."

"Fools," said Billy, who then got up and left.

Shortly afterwards, the eight men at the other table also drank up and went home, leaving Frank alone with Lisette another time. She poured herself a Dubonnet and sat down at the table with him.

"You don't mind if I take off my shoes?" she asked.

"No, of course not," he replied with a wide grin. "Please feel free to take off anything you like."

"Thank you, but I think the shoes will be enough for the moment. My feet are a little sore."

"That's not surprising. You've been doing all the work here by yourself."

"It won't be that way much longer."

"Wilt's coming back soon?"

"I don't know when he's coming back."

Frank detected a note of bitterness in Lisette's voice. The Wadleigh marriage was not in any better shape than the Canadian Confederation, he suspected.

"Anyway, it's just as well he won't be here tomorrow night," Lisette continued.

"It sure looks like there's going to be trouble."

"There's bound to be. All the hotheads are waiting for it."

"What a pity."

"You're right, it is a pity. *La St-Jean* used to be so much fun when I was a young girl."

"What was it like?"

"During the day there'd be a long parade ending with a float carrying a small, curly-headed boy and a lamb. Then at night there would be street dances everywhere. All of us girls would put on our prettiest summer dresses. Usually it was for the first time in the year."

"You must have been like butterflies emerging from a winter-long cocoon."

"I suppose we were. The boys generally seemed to be impressed. There was always a wonderful mood of abandon, as if we had all been liberated."

"In a way you were—liberated from the grip of winter."

"That's true. But it went even further. On *la St-Jean* we'd let the boys get away with a little more fooling around than usual. Couples would sneak off down the back lanes. There'd be quite a few rumpled dresses before it was all over."

"Sounds marvellous. Why did it change?"

"Politics and nationalism, I suppose. Back in the early sixties they decided that the lamb had to go, because it might be construed to symbolize Quebec—a submissive, docile, daisy-chomping Quebec. Some people even wanted a tiger, but you couldn't very well put a tiger and a little boy on the same float."

"No, I guess not."

"Anyway, some sculptor—Therrien, I believe his name was—came up with a papier-maché statue eleven-feet high, and it was supposed to symbolize power and dynamism and all that sort of stuff. They put it on the last float instead of the lamb and the little boy in the big parade in Montreal."

"Wasn't that statue finally destroyed?"

"Right. In 1968, when Pierre Trudeau and Drapeau and all the other bigwigs were on the reviewing stand and the parade turned into a riot. Since the mob couldn't get at Trudeau, they grabbed the statue and tore it apart. For weeks after that you could get little pieces of it—relics of the true St-Jean they called them—all over Montreal. But that was the last parade. Nothing has been the same since."

"It really is too bad. With the winters you have up here, you do need a celebration to welcome back the summer—a big, joyous occasion where everyone can let off steam. I'd much rather see rumpled dresses than heads bashed in."

"So would I. Do you want another beer, Frank?"

"No thanks. I can see that you're tired. I'll get out of here and let you close up."

Just as Frank rose to leave, Lisette's brother, Danny, appeared at the door carrying his guitar. He placed the instrument on a table and embraced his sister, then he shook hands with Frank. When he went back to his van to get his sound equipment, which he didn't want to risk leaving in the vehicle, Frank went along to give him a hand. Back in the bar-salon, Lisette had already placed two bottles of beer and a Dubonnet for herself on a table, and Frank decided to delay his departure.

"Danny's staying for a few days," said Lisette. "Wilt's away for God knows how long, and up in Montreal both the OUI and the NON people are giving Danny a hard time."

"Is that so?" commented Frank, looking at Danny and marvelling again at his remarkable resemblance to Elvis Presley, who, from all indications, probably was his father.

"All the singers and performers are expected to take sides, and most of them have," said Danny. "But I'd prefer to stay out of it. I've got enough problems of my own."

As Danny spoke, Billy Carcajou reappeared at the door. Frank detected what seemed to be a hint of disappointment in his expression on seeing that he and Danny were there. Billy must have been expecting Lisette to be alone in the bar-salon. Nevertheless, he came in and sat down at the table, accepting Lisette's offer of a beer on the house.

"Are you planning to watch the bonfire tomorrow night?" Frank asked the Indian.

"No. I plan to have my own ceremony," Billy replied, looking at Lisette rather than at Frank.

"What kind of ceremony?" she asked.

"An ancient, traditional Indian ceremony. I've found the sacred place just up the river, not far from this very spot, where my ancestors used to celebrate the summer solstice."

"Hey, I'd like to see that place," said Frank.

"How do you know it's the right place?" asked Danny.

"I know," Billy replied. "I've been studying the site, and I'm sure it's the one. I've found several artifacts and marks."

"But isn't it somebody's property?" asked Lisette.

"It's sacred Indian property. Nothing has been built there. It's an empty place along the shore."

"Afraid of spring flooding, I suppose," said Danny.

"Maybe," said Billy, emptying his glass.

He got up to depart again, followed by Frank, leaving Lisette to talk to her brother.

Chapter Nineteen

June 24th turned out to be a hot, humid day, the kind of day that wraps around people and keeps movement to a languid and sweaty minimum. Frank propped open the door to his room and let Mirabel and her litter wander in and out as they pleased. The kittens each ventured a few feet into the outside world then scrambled back inside the room, frightened by a dog's bark or the snap of a twig or some other unfamiliar sound or sight. Some went further than others, but as time passed, they all stayed out for longer and longer periods. It would not be long, thought Frank, before he had to start trying to get rid of the eight fluffy black balls of fur. As yet he had no idea what he would do about Momma Puss.

Frank persevered at the table in his room until nearly noon, unscrambling his stacks of notes and attempting to discipline the various items of information into connected paragraphs. By then he was sweating profusely from simply sitting in a chair and wielding a ballpoint pen. Not the slightest breeze could be induced to come through the open window or door. Finally Frank put on his bathing trunks and walked slowly down to the town park.

A crowd had already begun to gather. Several cars were parked along the lakeside road, and Frank wondered how many of them had baseball bats and lengths of lead pipe simmering in their trunks. Dozens of young men and women were sprawling on the grass or frolicking in the lake, and Frank noticed that they were divided into two separate groups. Overhearing a few words, he deduced that the English were on the right and the French on the left, leaving an empty no-man's land about twenty feet wide right across the middle of the park. A few people were sitting on the wooden railway bridge, which was only two or three feet above the surface of the water. It was fortunate, Frank reflected, that the sweltering weather dismissed any thought of activity other than immersing oneself in the cool water of Lake Missawappi, at least for the time being. Hostilities were obviously on hold until sunset. Still concerned to maintain a neutral stance in what he considered the ridiculous confrontation between Canada's two major linguistic groups, Frank chose to stroll right down the middle avenue, leave his sandals on the shore and wade into the water. After his swim, he took the same route back to the lake road and headed to the Inn for lunch.

To his surprise, Frank found the bar-salon empty of customers. Lisette explained to him that people who came to the park generally brought picnic lunches and coolers full of beer and soft drinks with them. He was also surprised and somewhat disappointed to see Lisette wearing a loose, smocklike garment rather than her customary figure-hugging top and slit skirt. It occurred to him that he had become almost addicted to a daily fix of hormone stimulation dispensed by the bar-salon hostess along with drinks and light meals. As if divining his thoughts—Frank had the disquieting suspicion that both Lisette and Norma were instantly and entirely aware of every lustful thought he had about them—she remarked that it was too hot a day to wear anything except a light caftan, sparking additional lustful speculations about whether or not she had anything on underneath it. Lisette also told Frank that she was thinking of closing the bar-salon that evening to avoid trouble, and he replied that he thought it would be a good idea to do so, even though it appeared that the expected brawl would take place outside, in the town park.

"Will you be going down to the park tonight?" Lisette inquired.

"I thought that I might take a peek," he answered.

"Then maybe I'll come with you, if you don't mind. I'd feel better having a man your size nearby."

The notion of being Lisette's escort and protector gave Frank an immediate twinge of pride. His experience as a football lineman should serve him in good stead if worse came to worst. Any son-of-a-bitch who tried to get to her would have to get by him first, he told himself, and he had stopped cold some of the toughest running backs in the Big Ten.

"I'd be happy to have you come with me, Lisette. And if they do start swinging, I'll make sure you get out of harm's way."

"Thanks, Frank. That's good to know. I'm feeling very vulnerable these days, like an abandoned waif."

"I understand."

"I'm caught in the middle of all this madness, you know. I'm at least half French Canadian, and I'm married to an English Canadian."

Frank was momentarily struck by the "at least half," then he reflected that in view of her mother's supposedly extensive community involvement, Lisette quite likely had no idea who her father was.

"Did you know that I'm part French Canadian too?" he asked her.

"You are?"

"That's right. My grandfather came from up around

St-Jean de Matha. His name was Telesphore Cyr."

"Cyr! Mon Dieu, Frank! My mother's maiden name was Cyr, Madeleine Cyr. I went by that name myself until I got married."

"No kidding? Then maybe we're related."

"We may well be."

"It's amazing how small the world is."

"You know, Frank, when you think about it for awhile, we're all related, everybody on the planet. I probably have Indian blood too, and God knows what else. That's why I hate all this bickering and fighting."

"I'm afraid it's a defect in human nature, Lisette. The bitterest conflicts, in fact, are often between peoples who are closely related. Take the Arabs and the Jews, or the Irish, or the North and the South in the American Civil War."

"If only there was some way to get peoples' minds onto other things."

"I know what you mean. With just a small fraction of the billions being spent on weapons, we could turn the Sahara into a garden."

Lisette seemed lost in thought for a moment or two.

"You know, Frank," she said finally, "Wilt has made a deal with Gabib. He's going to sell."

"But I thought that you owned fifty percent of the Inn, Lisette."

"I do. But Wilt intends to sell his half anyway, and I don't know where that leaves me."

"I imagine that Mr. Gabib will be making you an interesting offer."

"I don't want to sell, Frank. And owning half a hotel is like being half pregnant. I don't know what I'm going to do."

"I think you should see a lawyer, find out exactly

where you stand. Maybe there's a way that you can block the sale."

"I think you're right. Well I'd better get you something to eat."

"By the way, where's your brother, Danny?"

"He's still in bed upstairs. I guess he's into the habit of sleeping late when he's working in clubs till early in the morning all the time."

Unable to work in his room because of the heat, Frank spent the afternoon wandering around town. He visited the Murphys and marvelled at their house, the interior of which was now almost finished. As he inspected the place, he could not help thinking how the new house stood as a symbol of what could be accomplished when people worked together. It also occurred to him that the town brawl shaping up for that very evening would be an ugly example of what happens when they don't. Murphy and his wife told him that they would like to take the children to the park to see the bonfire, but they were not sure that it would be a good idea. They were thinking of having a bonfire of their own with the scrap wood from the recent construction and inviting all the village kids, which would get them away from the park. Frank was depressed to think that such a precaution should be necessary in a small town like North Chadley, but he had to agree that it made sense. If the adults were beyond redemption, then at least the children should be shielded from the conflict, in the hope that they might grow up a little smarter than their parents. Prejudices, Frank reflected, were not inherited but learned. They were part of the education process. The bitter irony of it all was that ignorance could be passed down through the generations far more effectively than tolerance, and throughout the world it generally was.

Toward the end of the afternoon, Frank found himself sitting on Norma Duffin's front porch sipping a rum punch. Her apartment was the ground floor of a house located right on the town's main street, with a view of the lake and the park. No doubt because she too was apprehensive about the explosive situation, she had arranged to have her children visit their father on the West Island of Montreal, an English residential enclave far from the rumbling East End of the city. Frank was delighted to have Norma, her lush figure positively ravishing now in tight black shorts and a halter, all to himself. He was even happier when she offered him a drink, and he began to edge toward a state of high excitation when she suggested that he stay for dinner. The two of them alone at last, he mused, on a warm summer evening, their inhibitions suppressed by a few rum punches, after dinner there was bound to be apple pie for dessert.

In the next two or three hours, however, Frank found himself cursing the Quebec troubles. Despite the privacy, despite the summer heat and the drinks, despite Norma's apparent fondness for him and his own quiet desperation, despite the damned rightness of it all, there was no way to transform the mood of the evening from sombre and foreboding to even mildly romantic. From the veranda they saw cars loaded with stiff-jawed young men heading toward the park. They watched as the boat trailer with the bonfire raft was backed down a ramp to the edge of the lake. Once afloat, the raft was stacked high with wood and towed to a spot thirty or forty feet from the shore of the park, where it was anchored with a length of rope.

Frank pondered the situation as he sipped his drink

and Norma gazed forlornly at the ominous passing scene. After all, he told himself, women were supposed to be hyper-amorous and abandoned in times of stress. It was one of nature's survival mechanisms to compensate in advance for a possible decrease in population. In the subway air-raid shelters of London during the World War II Blitz, Frank had once read, you couldn't hear the bombs for the panting and sighing and rustling of skirts. Nine months after the big power failure in New York City, the maternity wards were registering a production hike of several percentage points. Squirming in his seat while trying to adjust to the unfamiliar sight of Norma's splendid hips in tight black shorts, as she bent over to get the fruit juice jug from a shaded spot on the porch floor, Frank knew that nature's survival mechanism was working well enough on him—why the hell wasn't it working on her? But no matter how much he pondered and plotted, he could not hit upon a way to get his hostess into his eager, twitching arms, to be gently carried over the threshold into the damned empty house. With her three kids around most of the time, he might have a long wait for another such opportunity. Quebec, Frank decided, was turning into a rotten place to be. Even in darkest downtown Detroit, they took time out from murdering each other to make love once in a while.

After dinner, as the sun was setting behind the hills on the west side of Lake Missawappi, Norma suggested that they walk down to the park to see what was happening. Frank immediately recalled that he had promised to escort Lisette to the park, and he and Norma set off for the Inn. Still attired in the caftan she had been wearing earlier in the day, Lisette was standing with Billy Carcajou, and Danny was sitting on a bar stool with a beer when Norma and Frank arrived. Danny was obviously not going anywhere, but Billy was wearing an Indian costume—loin cloth, ornaments on his wrists and ankles, a large feather in a head band—and Frank recalled that he was planning to have his own ceremony to celebrate the summer solstice at the sacred site he had located. It appeared that he had been trying to persuade Lisette to join him. Frank would have liked to do so himself, rather than go to the park, but he doubted that he would be welcome.

"I'll be over a little later," Lisette assured Billy. "I'm just curious to see what happens in the park."

"You're a damned fool not to stay away from there," Danny muttered to his sister.

Billy nodded to Lisette and the others, then he headed out the door. He was a tall, square-shouldered man, and the brief costume he had on revealed that he was well muscled. Frank noted that both Lisette and Norma followed him intently with their eyes until he disappeared from view. I guess it works both ways, he reflected. When Billy was in North Chadley, Frank had heard, he lived in a camper parked someplace behind the Inn.

The scene at the park made Frank think that both Danny and Billy had the right idea to stay away. The crowd on the left side of the park, the French, was now much larger than during the day and was overflowing onto the low, wooden railway bridge. They were all staring silently at the anchored raft, where two men in a rowboat were apparently about to light the floating bonfire. The English group on the right, equally silent, were watching the raft and the French.

Both gangs were concentrated near the edge of the water, and there was still an empty avenue between them, leaving a clear view of the raft for the third concentration of observers now gathering on the sidewalk along the inland rim of the park. Frank recognized many people, including Paul Larose, Tremblay, Bertrand, Bourgault, Carson and his sidekicks. There were fewer women than men, especially among the English, but Clémentine and Marie-Ange were there. Frank also spotted Margery Miller. Murphy, Frank concluded, must have gone through with his plan to have a bonfire of his own, because there were no children in sight. Nor were there any of the older people of the village. In his immediate vicinity, on the presumably neutral space of the sidewalk, Frank likewise recognized a number of people. Bill Martin and his wife were there, three of the Arab associates of Gabib, Gordon Jackson, but none of the American summer people.

Although the sun had set, the still hot and humid air hung heavily over the tripartite gathering. Gazing skyward, Frank noticed that clouds had formed, accounting for the rapidly thickening gloom, and he began to hope for a storm, a monumental storm with great rolls of thunder and bolts of lightning which might cleanse the assembled mob of its sinister inclinations. Perhaps nature would save the Canadians in the end, he speculated, just as it had saved the Russians on at least two occasions.

Then a flash of light illuminated the park. Apparently gasoline had been thrown over the wood stacked on the raft, and the bonfire started with a burst of flames. The French Canadians at the left of the park and on the bridge all began to clap and cheer. A few of the English also clapped their hands, but this initial spontaneous reaction soon transformed into loud booing and shouts of "Get the fire engine."

Frank and the sidewalk people simply watched in silence. Norma and Lisette had each grabbed one of Frank's arms and were holding tightly, and a few men from each of the gangs in the park were now slinking back toward the cars parked along the roadside. Frank looked skyward again, but he was disheartened to see a dim outline of the moon. The clouds were thinning. The storm would come from below rather than above. It would have a "Made in Quebec" label for sure.

"Frank," said Bill Martin in a low voice, "I think we should get the women out of here. Why don't you take them back to the Inn. I have to stay because of the volunteer fire brigade. I have a feeling we're going to need our hose. But not for the bonfire."

"No, I don't want to go yet," said Lisette.

The flames were now leaping many feet into the air. The rippling water around the raft glittered brightly, as if it were being sprinkled with diamonds. Sparks were flying.

The three Arabs had bunched together and were backing into the street. They had obviously noticed the men edging toward the parked cars and divined what was going to happen. Frank also backed into the street, drawing his two charges with him. The country may smash itself to pieces, he told himself, but I'll at least preserve two of its best resources. The Referendum nastiness had doused the population in gasoline just like the bonfire, and now it would take only one idiot with a baseball bat to provide the spark. Looking behind him, Frank plotted an escape route between two parked cars. If necessary, he would carry Lisette under one arm and Norma under the other.

Suddenly there were shouts from the shore.

"The anchor rope's burned!"

"The raft's heading for the bridge!"

"Oh my God!" exclaimed Bill Martin. "I better get to the fire truck."

He and his wife rushed off as everyone else now stared at the tower of flames floating slowly toward the wooden railway bridge.

"*Laisse bruler le maudzit pont!*" someone shouted. "*C'est un pont fédéraliste.*"

For a moment Frank puzzled over how a bridge could be federalist, then he remembered that it was the property of the Canadian National Railway and would therefore be regarded as a symbol of the Ottawa Government. And one thing was now certain—if the volunteer fire brigade did not get there soon with a hose long enough to reach to the middle of the bridge, it would soon be a federalist contribution to a St-Jean Baptiste bonfire.

Since the brigade had been on standby all evening, the fire engine did appear within a minute or two. The raft was still about twenty feet from the bridge, and it appeared that the problem could now be brought under control within a short time. But an obstacle suddenly arose in front of the firemen—the French had formed a line at the end of the bridge and were blocking access. Bill was shouting at them to get out of the way, and others were shouting at him to turn the hose on the French. Obviously reluctant to hose the crowd, Bill was screaming at the top of his lungs.

"*Otez-vous de la, maudzits fous!*"

But the bridge blockers were not budging, and the flaming raft was now only a few feet away. Taking each by the arm, Frank pulled Lisette and Norma across the street to the sidewalk in front of the Café Québec Libre, away from the mob.

"Get a couple of Clémentine's tables and an extension cord out here," he told the two women. "I'm going for Danny."

Both Lisette and Norma stared at Frank for a moment, then they rushed inside. As he reached the door of the Inn, Frank noticed Billy Carcajou trotting toward the park. Still in his native costume, the Indian was carrying a length of rope and a cross-shaped lug wrench normally used to change tires.

"Come on, Danny, grab your guitar! You've got to play!" Frank shouted at Lisette's brother, who was still sitting on a bar stool.

Before Danny could respond, Frank grabbed the sound equipment and microphone on the small stage in the corner of the bar-salon.

"Come on! Move!" he ordered. Danny was confused, but he picked up his guitar and, pushed by Frank from behind, headed out the door.

When they reached the sidewalk in front of the café, Lisette and Norma, aided by Giovanni, had already brought out the two tables. Frank placed the sound equipment on top of one, then he picked up Danny and hoisted him on top of the other, at the same time telling Giovanni to hook up the sound equipment to the extension cord as quickly as he could.

The word that "the big Indian" or *"le grand Indien"* was swimming out to the raft rippled through both segments of the crowd and converged on the neutrals at the fringe. With Lisette and Norma now clinging to his arms again, Frank moved forward across the road into the no-man's land between the English and the French.

In the glare of the flames, Billy was clearly visible as he took a deep breath and dove beneath the floating bonfire. The men who had been blocking the bridge now merged with Bill Martin and the volunteer firemen to watch the drama unfold. The only sound was the crackling of the flames as the people on both sides of the park crowded the shore.

Frank turned briefly to note that Danny was now adjusting his microphone. He reasoned that Billy Carcajou would use the lug wrench as a grappling hook and jam it through a gap between the logs from underneath the raft. Evidently that was exactly what Billy did, and a cheer rose from the English, French and neutrals alike as he resurfaced with the rope in his hand and began to tow the raft back to where it had been anchored. Once again he dove underwater, this time to tie together the ropes attached to the wrench and the anchor. Then with the union accomplished and no danger of the connecting rope burning another time, Billy waded back to shore.

Apart from the headband and drooping feather, Billy appeared to be naked. The park was now flooded in moonlight, but the flames from the bonfire kept him in silhouette, and it was impossible to tell if he was still wearing his loin cloth. At the very moment he stepped on shore, while all eyes were fixed on the tall, glistening figure, looking like some Greek god emerged from the mists of time, music suddenly burst forth from the loudspeakers on the table in front of the Café Québec Libre.

All heads in the crowd turned. People stared in astonishment. Danny too appeared to be a reincarnation, or else Elvis Presley himself back from the dead. The song he was playing and singing half in English and half in French was a rhythmic ballad, a sort of blend of Gaelic, Celtic, and African-American folk music.

Shouts of "ELVIS! ELVIS! ELVIS!" now rose from throughout the crowd.

Frank felt Lisette stir, then release her hold on his arm. He thought that she was going to run off, but instead she began to dance, moving forward in the avenue between the two groups in the park until she reached Billy Carcajou. The Indian gazed at her for a few moments. Slowly, as if performing an act of worship, he stretched out his arms and took hold of her caftan. As the now mesmerized crowd stared, Lisette raised her arms, and in the next instant the caftan was being flung to the grass, resolving Frank's speculations of earlier in the day. She was naked.

The flickering light stroked her undulating hips as she took both of Billy's hands into her own. While the crowd pressed forward into the dividing avenue, Billy began to dance, complementing the movements of the nubile beauty in front of him, and a new, lusty cheer arose from the now-mingling crowd. In the next few moments, other people stripped off their clothes and joined the dance, forming a circle of vibrating, unencumbered humanity around Billy and Lisette.

Then Norma also let go of Frank's arm. He felt a twinge of alarm as she started moving toward the group of dancers in various states of undress. But before Frank could do anything, Gabib appeared and was taking Norma by the arm. His limousine was stopped in the street with the door open. Without thinking, Frank stepped forward and inserted himself between Norma and her boss, bodying the latter back into the street. Norma stood for a moment and observed the two men. Most of the people in the crowd were now dancing to Danny's music, pairing off throughout the park. Then Norma turned to Frank and held out her hands. As they began to dance, a glowering Gabib got into his limousine and drove away.

Frank and Norma soon found themselves close to Billy and Lisette in the middle of the park. Now all the people, English, French, Arab or whatever, indistinguishable from one another, were swaying and whirling with total abandon. Soon the bonfire sputtered and gave off its last flashes of flame, but the park remained illuminated by the soft glow of moonlight. Frank had no idea what dance he was performing. He simply let his body flow to the rhythm of the music, as all the others were doing. The harmonious motion of the figures gliding around him seemed to have been choreographed in a distant tribal past and imprinted in the genes of all members of the human race.

The dancing continued into the night. Then eventually couples began to lie down on the grass or to wander off into the shadows. Billy and Lisette appeared to be gone, and Norma suggested to Frank that it was time to go home too. Danny had just stopped playing and had retired inside the Québec Libre with Clémentine and a few others.

As they stepped onto Norma's porch, Frank's pulse, already exercised by the spectacles he had witnessed during the last two or three hours, went into overdrive. The good St-Jean Baptiste was looking after his own after all, he mused, even unto the third generation of American grandsons, who deserved a break once in a while. In a few moments, he and the new, miraculously unwound Norma Duffin, who had that night made a clear decision in his favour, would be behind the closed door, alone, in private, with no kids around, and the pleasures of the flesh would abound without limit. It was fitting that it should happen that way, Frank told himself, as if preordained by the cultural evolution of humankind, by fertility rites reaching back to the foggy dawn of communal living, by a veritable consortium of pagan deities and Christian saints. Only someone versed in the finer points of anthropology could fully appreciate the appropriateness of what was about to take place. Frank felt his frame actually shudder in anticipation.

Once she had stepped into the doorway, Norma turned to face him. He was therefore obliged to stop before stepping into the house.

"It was truly amazing, Frank," she said. "And you were the one who started it off by thinking of Danny and his Elvis Presley routine."

"It wasn't me, Norma. It was Billy Carcajou rescuing the raft. Then Lisette doing her thing. I hope I didn't make trouble for you and your boss."

"Don't worry about that. He has no right to try to run my life."

"I imagine that he simply wanted to protect you."

"I was well enough protected."

Norma smiled her appreciation, and Frank took the smile as a cue to advance into the doorway. Then to his utter consternation, her expression abruptly turned serious.

"I can't invite you in, Frank," she said.

"You . . . can't?"

"It's too soon. I have to have time to think. I'm in such a giddy mood tonight that I don't know what I might do."

Reflecting on the possibilities of what Norma might do, could do, in fact by rights should do, Frank simply looked at her forlornly.

"But I would like to get together with you tomorrow. Perhaps we can make plans about what to do . . . to stop Mr. Gabib, I mean."

"Yeah," said Frank, thinking that if Norma Duffin

were only half as successful in thwarting Gabib's plans as she was in crushing his own, the poor guy didn't stand a chance.

"Good night, Frank," she said.

"Good night, Norma," he replied as she closed the door.

Two or three couples were still sporting in the shadows when Frank passed by the park. Along the side of the road, he spotted a few items of outer and underwear, and for an instant he wondered if Lisette had recovered her caftan. Gazing out at the lake, he saw that the raft had disappeared. Anyway, St. John the damned Baptist didn't deserve to be honoured in the first place, Frank told himself. He was a common trickster in the end, the saint of unfulfilled expectations.

As he wandered toward the Inn, Frank noticed that a dim light was still on in the upstairs living quarters, and he wondered what Lisette was up to. No doubt entertaining that wretched Billy Carcajou, he speculated bitterly, the crazy bare-assed Indian who had touched off all the frustrating madness. Canadians were reputed to be a conservative, undemonstrative people. That's what it said in the books. What a laugh. Anyone who believed that should have seen the bunch of them cavorting around the park naked and half naked, English and French alike.

Then suddenly it occurred to Frank that the brawl between the English and the French which everyone had regarded as inevitable had not taken place after all. It had simply been forgotten. People had tossed off their prejudices and animosities with their clothes. And as with the various items of clothing scattered in the vicinity of the park, they might not be able to find them again.

Frank was greeted by a cacophony of raucous meows when he opened the door to his room, demonstrating that the kittens had all inherited their mother's sound system and reminding him that soon he had to find takers for the little cats and get Mirabel fixed before she deposited any more on his shoes and socks. Perhaps, he thought as he tossed his shirt on the dresser, he should get himself fixed at the same time.

Chapter Twenty

Within a few days after the night of the floating bonfire, Norma and Frank had their scheme to save North Chadley in full operation. For his part, Frank had briefed Bill Martin on cases he knew from his studies in anthropology of small communities which had battled the development plans of corporations, governments and powerful individuals. Some, of course, notably Indian bands and other groups for whom being kicked around had become an established pattern of life, had failed. But other groups, notably those which marshalled legal expertise and public opinion, had succeeded. Frank also spoke to Marcel Tremblay, Mayor Richmond, Jeannie McVicar, and Paul Larose, and he knew that Bill was meeting with other townsfolk to draw up a strategy.

For her part, Norma had carefully planted in Mr. Gabib's mind the idea that he and his associates should formally present the complete development project for North Chadley at the next town-council meeting. Leery at first, Gabib had soon become obsessed with the idea and was even rushing to have an elaborate scale model built in time for the council presentation. He was blindly proud, Norma told Frank, totally convinced of the magnificence of his baby. Thus he had no doubt that all other reasonable persons, once they could actually see what was to be, would be likewise convinced.

"It would be so much easier, sir, if you had the town behind you," Norma had truthfully told her boss.

"Yes, of course, Madame Duffin. But how? Many seem to be suspicious of me."

"Because they have no clear idea of what you intend to do. And since they don't know the facts, all kinds of wild rumours are spreading."

"What rumours, Madame Duffin?"

"The other day in the grocery store I overheard someone say that you planned to bottle the lake water and send it back to Saudi Arabia. Somebody else spoke of a camel-breeding operation. There's even been talk of you scouting local girls to stock harems."

"I see, I see. Thank you for telling me this, Madame Duffin."

As Frank knew, Norma had managed to regain Gabib's confidence after her rejection of him on the night of St-Jean Baptiste, for he had been the lever on both occasions. Two days after the bonfire, he and Norma had been talking in the park while her three children swam in the lake. When Gabib had arrived in his limousine to tell her that he needed her immediately to attend to urgent business, Frank had offered to take the children out for dinner. Norma had then gone off with her obviously reassured boss, and Frank had ended up with the three kids at McDonald's in Brooke. Fortunately, he got along well with the Duffin children, and like most youngsters, they seemed to take to him.

By arrangement with Mayor Richmond, Gabib and his two architects or engineers, accompanied by Norma with her stenographer's pad, arrived in the town hall before the council meeting to set up their scale model. Then they covered it with an embroidered piece of cloth in order to have a proper unveiling at the appropriate time.

That time came, or at least seemed to come, after the council had finished with routine business and Mayor Richmond mumbled a few token words of introduction and sat down. The hall was packed with townspeople, and once the unveiling had taken place, everyone in the room got up and crowded around the conference table to get a glimpse of the construction projected for the various downtown properties purchased by Gabib.

The model was elaborately detailed, with a pastel-coloured fifteen-storey hotel and convention centre on the spot where the old wooden sheds of a marina now stood. The luxury hotel would provide, Mr. Gabib himself explained, harbour facilities for speedboats, yachts, and motor launches underneath the mezzanine floor. On the present site of the town's snack bar was an exclusive boutique, which, according to one of the Arabian architects, would feature exquisite jewelry selected by expert buyers and a choice of the finest furs, the sales of which, the man added, were intended to boost the Canadian economy and assist beleaguered native trappers and hunters such as "Eskimos, Red Indians, and Newfoundlanders." The location occupied by the town's other marina, up the river a little way, had a model of a futuristic helicopter and STOL aircraft pad atop a travel bureau, which would offer the latest in computerized services.

The homeowners, back in their seats again, sat in mystification as the three swarthy outsiders, flashing broad, toothy smiles and bubbling with excitement, expanded further on what was in store for the sleepy village of North Chadley. All three chuckled and winked at each other and at the men in the audience when they described a massage parlour, complete with saunas, whirlpools and hot tubs, as well as mud baths with therapeutic mud imported from California, to be staffed exclusively by buxom young blond masseuses brought all the way from Sweden. There would also be a limousine service, a special coffee and smoking salon, a beauty parlour for men, women, and other, a highly sophisticated haberdashery, and eventually an international centre for Islamic studies. The whole downtown area would be interconnected by a suspended electric tramcar system along the lines of Disneyland.

Mr. Gabib himself, oozing confidence and sincerity in the manner of a television evangelist, concluded the presentation by proclaiming that he was firmly committed to "putting St-Alphonse de Chadley Nord on the map." Businessmen, scholars, presidents, princes and sheikhs would jet in to an enlarged and improved Brooke Airport from around the globe, then be whisked by choppers to "Bagdad-sur-le-lac." Tidal waves of money would flood the town, thousands of jobs would be created, gorgeous women in the latest fashions parading the avenues would be more numerous than the birds in the sky, condominiums would tickle the clouds, the entire circumference of Lake Missawappi, now mostly a wasteland of forest and wild flowers, would be developed, would be transformed into a vast, vigorous caravansary, would blossom like an oasis in the desert.

Mr. Gabib, Frank noted from his seat at the back of the town hall, continued to smile gleefully as he sat down, but his two companions developed puzzled expressions on their faces as they apparently were waiting for an explosion of applause. After a few moments of utter silence, they both stood up and applauded themselves, no doubt presuming that the audience of undemonstrative Canadians simply needed a cue. The assembly, however, did not follow suit. Their response was a deep-freezing, collective stare of disbelief.

The next thing the three gentlemen from the Middle East knew, the president of the recently formed Ratepayers Association des Propriétaires, Bill Martin, rose to propose the adoption of new zoning bylaws, which he read out in French and then in English. The first of the proposed new bylaws prohibited the construction of any edifice within the territory of St-Alphonse de Chadley Nord more than two storeys high or which obstructed the view of the lake from any existing home. The second regulation prohibited any commercial enterprise except on sites already being used for commercial purposes, and a third required all new buildings, including those erected after the demolition of an existing structure, to occupy not more than one third of the area of the lot and to be set back at least fifty feet from the street. Martin then added a fourth zoning bylaw, which Frank suspected had been tagged onto the list at the last moment. This final regulation prohibited landing facilities for helicopters, STOL planes or any other flying machine, massage parlours however staffed, electric transportation systems and academic institutions, apart from the existing public elementary school.

When Bill Martin sat down, Mr. Gabib and his two associates finally heard the explosion of applause they had been anticipating a few minutes earlier. They sat like three stone sphinxes, immobilized and uncomprehending. The mayor, Reginald Richmond, then stood up to ask if there was a seconder for the motion on the floor.

"*J'appuie*" and "I second it" rang out from around the room. Since Clémentine's voice was the loudest, she was officially recognized and a vote was called for. It was only after the motion had been carried unanimously that Gabib seemed to grasp the implications of what had happened. His dark eyes now sparking like the orbs of a toy robot, he jumped to his feet.

"You fools! You stupid fools!" he screamed. "It is true what they say about Canadians. Don't you understand? I am here to save you. I am here to put you on the map ..."

"We're already on the goddamned map!" responded a loud voice from the back of the room.

"No! No! No! Nobody knows about this place," shouted Gabib.

"Mais alors, comment se fait-il que vous le connaissez? How come you know?" another voice shouted.

"I found out by accident. For you, a fortunate accident. But that does not matter. I am here to offer you prosperity—jobs, money, progress, prestige, high-class people, beautiful women. Are you all too stupid to understand?"

"Mange la marde!" yelled Clémentine in her diva decibels, voicing the sentiments of the assembled townspeople.

Gabib and his two aides and Norma then gathered their materials and left the council meeting, but not before he had promised that his lawyers would be investigating the legality of what had taken place at the meeting and would also be consulting certain government cabinet ministers who happened to be friends of his. He concluded by stating that he would put North Chadley on the map whether North Chadleyites liked it or not.

The mood in the bar-salon later that night was quite triumphant, although Bill Martin repeatedly cautioned that the battle was not over yet.

"But at least we've got the townspeople pulling together," he said.

Frank noted that Billy Carcajou was working as bartender, helping out Lisette, who seemed to be in a particularly cheerful humour. The new zoning bylaws adopted by the town council would not prevent her husband from selling his half ownership of the Inn to Gabib, but she felt that they would certainly dampen the latter's interest. She also hinted to Frank that another possible resolution to the problem was in the wind, and he suspected that it had something to do with the big Missawappi Indian who was giving her a hand in the bar-salon. Whatever the case, clearly Wilton Wadleigh had dangled his tempting wife in front of other men once too often. Frank noted that Lisette was wearing comfortable medium-heeled rather than her usual high-heeled shoes.

Sitting with Bill Martin and Gordon Jackson, Frank kept looking toward the door and hoping that Norma Duffin would show up. He was worried that perhaps Gabib might blame her for the debacle in the town hall. On the other hand, perhaps Gabib might not blame her. Perhaps he would transfer his operations elsewhere and make her an offer she couldn't refuse. She had never indicated any dislike for the man personally.

Norma, however, did not show up, and when the others began to leave, Frank too went back to his room and his black cats.

Chapter Twenty-one

Although it climaxed feverishly in the rest of the province, with rallies, parades, accusations, proclamations, and widespread frothing at the mouth, the final days of the Referendum campaign were remarkably defused in St-Alphonse de Chadley Nord, largely due to the St-Jean Baptiste get-together in the park, Frank thought, but also because of the cooperation between French and English to block Gabib's grandiose plans for the town. Two other developments, however, also contributed to the easing of tensions.

The first, like the park love-in, was sparked by Billy Carcajou. It turned out that the briefcase he often carried with him was packed full of maps, letters, copies of colonial government papers and various other documents, and that his visits to the town and to neighbouring counties were primarily for the purpose of surveying the territory, at least until the moment when his mind was boggled by the sight of Lisette writhing up to him in the park. On behalf of himself, he being a hereditary tribal chief, and a dozen or so other surviving members of the Missawappi first nation, Billy had started court proceedings to reestablish title to 21,310 square miles of the Eastern Townships of Quebec, an area larger than the Province of Nova Scotia.

Billy explained to Frank that neither the French nor the English colonial governments had bothered to negotiate rights of any description to the territory traditionally occupied by the Missawappi nation; therefore, all the land grants so generously bestowed upon friends and relatives, mistresses and manipulators, retired officers and younger sons, eventually to pass into the hands of unwitting settlers, were null and void. With the help of several lawyers and archeologists, Billy, who was himself a graduate of the McGill Law School, had been preparing his case for years. What Lisette had hinted at regarding the ownership of the Inn, as Frank had suspected, was indeed connected with Billy Carcajou. Apparently the site of the Inn and the surrounding area by the river outlet of Lake Missawappi, including the sacred ceremonial ground Billy had located, were of special significance, having been where the main Missawappi Indian village had actually stood for centuries. Archeological evidence abounded. This area was clearly identifiable as compared to the wide-ranging, seasonal hunting grounds of the tribe. Any proposed sale within its boundaries would now be blocked until Billy's claim was settled in the courts, and there was a good chance that he and his fellow tribe members would end up owners of at least that tract of land.

"I don't care about the Referendum," Billy told Frank. "The English and French can fight with each other as much as they like. But they are fighting over nothing, because this land is my land."

Frank was naturally intrigued by the affair, especially after he was able to persuade Billy to let him examine the documents he had collected. The opening section of his doctoral dissertation, he speculated with unmitigated glee, would now be nothing short of sensational. And the conclusion as well, no matter what the courts decided.

The residents of North Chadley, on the other hand, were stupefied. Property deeds were dug out of safety deposit boxes and secret drawers to be woefully contemplated, nominal landowners wondering if the papers were worth no more than last week's losing lottery tickets. All that could be done was to wait and see, and to hope that the damned upstart Indian, who was now living in an upstairs apartment of the Inn, within easy pouncing distance if not in the very quarters of the innkeeper's lusty wife, at the moment without benefit of husband, might be driven to distraction. It was bad enough, some villagers told Frank, to have to deal with the Arabs.

Billy's claim, thus, had the effect of taking minds off the imminent Referendum, of changing perspectives. Meanwhile, Frank learned that other native peoples were further complicating the political situation—the Cree and Inuit of the North, fully two-thirds of the area of the Province of Quebec, held a referendum of their own and voted almost unanimously to secede from Quebec if Quebec opted to secede from Canada.

The second event to divert attention from the Referendum was the surprise wedding of Jeannie McVicar and Joe Larose. After being engaged for more than half a century, they decided to get married on July 1st, Canada Day. Everyone in the village was invited, and just about everyone attended. The wedding itself was a simple, non-denominational ceremony performed by the Unitarian-Universalist minister in the park. Paul Larose was Joe's best man, two of the Murphy daughters were flower girls, and Mayor Reginald Richmond gave away the bride.

The vast reception, however, was held in the Missawappi Club, which Jeannie had apparently rented for the occasion. After the park ceremony, two bagpipers and a drummer led a parade of the wedding party and guests along the lake road to the clubhouse. Bill Martin quipped to Frank that the reason for the loud music was to drown out the subterranean rumblings of Jeannie's reverend uncle and other Presbyterian forebears, as well as generations of deceased papist Laroses, turning over in their graves.

The reception was launched by a barrage of champagne toasts in French and English, with Bill Martin, Billy Carcajou and Mr. Gabib himself then delivering one each in Gaelic, Missawappi Indian and Arabic for variety. The buffet dinner, including shrimp, tourtières, roast beef, lamb, poached salmon, beans baked in maple syrup, and a variety of other fare, was spread over several tables, and three bars were like beehives at the peak of a nectar flow. To the music of a five-man orchestra, which mixed old-time favourites with the current disco beat, dancing continued long into the night. Every hour or so the pipers played for a square dance which rattled the window panes and shimmied the timbers of the large hall.

Frank escorted Norma Duffin. She had actually come to his room behind the Inn two days earlier to ask him to accompany her to the wedding, and he had, of course, immediately accepted to do so. When he inquired how things were going with her boss, she told him that Gabib had been greatly disturbed by the council meeting and was now holding consultations with his lawyers, his father, and anyone else who seemed to be consultable. But he didn't blame her at all, she said. In fact, he was being especially friendly toward her and had even given her a gift of exquisite silk lingerie imported from Paris.

Delighted to see Norma at his door just a few moments previously, Frank's morale now hit the floor like a dropped egg. Holy Mary, he reasoned, no man gives a woman fancy underwear unless he figures there's a fair chance that he'll see her in it and then out of it pretty soon. The situation was hopeless after all. He should have realized as much when she wouldn't let him an inch inside the front door. She wanted his help to keep the Arabs from messing up her miserable little town, but that was so she wouldn't have to risk her job. She didn't give a damn about him personally. She was an independent cuss all right. It was a great shame. Something was terribly amiss in the whole sociocultural system, Frank concluded sadly. The Lapps of Norway and Sweden, the Maoris of New Zealand, the Sioux, the Comanches, the Perce Nez, and the dozens of other Amerindian tribes never had these problems. They had simple mechanisms to assure that a resource like Norma Duffin, a beautiful unattached woman in her prime, would not be wasted. North America had definitely developed into a society of monumental waste—of food, of manufactured goods, of raw materials, and of women.

"By the way, Frank," Norma said before she left, "the kids are just dying to go out for hamburgers with you again. You certainly made a hit with them. That's all I hear about at home."

"Is that right?" he responded flatly, thinking that's about all I'm good for, keeping her kids amused while good-looking momma entertains her boss in her exquisite silk lingerie imported from Paris. Nevertheless, Frank did end up offering to take Norma's three children out to eat the following night as well as Norma herself to the wedding one night later. Norma took home one of the kittens, leaving him with six to place. The young Murphy girl had already picked up one that afternoon.

The wedding reception proved to be a bonanza for Frank. He slipped off during the dancing and brought over the kittens in a large cardboard box. Four of the remaining six were soon chosen, and Jeannie McVicar herself said that she would take one of the two left. Frank felt a sense of relief. Now the challenges in his life had been reduced to one black kitten, an acceptable doctoral dissertation, one potent female cat, and one potent female person.

The latter was wearing a light blue party dress which accentuated her full figure and blond hair, and she looked as majestic as the bride as she glided over the dance floor with old smoothie, Joe Larose, who was making the rounds of his lady guests. As the evening progressed, Frank felt Norma clinging to him more and more amorously, their two bodies merging into a quivering blob of provocation during a slow waltz. But he steeled himself for the inevitable derailment, even when Norma whispered to him that her three children were off with their father in Montreal for the weekend, leaving her alone and lonely in the house by herself. He replied that he would have to get the two remaining kittens back to his room, but she simply said, "Okay, let's go."

Norma hurried Frank along as they dropped off the kittens. When they got to her house, she opened the door, then she took his hand and ushered him into the house. He was not sure what to make of this gesture, but he did not resist. Nor did he hesitate when she took him into the bedroom and asked him to undo the buttons on the back of her dress. That night, in the early hours after Canada Day, whether because of the mood of romance engendered by the wedding, the maturing of their relationship, or sheer mercy on the part of Norma, the four challenges in Frank's life were gratifyingly reduced to three.

Over the next few days, Frank's bulky frame floated around the town like a tumbling tumbleweed. Even the discovery of the grey pick-up camper with red fenders which had forced him off the road during the snow storm on the day of his arrival in North Chadley did not stir him to anger. It was parked behind the garage not far from the Inn, and Frank simply sat down on a fender and waited for the owner to show up. And who should it turn out to be but Billy Carcajou.

"Billy, you're a lousy driver," said Frank.

"Why do you say that, Frank?"

"Because you turned onto the highway last January right in front of me without looking and nearly wiped out the both of us."

"I did?"

"You did. I know it was you because of those red fenders. And just think what we would have missed in life, you and me."

"Got those fenders in a junk yard."

"After the original ones were mangled, I'll bet."

Billy nodded his head.

"I'm sorry, Frank," he said. "I guess we Indians have a bad habit of not looking too carefully before we do things."

"I have to admit that's true, when I think of some of the treaties signed and various other deals. But you seem to be cured, except for the driving."

"How can I make it up to you?"

"I was hoping you'd get around to that. Let me photocopy those papers you've collected. Then I can take my time going over them. I'm not in any hurry any more."

"Okay, it's a deal."

"And one more thing—I need to find a home for a

black cat."

Frank had decided to concentrate on Mirabel herself, because he was confident that someone would take the last kitten if he showed it around. People, he knew now, had trouble resisting kittens when they actually laid eyes on them, which explained why the world was overrun with cats.

"What cat are you talking about?" asked Billy.

"A black female alley cat that's been living in my room."

"Fluffy tail, with a few white hairs under her chin?"

"Yes. How do . . ."

"I think that might be my cat, Frank. I lost her when I came here last January. She used to keep me company when I travelled around in my camper."

The two men went immediately to Frank's room, and sure enough, Mirabel was Billy's long-lost pussy cat Memphremagog, or Maggie for short. She had evidently decided to find some warm, stationary place to have her kittens, and Frank's room happened to be convenient. And just as Lisette had done in the park, she quite blithely abandoned his protective custody and jumped into the arms of Billy Carcajou. The son-of-a-gun has a way with females, Frank observed to himself, taking comfort, however, in the thought that of late he was not totally devoid of such talents himself.

Jeannie and Joe Larose had told everyone that they were going to spend only a short honeymoon of two or three days at the seashore in Maine, intending to have a proper and extended one in the form of a Caribbean cruise during the winter. About ten days after the wedding, therefore, Frank set off to deliver their kitten, but he didn't quite complete the mission.

It was a hot July night, and a scented mist hung over

the roadway up to the McVicar house. Carrying the little cat in a cardboard box under his arm, Frank strolled along slowly, letting his mind wander among the experiences of the last few days. The Referendum, he reflected, had been threatening to tear the town apart, but now people seemed almost to be more closely united than ever before. Elvis, or at least a good facsimile, had saved Quebec so far as North Chadley was concerned, turning what was shaping up to be a bloody brawl into a multicultural love-in. Billy Carcajou had also been a significant factor, putting the whole situation into perspective with his land claim, which took the wind out of the sails of both English and French sovereignty champions. Then the fact that the English and French had to work together to save the town from Gabib was an additional helpful circumstance.

Frank had heard about a number of aftermaths of the bonfire party. George Carson was seen paddling off in a canoe with one of Marcel Tremblay's daughters, neither one of them having taken the trouble to recover their clothing jettisoned earlier in the park, and they had not been seen since. His mind apparently unhinged by staring too long at Lisette in the moonlight, Gordon Jackson had ended the evening pressed to Marie-Ange's ample bosom, from which he had not yet been able to wean himself. There were rumours of various other developing liaisons. It was truly amazing, Frank mused, when people let their hair down, as it were, and followed their basic instincts, how different they could be from their usual selves. The extent of the difference depended on how much an individual was inhibited or suppressed in the first place. It was the same with collectivities. Both English Canadians and French Canadians were peoples who had long been suppressed, by their respective notions of duty, by the Church, by various authorities, even by their efforts to be different from the rebellious and undisciplined Americans next door. Politicians had quickly learned to exploit these complexes. The people had been conditioned to do what they were told, and that's exactly what they did for generations. But now Canadians were finally daring to be themselves, and certainly there were a few surprises in store.

Every social system, Frank reminded himself, was a means to control the innate destructive urges of human beings, or at least of some human beings, so that communities could exist with a tolerable minimum of physical violence. The trouble was that once in place, the social systems themselves often evolved out of control, becoming too complex, too repressive, even too violent. Sometimes they aggravated what they were originally intended to control, the hunger for power and the megalomania of aggressive individuals. Frank resolved to provide a detailed analysis of the changes taking place in the Canadian social system in the conclusion of his dissertation. In fact, he had no choice but to try, although he realized that it would be largely guesswork, because nobody could know for certain how extensive the changes would be and whether they would improve or worsen the quality of life in the country. At least there was no immediate danger of Canada becoming a Marxist "paradise" like Ethiopia or a garrison for the privileged few like Saudi Arabia. On the other hand, if the results of the Referendum set off the disintegration of the nation, then who could say what would happen to the pieces? That would mean a whole new ball game, quite probably with Uncle Sam acting as referee.

Anyway, to hell with it for the time being, thought Frank as he neared the sprawling, white-clapboarded McVicar house. The mist still hung heavy on the hillside, and he felt as if he were moving in a twilight zone. The mood was heightened when his ears began to pick up the faint music of a Viennese waltz. Frank stepped softly onto the veranda of the house, and through the picture window he could see most of the huge living room. Jeannie and Joe were dancing, gliding and pirouetting gracefully around the room to the music of the waltz, now passing by the 1933 Quebec Championship cup and the photograph of themselves on the mantelpiece.

Then, to his astonishment, as he stood and stared at the dancing couple, Frank was not seeing two septuagenarians but a young man in a tuxedo with a mass of black, wavy hair and huge shoulders and chest. He was holding in his arms a tall, statuesque strawberry blonde in a ballroom dress.

Frank closed his eyes, which he knew were playing tricks on him. He was seeing a photograph come alive rather than real people. But when he opened his eyes again, the young couple were still dancing, gazing into each other's eyes, preoccupied with each other.

Frank backed up and stepped down from the veranda, tightening his grip on the cardboard box with the kitten. He hesitated for a moment, was about to step up again, then he turned and walked slowly away. He admitted to himself that as a man presumably committed to scientific research, he was not acting rationally, but he wanted to preserve his hallucination for a little while.

Back at the Inn, after putting the kitten in his room with its one remaining littermate, Frank went to the bar-salon. Marge Miller and Billy Carcajou were there, four

Arabs were sitting at another table, and two couples at a third. Despite the presence of the Arabs, Lisette had not changed into her California scanties. She was wearing a new loose skirt and low, comfortable shoes.

Frank sat down with Marge, and before long they were joined by Bill Martin and the elder Murphy. Frank wanted to tell the others about his strange experience at the McVicar house, but he was afraid that he might destroy his credibility. They would think that he had lost what feeble grip he had.

"When did Jeannie and Joe get back?" he eventually asked.

"Oh, they're not back yet," replied Murphy. "Joe phoned me from Cape Cod this morning. He wants me to deliver his eggs for the next few days."

"Imagine! At their age!" said Marge, and everyone laughed.

Except Frank, who was lost in thought.

Chapter Twenty-two

Despite a last-minute frenzy across the province, marked by promises of terrestrial paradise and prophecies of instant disaster, Referendum day was uneventful in St-Alphonse de Chadley Nord. Everyone wandered over to the polling station in a leisurely manner, as if to vote on a new sidewalk or whether to install flower boxes on the rails at the sides of the bridge. In the evening, Frank watched the results on the television set in the Inn, where a crowd of NON supporters had gathered.

Apart from Bill Martin and Lisette, who seemed confident, the rest of the group were obviously nervous before the reports from the polling stations started to come in. Many sat and stared at the television screen in silence, their fingers white as they gripped glasses or the edges of chairs. Frank did not share but could understand their anxiety, because in effect the fate of the whole country was about to be decided. A win for the OUI, despite the ostensibly non-committal nature of the Referendum question, could trigger an irreversible process of national disintegration. Once the cookie started to crumble, it was only a matter of time until crumbs were all that was left. Since he had carefully monitored the Referendum campaign with respect to the involvement of various community institutions, Frank realized that from a purely selfish point of view, he should be rooting for the OUI side. A Separatist victory might transform his doctoral dissertation from a scholarly exercise consulted every ten years or so by other Ph.D. hopefuls into a timely best-seller. Newspapers, magazines, publishers would be banging at his door. It would be as if he had been an eye-witness at the signing of the Magna Carta or the doing-in of Julius Caesar. He would make money, become rich, and he would be able to propose to Norma Duffin on one symbolic bended knee rather than on all fours.

Frank was jolted from his reveries when the crowd in the Inn spontaneously broke into the Canadian national anthem, "O Canada." As he listened and watched the faces, it occurred to him that perhaps the OUI people had made one big mistake—they had presumed that they had a monopoly on emotional involvement. Nobody, either English or French, was supposed to feel any more strongly about the Canadian Confederation than they would about the galactic splatter of the Milky Way. But obviously, Frank decided, however undemonstrative they were supposed to be, Canadians did give a damn after all. They had deeper feelings about their country than he had been led to believe.

The Referendum results soon confirmed Frank's speculations. The NON vote climbed to over fifty percent and held. Victory was assured. As the crowd in the Inn began to celebrate, Frank slipped away to observe what was happening in the Café Québec Libre.

The group gathered there in front of the television set were subdued. Curiously, however, Frank detected a sense of relief rather than defeat. Many of the OUI people, he began to realize, had supported the cause out of feelings of duty to the collectivity, but deep down they had no wish to go all the way. Apart from the CNR one beside the park perhaps, they did not want to burn their bridges. Clémentine seemed to capture the mood when she got up and turned off the television set.

"Alors, c'est fini tout ça," she announced. *"On a*

d'autres choses à faire."

Paul Larose asked Frank what he thought about the outcome, and Frank replied that time would tell. He suggested to Paul that Quebec would emerge the winner in the long run, because now the rest of the country was aware of its distinctiveness and would henceforth be less inclined than in the past to ignore the rights of French-speaking Canadians. Paul allowed that if *les Anglais* had learned something, then the Referendum may have been a success after all, and several others agreed with him. Frank added that not only the English but many Americans and people in other countries now recognized the French fact of Canada, so the Referendum had certainly produced positive results, however disheartened the OUI people might feel for the time being. Just then Bill Martin arrived in the Café Québec Libre. He walked right over to Clémentine, and the two embraced.

"Finies les folies," he announced. *"Désormais on va travailler ensemble. Vive le Québec!"*

The reaction was not thunderous, but everyone cheered, and Clémentine embraced Bill again. Frank concluded that the wounds of the Referendum campaign might not take so long to heal as he had feared at various times over the past few months.

In the weeks that followed, North Chadley reverted to a sleepy little village on the shores of Lake Missawappi. There was excitement in town when the news broke that Margery Miller had finally won $100,000 in the Quebec lottery. Within hours of receiving the money, she had quit her cleaning-lady jobs, bought a new colour TV with a VCR, and headed to Montreal in a taxi, reportedly to try her luck at the Blue Bonnets race track.

The other event to cause more than a ripple of attention was the erection of a statue in the park. One of St. John the Baptist would have been less controversial, thought Frank, and appropriate in a way, but not quite so eye-catching. The town council, after long deliberation, had finally accepted the proposal by eccentric Morton Wadleigh to erect the bronze statue. Entitled "Madeleine the Divine," but bearing a striking resemblance to Lisette of the Inn, it was a life-size nude bending slightly forward and with arms thrown backward as if she were about to dive into the lake. How Wadleigh had created it was a mystery to many of the townsfolk, but Frank guessed that apart from the sketches he knew she had posed for, Morton had probably made plaster casts of various parts of Lisette's anatomy then put them together to form a complete mould. Apparently the mayor himself, old Reginald Richmond, had pushed the bizarre project through council, and his wife had not spoken to him since, explaining why he spent a lot of time wandering the park.

As for Lisette herself, she began divorce proceedings against Wilt, who had decided to stay in Florida with a new restaurant and a new woman. Lisette intended to keep the Inn, but she did close the bar-salon for a few days while she toured the district with Billy Carcajou, who was surveying his possible future domain pending the outcome of his lawsuit. After a talk with F.R. Scott, Frank concluded that Billy certainly had a case, but it would probably be settled by a sum of money and only after years in court. In the meantime, however, Billy could take comfort in the fact that he was staking his claim, presumably as often as he liked and she was willing, to a territory more highly coveted than any parcel of dirt. The day that Billy and Lisette wheeled out of town in his camper, Frank found Mirabel scratching at his door, exactly one hour after he had persuaded Marie-Ange and Gordon Jackson to take the last black kitten.

Before the end of July, George Carson and the Tremblay girl finally canoed back to town, fully dressed, and took up housekeeping in the apartment above the garage. Not long afterwards, Mr. Gabib folded his tent, having decided, according to Norma, that North Chadley was beyond redemption. The last straw was the mayor's facetious offer to put a veil over the head of the bronze statue in the park, which Gabib had labelled an obscene affront to womankind, who were meant to be protected, kept sheltered in households as mothers or maids.

To Frank's profound relief, Norma declined the offer to work for Mr. Gabib in Jedda, Saudi Arabia, preferring to take her chances on finding another job in North Chadley or Brooke. She also began to type Frank's dissertation, and she was proving to be a highly efficient editor, eliminating his spelling and grammar mistakes and questioning any weakness in logic or clarity. Thanks to her, Frank acknowledged with wonder and gratitude, there was now a good possibility that he would complete a doctorate rather than turning into a package of blubbering frustrations, fantasies and anthropological debris.

He was also eating well, having dinner regularly at Norma's place. Since she was busy winding up Mr. Gabib's affairs in the village, Frank often did the cooking, and his meals seemed to be highly appreciated not only by Norma but by her three children, who were quickly adjusting to the presence of the large American graduate student. He went with them hiking and canoeing. When the girl was invited to go on a week-long trip with her father to a conference in Vancouver, the two boys pleaded with Frank to take them on a camping expedition down the lake. With the proviso that at some convenient future date he would also take her on a camping trip, Norma happily agreed, and the boys jumped into Frank's arms in their excitement.

Sitting on the veranda while the youngsters scurried around town gathering the camping equipment Frank had listed for them, Frank remarked to Norma that he would be forced to compete with her children for her affection. She replied that the situation seemed to be reversed—she would soon be forced to compete with her own children for Frank's affection. Either way, they agreed, with a little luck it would all work out, so long as there was enough affection to go around.

Gazing out over the still waters of Lake Missawappi now gleaming in the twilight, then up the hill where the old McVicar house was visible through a vista of trees and where Jeannie and Joe might at that very moment be performing their magical waltz, it occurred to Frank that the same simple formula applied not only to Norma and himself and the children, but also to the whole village of St-Alphonse de Chadley Nord, to the entire province, to the country, to the continent, and to the world.

GLOSSARY OF QUEBEC FRENCH

Assieds-toué—you sit down; fr. *asseoir* (to seat, sit down) and *toué* (pronounced tway) fr. Std. Fr. *toi* (you).

Asteure—now, these days; fr. Std. Fr. *à cette heure* (at this hour, time).

Ben-stackée—well-stacked, busty; fr. Eng. *stack* and *ben* fr. Std. Fr. *bien* (well, very).

Bien entendu—(lit. well understood) of course, indeed; fr. *entendre* (to hear, to understand).

Ça coûtera ben cher—it'll cost a bundle; fr. *coûter* (to cost) and *cher* (dear) with *ben* fr. Std. Fr. *bien* (very, well).

Ça fait rien—(lit. it makes nothing) it doesn't matter, forget it; fr. *faire* (to make, do) and *rien* (nothing).

Ça suffit—(lit. it suffices) that's enough, that'll do; fr. *suffire* (to suffice, to be sufficient).

Caribou—a potent hooch, perhaps moonshine with maple syrup.

C'est pas grand chose—it's no big deal, thing; fr. *chose* (thing).

Chaton—kitten; which eventually becomes a *chat* (tomcat) or *chatte* (pussy cat).

Chauffer cette maison—heat this house.

Comme tout le monde—like everybody else; fr. *comme* (like, as) and *monde* (world).

Comment?—what? how? what do you mean?

D'autres choses à faire—other things to do; fr. *faire* (to do, make).

De retour—back home again.

Désormais on va travailler ensemble—from now on we're going to work together; fr. *désormais* (henceforth), *on* (one, but often with the sense of we or they), *va* 1st per. sing. of *aller* (to go) and *ensemble* (together).

Encore tout équipé—uncastrated; fr. *encore* (still, again) and p.p. of *équiper* (to equip).

Fête de la Saint Jean Baptiste—St. John the Baptist Day; fr. *fête* (feast).

Finies les folies—Enough of this foolishness; fr. p. p. of *finir* (to finish) and *folie* (folly, foolishness).

Fou—fool, nut.

Je me souviens—I remember; fr. *se souvenir* (to remember).

Laisse brûler—let burn; fr. *laisser* (to allow, let) and *brûler* (to burn).

Mange d'la marde—(lit. eat shit) go to hell, screw you; fr. *manger* (to eat) and *marde* fr. St. Fr. *merde* (excrement).

Maudzit (te-s)—damn, goddamned; fr. p. p. of Std. Fr. *maudire* (to damn, curse).

Glossary

Même chose—same thing.

Mon vieux—my old friend, buddy.

N'est-ce pas?—(lit. is it not?) right? eh?

Ote-toué de là—get out of there; fr. *ôter* (to take away, remove).

Partout—everywhere.

Pas catholique—not normal, acceptable, kosher.

Pas encore—not yet.

Pont—bridge.

Qu'est-ce qu'il a dit?—what did he say? fr. *dire* (to say, tell).

Sais-tu combien il a payé?—do you know how much he paid? fr. *savoir* (to know), *combien* (how much) and *payer* (to pay, pay for).

Sais-tu que M. Gabib a acheté . . .?—do you know that Mr. Gabib bought . . .? fr. *acheter* (to buy).

Sauve-moi—save me; fr. *sauver* (to save).

Selon les nouvelles—according to the news.

Tabarnac!—(lit. tabernacle) a strong curse, equivalent to Jesus Christ!

Tellement beaux—so beautiful.

Tout-foké—wrecked, totalled; fr. *tout* (all) and the old

four-letter word borrowed from Eng.

Tout-jammé—all jammed up; fr. English jammed.

Va-t-en, minou—get away, cat; fr. *minou*, a common name for cats in general and *va*, the imp. of *aller* (to go).

Vieille Anglaise—old English woman.

Voilà—there, there you are, see.

Vrai—true.

Vraiment—truly.

Voyons—(lit. let's see) come on now, no kidding; fr. *voir* (to see).

Whisky blanc—(lit. white whisky) moonshine or "white lightning."